LAST CHANCE
VOLUME 1
THE LEGEND OF
THE HATHMEC

To Harry,

Thank you for your support and I hope you enjoy the story.

Bradley Boals

BRADLEY H. BOALS

Cover art by Les McDermott.
For more information on this and other books in this series, visit hathmecbook.com.
Copyright © 2014 Bradley H. Boals

ISBN: 1500416460
ISBN 13: 978-1500416461
Library of Congress Control Number: 2014912169
CreateSpace Independent Publishing Platform
North Charleston, South Carolina

Dedicated to a good man and friend, Casey Dunagan. You lived life to the fullest and were never afraid to take a chance. Thank you for the passion that you had for life.

Special thanks to Rose Mary, Benny, and April. No one could ask for a better mother, father, and wife. I am blessed with a wonderful family and friends and truly appreciate your support.

Thank you to Amanda Banker Schaser and Rob G. I couldn't have finished this without you.

Thank you Lindsey and Shelby; I'll work on your request.

CONTENTS

CHAPTER 1
A Mosquito Bite 1
CHAPTER 2
History Lessons 15
CHAPTER 3
Beamball 29
CHAPTER 4
Meet Mr. Kellington 43
CHAPTER 5
Room 1313 55
CHAPTER 6
The Hathmec 67
CHAPTER 7
The Rorimite Tunnel 81
CHAPTER 8
Will Work for Food 97
CHAPTER 9
I'm a Sophomore 111
CHAPTER 10
Pity Date 127
CHAPTER 11
Girls and Gadgets 141
CHAPTER 12
Mirror Mirror 157

Contents

CHAPTER 13
Aliens Among Us 173
CHAPTER 14
Trust Me 185
CHAPTER 15
The Strength of Many 199
CHAPTER 16
Road Trip 211
CHAPTER 17
What Are You Thinking? 223
CHAPTER 18
Hit Like a Girl 235
CHAPTER 19
Change of Heart 249
About the Author 257

Chapter 1

A MOSQUITO BITE

The lights from the four-door sedan began to fade away from the banks of the Potomac as the car made its relaxed exit from the secluded and wooded opening. The sun was several hours away from making an appearance as the moon dominated a dark sky. Blood continued to mix with the murky waters of the river. The soul of a man faded as quickly as the lights from the car disappeared. The bullet hole in the forehead of the unknown body floating away gushed free of restriction. As the man's final breaths struggled to reach his lungs, his life passed before his eyes, with a focus on the events that occurred a few hours earlier.

It was about midnight when Mr. Elliott's stretch limousine pulled up to the front door of Club '84. The club's main building was previously used as a warehouse in the Washington, DC, downtown area, but now it's the hottest club in town. An observer might see celebrities, politicians, or even the occasional dignitary at a club like this. The lights outside the front entrance were bright as they ran up the three-story structure's brick face. Like any good club, outsiders can't see what is going on inside, but they can hear the beat of the music pulsating through the walls. A line formed around the block of hopeful entrants to the front door, but few would see any more than the back of the next person in line. Only the truly privileged, famous, or powerful are allowed into this particular club. Mr. Elliott fits all those categories.

Leo, the club's doorman, came to the limo's back door and opened it, expecting to see a few young ladies crawl out, the norm when Mr. Elliott arrived. This was not the case this evening, as the normally brash

Chapter 1

and cocky Mr. Elliott simply got out and made his way to the door. A bit confused, Leo asked, "Sir, where are your companions this evening? You're not losing that golden touch, are you?"

Mr. Elliott looked back as he entered the club and chuckled to Leo. "There's nothing golden about my touch; I just know how to get what I want. Right now, I want you to make sure that my car is ready to go when I am. I don't plan on staying long tonight."

With a hop in his step, Leo ran back to the club door and held it open for Mr. Elliott, and promised to take care of it. Mr. Elliott, in turn, slipped Leo a nice wad of cash and told him not to mess with his radio stations.

The inside of the club screamed of the excesses of the decade. The multiple dance floors and lounge areas were first class. From the pure crystal glasses that lined the length of the bar to the custom marble dance halls, there was no expense spared. Top-of-the-line sound systems covered the walls; DJs in every corner spun the latest tracks. The sheer size of the building would cause many to get lost in the darkness and heat of the night. The gold-inlay disco balls had been placed just a week earlier to accentuate the exclusivity of the club. No Joe Lunchboxes wanted here.

Mr. Elliott walked the length of the main floor and passed by the VIP booths. Some local politicians were hamming it up in one booth, and a couple of Grammy winners were in another booth debating why hip-hop would just be a fad. The bars were fully stocked, and the drinks flowed as quickly as the scantily dressed waitresses could deliver them.

The music pounded, hundreds filled the dance floors, and the smell of smoke and drink overwhelmed the senses. The multicolored lights of the hall flashed and moved throughout the floor as chants of "Go Stacey! Go Stacey!" resonated against the walls. Mr. Elliott knew Stacey quite well, and without even looking at the dance floor, he knew that she had removed some clothing and was dancing in one of the floor's several cages.

He thought, *How proud her parents must be!* Turned out her mother was in the cage next to her. Things had changed since Mr. Elliot was a kid, or maybe he just didn't know they existed back then. Regardless, they were part of the norm for him now, at least until he could do something about it.

Daniel Elliott was a regular at the club. So much so that he always had one of his many cars parked in the lot behind it. Waiting for a car to pick him up at the end of the night just wasn't his style. He enjoyed the attention that he received when he arrived to the club in a limo, but when he was ready to go, he wanted to control the exit.

At first look, there wasn't much about Daniel Elliott to get excited about. He was in his mid thirties, not a large man, thick black hair pulled back into a ponytail. His dress was conservative for 1984, custom business suit, tie, and black leather shoes. He stuck out like a sore thumb in a club full of pastel blazers, multicolored headbands, and sparkly gloves. There was nothing special about Mr. Elliott, except for the fact that he was rich, powerful, commanded respect, and everyone knew who he was—or at least they thought they did.

Daniel Elliott continued his walk to the far side of the building, where he planned to have a talk with the owner of Club '84. This was nothing new for Mr. Elliott. He had completed this walk many times in the past and had never had a second thought about it, but this time was different.

"Daniel, Daniel, over here!"

Daniel turned to see a lovely brunette making her way over to him. Daniel, a puzzled look on his face, asked the young lady, "Can I help you?"

"It's me, Ashley. We met last week." Daniel, still confused, shook his head and raised an eyebrow. "We met by the bar. You bought me a drink."

Daniel responded, "And then?"

"Then you complemented me on how limber I was."

As if struck by lightning, Daniel remembered, "Oh, Ashley, of course! How could I forget?" Daniel removed a one hundred dollar bill from his jacket pocket and handed it to the young model. "Go grab yourself a few drinks and I'll track you down later."

Ashley took the hundred and responded, "Sure thing. I'll see you later then."

Chapter 1

Daniel had no intention of finding Ashley again that night, but it was easier to hand over some cash than to deal with her. There were fifty other young ladies in attendance that night who could make claim to a similar scenario with Mr. Elliott. Luckily, Daniel always carried several Ben Franklins in his jacket pocket.

For all of the confidence and swagger that Mr. Elliott displayed on a nightly basis, his demeanor was different this time. His palms were sweating, his breathing was heavy, and he could feel his own heart beating louder than the bass of the music that streamed around him. To say that he was scared would be an exaggeration. Fear was an emotion that Mr. Elliott had not known for several years. This was an anxious feeling of the unknown, a feeling of uncertainty that didn't belong and needed to be taken care of.

The club's front office contained two rooms: the boss's main office and the waiting area, which was controlled by his personal secretary, Ms. Connie Bowers. Ms. Bowers was a lovely young lady, perhaps so young that she didn't belong in an over-twenty-one establishment, but she was committed to her employer. Despite her age, she didn't take any lip from the visitors who wanted to speak with her boss. Daniel prepared himself for the sharp shrill of the young lady's voice.

"Mr. Elliott, fancy seeing you here tonight. What can I do you for?"

Mr. Elliott replied, conjuring a wry smile, "I need to see him Connie, so don't give me any garbage about him being too busy or being out of the office. Use those pretty little fingers and buzz me through."

"Wow, you just get straight to the point, don't you, Mr. Elliott? I'm sorry, but he isn't seeing anyone tonight, and he specifically mentioned you by name. He told me to tell you to have a few drinks, relax, and he'd call you in a few days."

Mr. Elliott didn't like to be told no, so he repeated his request, but this time, he added that it was very important that he talked with him tonight. Connie replied, "Everyone always needs to talk to him tonight, or right now, or it's life or death. Regardless of your extreme need, you're not getting back there tonight. So please, go have a drink, and if you have trouble relaxing, I'm sure I can help you get very relaxed later."

Connie flashed a quick wink at Daniel and fluttered her hand toward the door. "I'll let him know that you came by."

Mr. Elliott, a master at getting what he wanted, decided to take a different approach. "Well, Connie, I can see that you won't budge tonight; so I guess I'll take your advice and head down to the bar. I may take you up on your offer later. Just make sure you tell him that I came by."

Grinning from ear to ear, Connie replied, "Sure thing, Mr. Elliott."

Mr. Elliott began to make his way back to the door, but then quickly spun around and looked back at Ms. Bowers. "Is something wrong, Mr. Elliott?" asked Connie.

Mr. Elliott responded with a comment about the bracelet that she was wearing. "Where did you get that lovely bracelet?"

She explained that it was a gift from her mother after she had graduated from high school. Mr. Elliott thought that it must have been a gift from last year.

"Would you mind if I took a closer look?"

Connie removed the bracelet, surprised that Mr. Elliott was so impressed with it. "It's really nothing special, just a nice keepsake."

Mr. Elliott held the bracelet in his hand for just a few seconds and handed it back. "It is just lovely, Connie; you should be proud of it."

Ms. Bowers took the bracelet back, placed it on her wrist, and replied, "Thanks. Will there be anything else?"

Instead of leaving, Mr. Elliott just stared back at Connie Bowers and said, "Connie, I want you to buzz me in and then finish painting your nails." Ms. Bowers didn't say a word; she reached down, buzzed the door open, and went about painting her nails.

The adjoining office was twice the size of Ms. Bowers's area, with a large collection of books lining the walls and a large gold-laced chandelier hanging from the middle of the ceiling. The room was unseasonably hot, kept that way to keep meetings short. Though hot, the office had the smell of a doctor's office, mixed with a hint of brandy and cigar smoke.

A couple of video monitors were located behind the main desk situated at the far end of the room. Daniel noticed the chair turned in the monitors' direction. A lump formed in Daniel's throat as he began to

Chapter 1

speak, but before he could get any words out, he was interrupted by a deep baritone.

"You just can't help yourself, can you?"

Trying to mask his nerves, Daniel replied, "I only use it when I have to. Besides, I knew you would try to avoid me tonight."

The owner of Club '84 turned his chair toward Daniel and said, "Avoid you? Don't be ridiculous. Why would I want to avoid the most important person in my life?" The sarcasm oozed from the owner as strong as his celebrity-endorsed cologne oozed from his pores.

The owner of the club was a large man, but in shape. He looked like he could play linebacker for a professional football team. His fingers were well decorated with several gold rings. They complemented the gold chains around his neck. A faint grin spread across his mouth as he responded to Mr. Elliott's remark, but it was clear he was not happy to see him.

The feeling was mutual for Daniel Elliott. This was not a conversation that he looked forward to having. In his heart, he wanted to believe that he could convey a message of reason, but in his mind, a fear started to grow that he never knew existed—a fear of the unknown that seemed like a distant dream from another lifetime. Regardless of the outcome, there was no turning back.

Daniel, whose face was beginning to bead with sweat, snapped back, "You know damn well why I'm here, Evan. You lied to me. We're supposed to be in this together."

The large owner of the club stood up and slowly moved away from his chair. He made his way over to Daniel and calmly put his arm around him. Then, in a very low and deliberate voice, he told Daniel that it was his responsibility to make the final decisions when it came to their ventures and that is what he had done.

"You knew what you were getting into when we started this, and I'm not about to change course now."

Daniel Elliott and Evan Elliott were brothers. They were not only bothers, but they were partners. They were partners in a venture that could define how everyone saw the world. They were partners in a venture that could change the way everyone lived in the world.

Daniel pulled away from the large arm of his brother and replied, "This is not what I signed up for! I certainly don't remember agreeing to go along with anything that you put your mind to."

Daniel composed himself as his brother walked away and said, "I've always gone along with your ideas and your plans because I thought we were both looking to accomplish the same goals. The things that Dad wanted us to do."

Evan, now pacing around the room, responded to Daniel, "We are still working toward the same goal; that hasn't changed. Sometimes things don't go the way that you expect and you have to make decisions for the greater good. Dad understood that."

"The ends don't always justify the means," replied Daniel. "We have plenty of time to do what needs to be done; we don't have to resort to these types of tactics."

Evan turned around and made his way back to his desk. His baritone, stern voice lightened to an almost comforting level. He politely turned back to Daniel and said, "We've been locked at the hip for a long time. Maybe you should take a little time to figure out if you want to continue working with me on this."

Evan grabbed a cigar that had been sitting on his desk, took a couple of puffs, and said, "You are just as talented as I am; you can go do your own thing. No hard feelings."

Daniel sensed the change of tone in his brother's voice and decided that this was a good time to make his exit. He watched his brother spin his chair back around to look at the monitors, a clear signal that he was done talking.

Before Daniel left, he looked back to the chair and placed his right hand on his chest. Just as calmly as his brother had spoken earlier, Daniel said, "I am the only one in the world who understands the burden of the choices we make." He began to open the door but quickly turned around and said, "Brother or not, I'll stop you from making the wrong choices if I have to."

Daniel Elliott left his brother's office and made his way back through the club to the rear exit, where he expected his car to be waiting for him. Evan Elliott watched him on those same monitors situated behind

Chapter 1

his desk and began to rub his chest. He began to tap and grab one of the chains around his neck. He talked to himself in a very low whispering voice. It was so low it was as much a thought as a statement.

The particular chain that he was handling had a small pendant attached to the end of it. The pendant had six small charms, each with a different shape inscribed into the face. His fingers picked up the slight indentations of the various designs that jetted just above the face of the item.

As he rubbed the pendant, he appeared to go into a light trance as thoughts and memories flooded his mind. He continued to watch Daniel on the monitors, as if waiting for a moment of clarity.

Daniel made his way through the club and reached the back exit where he was met by two of the club's bouncers, Scotty and Jimmy. "Ya leavin' already, Mr. Elliott?" snickered Jimmy.

"We can probably find ya some company for the night, since it looks like you struck out," added Scotty.

Daniel Elliott had never been a fan of Scotty or Jimmy. The clean smell of the office had been replaced by the bouncers' odors of sweat and cheap booze. He turned around, shot them an ice-cold stare, and said, "What I want you to do is go get my convertible and bring it to the door; I'm ready to leave. Leo should have it ready by now."

Jimmy looked at Mr. Elliott, got right in his face, and said, "I'm no gopher, Danny Boy. Go find your own damn car."

Red faced, Daniel responded, "You seem to have forgotten who you're talking to! Go bring my car around with a smile on your face, or I will make you go get it with a frown!"

Jimmy Lorenzen was approximately six feet eight inches tall and weighed about 280 pounds. He easily towered over Daniel Elliott, but Daniel would not back down. Jimmy began to remove the rings from his fingers and told Scotty to make sure no one was looking. "When I get done, you're gonna remember that I don't take orders from no rich pricks."

Daniel reached for Jimmy Lorenzen's arm and grabbed his shirt. He recovered his calm demeanor, because he knew that he had everything under control.

Jimmy looked at Daniel's hand on his shirt as Daniel said, "I didn't want it to have to be this way, but you forced my hand. Go pull my car around, now!"

Daniel couldn't believe that Jimmy Lorenzen, a minimum wage club junkie, had the nerve to pick a fight with him. Had he lost his mind? Was he drunk? Regardless, Daniel was confident that he had taken care of the situation.

As Daniel removed his hand, he relaxed and expected to see Jimmy make his way to the door, but he didn't. Jimmy's face was now red with rage and his fist was closed.

"You ignorant bastard, now I'm really gonna kick your ass," snorted Jimmy as he popped his neck and knuckles.

Daniel looked on as it was clear that Jimmy was about to take a swing at him. Daniel's pulse quickened and a sharp fear took hold. What was happening? Had he missed something? Was something different about Jimmy?

Just as Jimmy started to make his move against Daniel, Roger Timmons came around the corner. "What's going on, mates?"

Jimmy quickly stopped his movement toward Daniel, as he recognized Roger's Aussie accent.

Roger was the floor manager of the club. He was also Jimmy and Scotty's boss. Scotty began to slither away, hoping to avoid Roger completely. Jimmy, head and hands lowered, told Roger that he was about to go out back and get Mr. Elliott's car pulled around.

Roger responded, "Betcha were. I'm sure Mr. Elliott is ready to get out of here."

It was a strange feeling for Daniel having Roger Timmons, of all people, come to his aid. It was normally the other way around. Daniel was the one who had talked Evan into letting Roger run the floor of the club. Roger and Daniel had their moments of disagreement in the past, but for the most part, Daniel trusted Roger. Daniel knew that Roger wasn't a threat, so he had always felt comfortable with him.

Roger put his arm around Daniel and said, "What's up with you tonight? You don't look so good."

Daniel replied, "I'm fine; just tired, I guess."

Chapter 1

Roger, startled, said, "I dunno if I've ever seen you or your brother get tired; must be having an off day."

"Maybe you're right; everybody has an off day every now and then."

The problem was that Daniel Elliott didn't have off days, he didn't get tired, and he didn't have problems with guys like Jimmy Lorenzen. Something wasn't right. Daniel just wanted to get away from the club and go somewhere to think.

Roger walked out the back door with Daniel and asked him where he was headed. Daniel told him that he was going out to their spot on the Potomac to look at the stars. That spot was famous for the Elliotts' after-club parties, but it was also a place that Daniel could find the quiet that he needed. Roger told Daniel that he wished he could go out there with him, but he had to finish up at the club.

Jimmy pulled Daniel's car to the door and headed back into the club, but not before bumping into Daniel on the way. "Sorry about that, sir. I just don't know my own size," chuckled Jimmy. Daniel let it go and got into his car to begin his drive to the Potomac.

Before he pulled away, he yelled back to Roger, "Thanks for the help! I probably won't be seeing you for a while, so take care."

Roger, a partial smile on this face, yelled back, "No worries! I'm sure I'll see you sooner than you think."

As Roger watched Daniel pull from the parking lot, he was startled by a voice from the club. "Roger! You've got a call!"

Daniel had a good thirty minutes to drive before he reached his destination by the river. Daniel replayed his talk with Evan over and over in his mind. Would it really be that easy to move away from his brother? Was Evan going to take the talk seriously? Why did he suddenly have this strange feeling of dread, and why did he have such a problem getting Jimmy Lorenzen to do what he wanted him to do?

A lack of confidence and anxiety had never been problems for Daniel, but something just seemed different now. Daniel just wanted to get to his favorite spot on the river and figure things out. It was a nice clearing, far away from the heavy lights of the city, and it was the perfect location for spotting stars and relaxing. As he sped his way through traffic, he could see the small side road that would take him to the river.

A Mosquito Bite

Daniel was happy to see that he was the only one there. It was a cool, clear night and he could see plenty of stars in the sky. He could spend hours looking up at the dark and speckled nighttime sky and think about all that was out there. He stopped his car, turned off the engine, and decided to lie on the hood to get a better view. The warmth of the engine could still be felt on his back as he took his place. The rush of the water mellowed the sounds of the woods around him.

This was not a night to be pondering the universe; it was a night for decisions about his future. Was it time to break apart from his brother? He began to question himself. Maybe he shouldn't have threatened Evan before he left the club. The last thing he wanted was to start a war with his own brother; but he knew what Evan was capable of and that scared him.

As Daniel sat and watched the stars twinkle in the sky, he felt a small mosquito land on his arm. As he looked over at it, he felt a small tap where the bug had landed. He swatted the mosquito away and looked down at his arm. It began to swell around the area of the bite.

For most people, a mosquito bite and the light swell that it can cause would not be a big deal, but for Daniel Elliott, a sense of panic that he had never felt before engulfed his entire body. He now knew why he was so off and why Jimmy Lorenzen had caused him problems earlier in the night. Daniel began to rummage through all of his pockets. His manic search was no different than an asthmatic searching for his inhaler during an attack. Daniel mumbled to himself, "Where the hell is it?"

A bright light had sneaked up behind Daniel as he was searching his pockets. A black sedan had pulled up behind him and the headlights blinded Daniel. The car came to a slow stop, and Daniel looked to see who was driving. A man stepped from the vehicle and made his way to Daniel's car.

Daniel, his eyes now focused from the lights on the sedan, yelled to the man, "Roger, is that you?"

It was Roger Timmons from the club. Daniel, now relaxed, asked, "What are you doing out here? Decide to look at some stars with me?"

"No, mate, I'm not here to look at stars, just to take care of some business."

Chapter 1

"What kind of business could you possibly have out here?" replied Daniel.

Roger slowly walked toward Daniel while reaching for something in his pocket. He pulled the object from his coat and pointed it directly at him. It was a small revolver and the hammer was cocked.

Daniel mustered up as much confidence as he could and demanded that Roger lower his weapon. "Are you a fool? You know you can't hurt me with that thing. Who put you up to this?"

Roger, with a small smirk, stared back at Daniel and said, "What's wrong, mate? Can't you tell what I'm thinkin' or don't you have the juice anymore?"

Daniel responded, "I've always helped you out and this is how you repay me! Who is making you do this?"

Daniel knew that his threats were useless at this point, so he decided to make one last play. "I'm warning you. You don't know what you're doing, and I won't forget this." Daniel slowly reached his hand up to his chest and stared back at Roger.

"I'm not being controlled to do anythin'. I'm doin' this because I'm good at it and I get the job done." Roger shook his head as he saw Daniel's hand come up. "By the way, you can stop clutchin' your chest; it's nothin' more than a paperweight now."

Daniel's eyes grew large as the realization of what was happening took hold. Roger walked within a couple of feet of him and pointed the gun right at his head. Daniel moved back as close to the river as he could get without falling in. "You don't have to do this, Roger! We can work something out!" exclaimed Daniel.

"It's already worked out, mate, and it's no bull dust; you're gonna miss out on all the fun to come."

A shot rang out at the secluded location just beside the Potomac. Roger had squeezed the trigger and put a bullet between the eyes of Daniel Elliott. Daniel fell backward into the river, his limp body being dragged by the current. He slowly sank out of sight, blood pouring from his wound.

Roger walked back to his sedan and drove away from the crime scene. He wasn't in a rush or flustered at all. He knew that he would never be brought to justice for the murder that he had just committed, and he took a sick joy out of that knowledge.

Roger reached the edge of town and found a pay phone located at the corner of an old, closed-down gas station. He dialed the number he was instructed to use and waited for an answer. A deep baritone voice asked, "Is it done?"

Roger replied, "Yes sir, Mr. Elliott. I put a bullet between his eyes, just like you wanted."

"Good job. Did you tell him that I had sent you?"

"I didn' have to, boss. By the look on his face, he knew. He knew you were the only one that could do that to him."

Evan was silent on the line for a moment, and Roger asked, "You still there?"

Evan replied, "Give me a minute. It's not every day that you kill your own brother." There was another short pause before Evan added, "It's time to change the world."

Chapter 2

HISTORY LESSONS

"Ten minutes to shutdown. Finish your work and clean up your areas!" shouted the lead supervisor to his workforce. "No sneaking out early; we need to meet those quotas."

The last thing the lead supervisor for the largest uniform manufacturer in the South wanted to do was inform his bosses that they missed their quota for production. Luckily for Mr. Jim Dial, today had gone well on the shop floor and he had nothing but good news to report.

Mr. Dial was the lead supervisor for Assembly Area 12 at Manufacturing Hub 4 in Sector 37 of the South region of Continent 4, or C4 for short. Continent 4 was the term used to describe the area of the former United States of America. The year was 2185, and the world that Daniel Elliott knew in 1984 was all but gone.

"Stop loading those uniforms, 14561, and start cleaning up; this place needs to be topnotch before the next shift gets here!" exclaimed Mr. Dial.

"Sorry, I was concentrating on my work so much, I didn't realize it was so late," replied Ms. April 14561.

"No problem," said Mr. Dial. "Just hurry up and get your machine ready for the next shift."

April had worked at Manufacturing Hub 4 since she was nineteen years old. It was a modernized building, and the equipment was built with safety in mind for the employees. Rows and rows of equipment lined the aisles of the factory, and hundreds of personnel worked the cells along them.

Chapter 2

She had been loading cloth uniforms into a machine that would correctly size and mark them for the area of the world to which they would later be sent. It was an efficient setup where everyone had a job to do and it was expected to be done.

It was a meager job, but she did it to the best of her ability every day. April, now thirty-two years old, had become robotic in her daily tasks—the same work, at the same station, day after day. The same could be said of anyone at the hub.

"What are you having for dinner tonight?" asked Paula Anderson. Paula had worked beside April at station B42 for the last eight years. Paula was a friendly person and tried to talk to April as often as she could. April, on the other hand, was a quiet worker and would speak only when spoken to.

"Well, it's Saturday night, so I believe we're scheduled for sub-meal 16."

"That sounds good; I think our housing district is having sub-meal 11," replied Paula. "I can't stand roasted chicken, but I'll make up for it with Sunday's meal."

"That's not my favorite either, but at least it isn't one of those protein shake meals where you have to drink your dinner."

The protein shakes were only used when a district ran out of rations, and that was only toward the end of the month. For tonight, the ladies would be able to enjoy a nice mix of meat and vegetables, prepared by the chefs of their particular housing districts. They both needed to get a move on to make sure they didn't miss the dinner bell.

"Hope you have a nice day of rest, and tell the boys I hope they play well tomorrow!" exclaimed Paula as she made her way out the front door of Hub 4.

"You too, and I'll let Matt and Connor know you're rooting for them."

April made her way down the front stairs of the uniform plant that she had worked at for thirteen years and proceeded to make the 1.5-mile walk home to check on her two boys. Manufacturing Hub 4 was a large brick building with few windows and few distinguishing marks beyond the large stencils of "Hub 4 / Sector 37." The building was the same color and shape as the building beside it, a medical complex, and the same color and shape as the building across the street, a security station. In fact, the structure and style of all the buildings in Sector 37 were almost identical, except for their functional markings.

The walkways were packed with local citizens going to and from their respective jobs. It resembled a swarm of multicolored butterflies moving about in formation. Each citizen's dress was color coordinated to match the type of job he or she was trained to do. For example, a factory worker, like April, wore a darker gray, while doctors wore a traditional white. All was well organized and laid out for the citizens.

For someone who did not know this area, it would be very difficult to determine where you were or where you were going, but for April, it was no problem at all. She had lived and functioned in this area for a long time. She could walk to her housing complex with her eyes closed.

Any remnants from the world of the 1980s were just a distant folktale to the people of 2185. There were no personal vehicles, only sectional transporters. There were no personal residencies, only controlled housing apartments.

There was no choice in occupation. Residents were allowed to go to school until eighteen and were then separated into determined groups either selected for higher education or for labor jobs, like the one April had. Students who excelled in math and science might be forced into a medical profession or engineering profession. Students who had skills with the written word might move on to get an education in journalism, a controlled style of journalism where all printed writing was reviewed and validated for content before reaching citizens of a sector.

Strong or athletic citizens might be moved into security professions and dispersed among the many sectors. The disabled or those deemed a burden to society lived under a different set of rules. All roles were determined by an all-world governing power, with little concern for individual preference or desire.

April was forced to walk by a security post stationed just outside of her housing complex manned by two guards, Brett and Sam. The post was positioned so that anyone entering or leaving the building would

Chapter 2

be checked in or out. Multiple video cameras and windows lined the building's face, and the smell of coffee was always present.

Both guards were quite large, a prerequisite for a security guard, but their personalities were quite different. April had no problems with Sam. He was a respectful man and had always been very nice to her, but Brett was a different story. The small bit of power that he wielded went straight to his head, and he had no problem abusing that power whenever he felt like it. April dreaded having to listen to Brett's sarcastic, misogynistic comments.

"Planning to head on up for dinner?" inquired Brett.

April hastily replied, "Of course I am; the same as every day."

Brett, rubbed his chest, smirked, and offered his assistance. "Maybe I'll come up later tonight and give you some dessert. What time do your boys go to bed now?"

Sam stepped in and played interference, as usual. "Now Brett, you know you can't leave the post in the middle of the night. What if the sector leader comes by for a visit and sees you gone?"

Just as Sam finished his thought, a loud jingle filled the air. It sounded like giant wind chimes had flooded the area, and once it stopped, everyone stood at attention and looked to the sky. April was frozen, along with the guards, as they awaited the imminent announcement. It was like an echo from the past, but the comments were as clear as speaking to someone on the telephone.

"Let us take this opportunity to pause and give thanks to the Council of Compassion and World Order and our Supreme Leader Minister Hathmec. Without our esteemed leadership, where would we all be?"

A round of applause and cheering bounced from the walls of the buildings that made up Sector 37. April, with little enthusiasm, clapped her hands until the surrounding areas came back to normality. As if Minister Hathmec or the council needed more reassurance of their place in the world, they certainly didn't need the applause of the hardworking people of Sector 37. This was the CCWO's world, and everyone else just lived in it.

The daily affirmation was complete, and April slinked away from the security post and headed up to her apartment on the ninth floor of

Housing Complex 22. Before leaving, she gave a quick wink to Sam, just as a thank-you for getting Brett's attention away from her.

Not that she was interested in Sam, but he was one of the nicer men she had ever known. April tried to avoid most of the security personnel in her sector; they all seemed to feel privileged in some way, but Sam actually cared about people. As part of Sector 37's security team, Sam was never one to use force as a first resort. In a different time, Sam and April would have probably gravitated toward a relationship.

Relationships of any type were difficult in the year 2185. Conventional marriage was regulated. You were allowed to set up a contract between a man and a woman, but the government gave the final authorization to allow its completion. No unauthorized breeding would be tolerated. Couples were forced to go through a battery of physical and mental tests before permission would be granted to bring a new child into the world.

The CCWO had placed these restrictions on its citizens after years of population booms and the introduction of new strains of superviruses to its citizens. The system was very slow and cumbersome. Most couples waited up to a year to get permission to have a child. For couples that did not follow these guidelines, the repercussions were severe. This included sterilization, confinement, exile, and, in some cases, death. The unregulated child would be moved into a caretaker's home. In extreme cases, the child might be sent to a government citizen camp.

The concept of familial labels had also vanished. There were no longer the labels of father, mother, son, daughter, and brother or sister. Certain people were caretakers of younger or older persons as assigned by the government. For the most part, they did try to keep breeding partners and those offspring together, but this was not always the case, depending on the greater good. In fact, over the last thirty-five years, the idea of a last name had been removed as a social norm. April's full name was April 14561; a last name replaced by a random number.

For someone born within the last thirty-five years, having a random number for a last name was not a big deal. They didn't know any better. They went on about their predetermined lives and had no idea of what they might be missing. April, on the other hand, had an idea of what could be.

Chapter 2

April was a beautiful woman. Long blond hair accentuated her lean five-foot six-inch frame. She completed school and had expected her life to take the path of a scholar. She was a creative and fearless teenager. She excelled in math and science, an accomplished student. She was a bit of a troublemaker in her younger days, but she had the respect of her teachers and friends. Big things were expected to consume the life of April 14561, but they didn't. She was a factory worker with a desire for more.

She wanted more from life for her and her kids, and in her heart, she knew that life would eventually find her. April 14561 was a woman on a clock. She knew that her time was coming; she just didn't know when. For now, she just continued to live day-to-day, waiting for her chance.

As April opened the door to her apartment, she braced for the impending attack of two very lively and spirited young men. She walked into the main living quarters and noticed a pile of books lying on the small couch in the center of the room. She thought, *I know Connor's here.*

A dim light flickered just past a small bookshelf, illuminating a small kitchen and dining table. Just a few cupboards and a refrigerant unit to hold snacks were allowed in the housing complex apartments. April picked up the fresh aroma of pine and lemons as she made her way past the couch. The complex sterilization team had been there earlier in the day. She wasn't worried; the boys' natural stink would have it back to normal in less than a day.

April peeked into her bedroom to see if the boys were hiding in there, but no luck. The shades were pulled on her only room window and the clothes she had left out on the bed that morning had been removed by the same pine and lemon team. She looked across her small dresser and wondered what other items had been moved while she was at work. She didn't worry about jewelry or family heirlooms, as those were not permitted for a factory laborer. She left her one area of the apartment that was hers alone and proceeded to the far end of the home. The boys' room was the only other spot to check in the apartment, but before she could get to the door, it flew wide open.

"Where you been?" asked Connor.

"Yeah, dinner will be here any minute. You don't want to have to wait for the second go-around; it's always cold!" exclaimed Matthew.

April responded as any good mother—or in this case, caretaker—would have responded: she changed the subject to what the boys had been doing.

"Have you finished your schoolwork?"

Both of the boys responded, "Yessssss."

"Have you finished your chores?"

Another prolonged response: "Yessssss."

"Have you finished the reading I told you to have done before I got home tonight?"

The boys looked at each other and then back to April. Connor spoke up first: "Sure we have—a very interesting read about the things that we were reading about."

April replied, "That's a pretty pathetic response. Can you tell me what the reading was about or even the year that it refers to?"

Connor was a bright, energetic, and opinionated fourteen-year-old. People always mistook Connor for being older than fourteen because of his size. "You must be eighteen by now," neighbors told him. He was already six feet three inches tall and towered over April. His size got him into trouble at times.

Controlling his emotions was not Connor's strong suit; he had quite a temper. This temper had gotten him into trouble at school and with April more than once. He wasn't one to back away from confrontation. Connor's frustrations clouded his judgment at times, which led him to make bad decisions.

His short blond hair was combed just to the right of his freckled face. He was dressed in the standard school uniform that every student of the time was made to wear. Brown slacks, a red buttoned shirt, and brown ankle boots made up his look. The red shirt symbolized the district they lived in, similar to a high school's primary colors.

Connor enjoyed changing up his clothes to look like the people he had read about from the 1950s. He tried to turn the bottom of his pants legs up like the bikers from the era, and he even attempted to slick his

Chapter 2

hair back. This was unacceptable in school, so he would only wear those types of things at home.

"Come on, April," spouted Connor. "The 1990s are so boring."

"Yeah, can't we read some more about the 1960s or 1970s? Those decades are actually interesting," said Matthew.

"Or even something about the 1950s," added Connor.

Matthew was also an extremely intelligent, well-spoken, and handsome fourteen-year-old boy. No one would mistake him for an eighteen-year-old, but he was still a good size for his age. A very faint sprinkling of facial hair had started to pop up on Matthew's face, which didn't match the lanky legs and thin frame of his body.

Everyone thought that Connor was Matthew's older sibling, but they were only a couple of days apart in their ages. The extra head of height that Connor had on Matthew helped perpetuate those thoughts.

To talk to Matthew for an extended time, one would forget that he was only fourteen. It was like speaking to a thirty-year-old adult. He was the more timid of the two boys. He had always felt out of place at school, with his peers, and with the girls in his class. Matthew felt most comfortable when he was with Connor and April. It was like being in a family.

While Connor was still wearing his school uniform when April arrived home, Matthew had already changed into his assigned home clothes. Matthew's skinny legs poked out from the knee-length black shorts he was wearing. He also donned a skintight shirt that he normally wore only while playing ball in the park.

While most people believed that Matthew and Connor were brothers, Connor was the only true blood-son of April. Connor had always been the more confident of the two boys, and Matthew usually followed his lead. Matthew was handed over to April for her to act as his caretaker because Matthew was an orphan. He had been placed with April just a few months after she had given birth to Connor. April treated both of the boys as equals and never showed favoritism to either boy.

Connor and Matthew had a strong bond, regardless of blood relation. Matthew followed Connor's lead when it came to dealing with social situations and dealing with others their own age. Connor could physically overpower Matthew, but Matthew had the intelligence and emotional maturity to offset Connor's immature impulses. They made a good team, and whether they would admit it or not, they cared for each other.

While Connor felt that April took Matthew's side on too many issues, Matthew always doubted whether April could care for him as much as her real son. April never saw the distinction and loved both of her sons as if she had given birth to them. It wasn't a family of 1984, but it was their family.

"I told you that you could read some more about the mid-1900s next week. You need to finish up the books on the 1990s first," continued April.

A knock was heard at the door. Two quick knocks, a slight pause, and then another quick knock. April and Matthew made their way to the door and opened it to see one of the complex's servers with his dinner cart in tow.

"Those boys hungry tonight?" asked the server.

"Oh, I'm sure they'll clean their plates," replied April. "Will you be coming back around for seconds?"

The server looked at the checklist he always carried and told April that he doubted it. The complex had been running low on everything the last few weeks. He apologized and went about his route.

Each complex had a number of breakfast and dinner servers that brought around the designated plates to each apartment. The residents ate the prepared meal, based on a predetermined schedule, cleared their plates, and placed them outside their doors for pickup.

This particular meal consisted of a piece of baked ham, processed green beans, cheese pasta, a hard-shelled roll, and to top it off, an energy drink. The energy drink was a combination of flavored water and sweetener. Citizens either ate what was brought or they were stuck eating the limited rations in the apartment kitchen.

There were few options for citizens to buy their own food in Sector 37. Most kitchens had a small stock of drinks, bottled water, and juice. You could find some breakfast bars and snack items, mostly high-protein supplements and chewable tablets. The council did not believe in

Chapter 2

the distribution of fresh fruit or vegetables beyond those served in the daily meals. A public health issue was how they justified it.

"Sub-meal 16 again," complained Connor. "I hate ham and beans."

"It's better than that casserole stuff we had last night," replied Matthew.

"True, but I really wanted some zesty chicken or pizza tonight."

April interrupted. "Sorry boys, pizza and chicken aren't on the menu for another couple of weeks."

The three continued to eat their dinners and discussed the day's events. April told the boys about her day at work and how one of her coworkers had accidently come back from break three minutes late. Luckily, it was his first offense, so he only got a summons to appear before the district council.

"He got lucky. They could have sent him to one of those camps," said April. "What happened at school today?"

Before the entire question could get out of her mouth, Matthew responded, "Connor was sent to the principal's office for talking back to Ms. Beatle."

Connor grunted, "Thanks."

April frowned and bit back at Connor. "Please tell me you did exactly what the principal told you to do."

Connor, head dipped and still grunting, responded, "Yes, I always do exactly what I'm told to do by Principal Abbott, just like you told me. He didn't even try to use his pendant; he just gave me a lecture about not talking back to authority and made me polish his Educator of the Year award."

"You have to be more careful. If anyone ever finds out that you two are immune to the controllers, we will all be in big trouble. Next thing you're gonna tell me is you've been spouting off about the books I've been letting you read."

A wry smile came back to Connor's face as he glanced at Matthew. Matthew knew what was about to come and proceeded to tell April of his own mistake. He explained that he had mentioned to a couple of the guys in class that he had some old history books hidden at the apartment.

April raised her hands to her forehead and rested it on the table. She didn't say anything for a moment. "They didn't even believe him. They thought he was making things up to impress some chicks," said Connor.

Matthew interrupted and said, "I can't just sit there and let them say things that aren't true in class. The history books that you have us read just don't make any sense next to what we learn in school."

April, her head pulled back up from the table, glared at both of the boys and spoke with conviction. "I thought you boys were old enough to understand what I am trying to do for you. The greatest scholars and historians of our time would love to get their hands on the information in those books. It's the truth of our past, and we have it right in front of us."

She started to pick up the empty plates from the table and walked toward the front door, but she quickly turned around and with more force behind her voice exclaimed, "If anyone finds out that we have these books, we will get a knock at our door one night and be taken away! Is that what you want?"

Matthew understood the mistake he had made. "Sorry, I just got carried away; it won't happen again. You can count on us."

"Both of you go on to your room and get to reading tonight's lesson and I'll get dinner cleaned up. And another thing: we aren't called chicks; it is either girls or women. You've got to stop using slang words from those books."

The boys started to make their way to their room and heard April hand out one more order. "You have three hours before the lights are to be off, so don't dawdle."

The boys entered their shared room. It was twelve feet by twelve feet in size, with a bunk bed in the far corner. Connor had the top bunk because Matthew was afraid of heights. Across from the bed, just under the room's only window, sat an old wood desk with two swivel chairs, one for each boy. This was the hiding spot for the old history books that April presented to the boys every few weeks.

Neither boy knew where the books had come from; April said that it didn't matter, just that they couldn't tell anyone they existed. Both boys

Chapter 2

had been reading about American history from the start of the 1770s revolution up to the late 1900s.

It was so strange for them to read about patriots and civil rights leaders from the past. Everything they had learned in school about history had revolved around the Supreme Leader and the CCWO. It was clear to both of them that history was being altered in the classroom, and they both wanted to know why, but for different reasons.

Before the boys grabbed their books to start reading, Connor popped Matthew a good one in the arm. "That's for telling about the principal, you prick."

Matthew responded in kind, without near the pop, and backed away to the desk.

"Sorry, it just kind of slipped out."

Connor plopped down in his desk chair and shook his head. "I don't know why she gets so worried about this stuff. Does she really think masked men are going to come in here and take us all away?"

Matthew ignored Connor's question and said, "It says here that something called the Internet was really popular in the 1990s and people had their own computers at their homes."

Connor, perplexed, flipped over to the same page. "How did they have computers in their homes back then and we can only use computers at school? It doesn't make sense."

Matthew backed up in his desk chair and responded, "It makes sense if you listen to what April has been telling us. We're living in a time that is totally different from what our ancestors lived in."

Matthew paused a moment and then explained that he didn't think the government was set up the same way in the past as it was now. He couldn't find one thing in the history books about a Supreme Leader or any World Council.

Connor had no problems whipping Matthew in a physical altercation, but he struggled when trying to match his logic. He couldn't think of a good counterpoint to Matthew's explanation, so he repeated his standard responses. He reminded Matthew about all of the wars they had read about in the 1920s, 1940s, 1950s, and 1960s.

"They even had one in the 1990s. It was short, but we don't have people killing each other here for no good reason, and the government takes care of us. Based on what I've read, you were just on your own back then."

Matthew began to argue with Connor, but didn't see the point. They had disagreed on these books for months and he didn't want Connor to think that he was trying to outsmart him. Matthew could read and absorb information much faster than Connor, so he backed off.

Matthew continued reading for the next couple of hours about the 1990s. He read about the types of music people liked, the art that was popular at the time, and the clever inventions that were developed. Through the entire lesson, he could only think about what it would have been like to live in those times and why things were so different now.

Connor and Matthew finished up their lesson at 9:45, so they had only fifteen minutes to get ready for bed. It was lights out at 10:00 p.m. for Sector 37. The boys shared a bathroom, so it was always an all-out fight to be the first to use the sink and the toilet. Connor usually won, but for some reason, Matthew had a bit more fire tonight and he outdueled Connor for the sink. As Connor impatiently waited his turn for the bathroom, he decided to bother Matthew with questions that were difficult to answer with toothpaste in your mouth.

"So what are we doing tomorrow for the Day of Rest?"

Matthew responded as he had so many other times to the same question: "Sactor Perk fur some bawll." Matthew had actually said, "Sector Park for some ball."

Connor laughed and said, "Sounds good, but you know you're gonna get your butt kicked again."

After a moment of loud spitting and gargling, Matthew emerged from the bathroom and jumped into his bed. Connor looked over at him as he entered the bathroom, and Matthew whispered, "We'll see about that."

Both boys had been asleep for about an hour when Connor was awakened by a bright light coming through their bedroom window. He poured himself from his bed and made his way to the window. It was unusual to see any lights, besides streetlights, after the 10:00 p.m. curfew. As he reached the window, he looked to the warehouse building that was to the

Chapter 2

left of their apartment complex. This was one of the only buildings in the area that didn't look like the others. It was supposed to be torn down a few weeks before, but for some reason, it was still standing.

Connor could see a bright, yellow, pulsating light coming from the top floor of the old building. He could also hear sounds from the window, like a generator being cranked or the spin of a tire on the road.

"What are you doing up? We're supposed to be in bed."

"Shut up," responded Connor, as he intently looked to the old building as the light continued to pop from it. Matthew also fell from his bed and moved to Connor's side.

"What do you think it is?"

Connor responded, "I don't know, but I see four guards heading over there."

Connor grabbed Matthew by the shoulders and pulled him lower to the edge of the window. He popped him on the top of the head and told him that if those guards saw them up after ten, it would be their butts in a sling.

The boys looked back to the warehouse window and could see a man staring back at them. He had a bald head and was wearing black glasses. He kept his position, looking out toward the boys for several seconds.

"He can't see us, can he?"

Suddenly, the man in the window pulled down a shade and he was gone, along with the light and noise. Matthew looked at Connor and with a sigh said, "We could see him. Why wouldn't he be able to see us?"

The boys decided to stay up for another hour to see the man brought from the building by the four guards who had entered, but they never saw anyone leave. The boys wanted to know if the man had been arrested and what had created that bright light.

None of those questions would be answered that night, however, so they decided to go back to bed. They would have a big day at the park tomorrow and needed their rest. They both decided that they could do some investigating of the building tomorrow. For now, the boys were in bed, and another day in Sector 37 faded away.

Chapter 3

BEAMBALL

"Wake up, Matt! We're gonna be late for the game," said a wide-eyed and hyper Connor to the lump still slumped into his covers.

"What time is it?" asked a sleepy Matthew.

"It's nine, and our game starts at nine thirty. Get your clothes on, eat the breakfast bar April left for you, and let's get to the transport."

Matthew jumped from his bed and started rooting around in his closet for his best set of ball clothes. Today was a big game. This was a chance to make up for the repeated losses to Sector 39 over the last two years. As Matthew looked through the wreck of a closet that he and Connor shared, Connor made his way to the kitchen to get Matthew's pastry that the breakfast servers had left an hour ago.

Connor ran into the bedroom. "It's still pretty warm, and I only spit on it once, so it should be good."

Matthew struggled to pull his red ball shirt over his head, but he started to make his way to the front door, regardless. He did not want to miss this game.

Connor handed Matthew his breakfast, grabbed his key to the apartment and his sector ID, and made sure he had some credits for the transport, and the boys were out the door.

"Race you to the bottom," yelled out Connor, already halfway down the first flight. Matthew gave chase, but he was not as fast as Connor in a fair race, much less when Connor cheated.

The boys ran a couple of blocks to the closest transport station and saw their ride pulling up, just as they pulled out the credits needed

Chapter 3

for the payment to travel. A credit was much like a coin, but there was only one coin per person and a digital readout told how many credits you had. Kids the age of Connor and Matthew were given ten credits a month for travel on the sector transports.

As the boys loaded onto the crowded transport, Matthew questioned Connor about the credits left for the month. It looked like they had enough credits to get back to the park one more time that month. The boys always went everywhere together, so neither had any extra credits for the last week of the month.

Matthew asked, "How we gonna get to the park?"

Connor replied, "Walk, I guess."

The boys both laughed out loud, knowing it was a good fifteen miles to the park. It took two changeovers on the transport system just to get there. They hoped that the transports were all on schedule so they wouldn't be late for the game.

The transport system between the sectors was designed based on the old highway system. Instead of roads where cars and trucks had traveled between locations, there was a central system with thousands of interconnecting lines. Unlike the days of the old railroad system, these transports ran on magnetized plates and speeds of over one hundred miles per hour. Ninety-nine percent of the population used this for travel, so they had to be fast. They could best be described as an aboveground subway, without the graffiti.

The boys had rushed out of the apartment so fast they had almost forgotten about the mysterious man in the warehouse window. As Matthew reviewed his plans for the approaching game, it hit him that he and Connor had some detective work to take care of after the game.

"Are we gonna check out that warehouse when we get back home?" asked Matthew.

"Come on, do you really want to see if we can find some old guy that was staring at us through a window?"

Matthew was determined to find out what had gone on the night before. He wanted to know what that light was and if the old man had been taken by the sector security team. For some reason, he wanted to know who he was.

The transport came to an abrupt stop without making a sound. It was time to jump on the last connection to the park. The boys followed the mass of citizens to the adjoining transport. For the volume of people moving, there was not a lot of conversation. People knew where they were going and had little time to talk to each other. The prevailing sounds came from the monitors in the station that repeatedly showed the Supreme Leader and the World Council helping their fellow citizens.

"We'll take a look around when we get back," said Connor. "We're only a few minutes from the park and we need to concentrate on the game." With that, the boys stopped talking about the strange man in the warehouse and talked strategy for the game.

Connor, the gambler of the two, made the first suggestion. "We need to go long early and build up a lead. Sector 39 will start making mistakes if they think we're gonna run up the score."

Matthew, the planner and more analytical of the two, was not thrilled with the plan. "We can't go long early against these guys. We're not as athletic as they are. We need to start conservative and try to wear 'em down."

Connor punched Matthew in the arm and announced to the entire transport, "This guy is such a wimp! Good thing I'm the captain of the team." He got a couple of looks from girls at the front of the cabin, but everyone else ignored him.

The final transport pulled up to the last stop on the boys' journey. Just a quick sprint down to the corner and the boys would reach the park. They jockeyed around other passengers waiting for their rides and wound their way past the main transport station's building.

Suddenly, as if a pop-up book had been opened, the landscape turned from the brown brick and steel of a functioning city to the green and wide-open spaces of a national park. The boys ran through the main gate and were greeted with perfectly maintained green grass, large oak trees with extended limbs and lightly colored leaves, and a backdrop of rolling hills and stone peaks.

The park was a true escape from the day-to-day reality of school and work for the local communities, and today was no different. The

Chapter 3

park was packed to capacity with hikers, bike riders, and bird watchers, and of course the ball fields buzzed with anticipation awaiting the start of the weekly beamball matchups. The contradiction of odors from the sterilized district hubs of the city to the smell of fresh mowed grass, dandelions, and wood bark was inescapable.

The visual differences were not limited to the physical surroundings, as people in the park were allowed to wear clothing of their own. You couldn't tell a factory worker from an engineer on the Day of Rest. Security was tight at the park. They wanted to make sure that no one strayed too far from the community norm.

Beamball was the only government-sanctioned sport left for school-age young adults to play in the year 2185. It had been around for thirty years and was as popular as ever. The boys ran up to Field 12 and saw the rest of their team stretching and prepping for the game.

"Where have you two been? I thought we were gonna have to forfeit the game," said Coach Jenkins.

Matthew explained that the transports were running behind, and Connor explained that Matthew was running behind.

Coach Jenkins only took this job with the school to bolster his own work history, so he didn't take it too seriously. He never had the boys run laps or sprints as a punishment; he just wanted to look good for the Sector 37 school board. He wasn't much of a coach, and the small blue whistle around his neck didn't disguise that he would be more comfortable teaching an English class. His cardigan sweater and brown loafers did not match the athletic theme of the day.

"All right, boys, as you know, we are playing Sector 39's top team. They've beaten us three times in a row, so it's important to make me look good today." The boys looked at Coach Jenkins, and he revised his previous comment: "I mean, I just really want you guys to get that good feeling of a victory this time." Coach pulled out a clipboard and pointed it at Connor. "Now, you have to look out for 32451; he killed us last time."

Rocky 32451 was Sector 39's best disruptor. This was one large fourteen-year-old. He made Connor look small. Rocky was all of six feet five inches and 230 pounds of pure muscle, and he was as fast as a transport on All Hathmec's Day. He was, by far, the most feared disruptor in all of the age twelve to fourteen beamball divisions.

The field stands were full of onlookers, family, and fans of this division's teams. April was missing from that group. She had to get up early to run errands and would not make the game. She trusted the boys to get to and from the games on their own, and she had promised not to miss any of the championship tournament games that would be played in a few weeks.

Coach Jenkins gave his final instructions to the boys of Sector 37 and then read off the lineups for the start of the game.

"42713 and 21874, you are marksmen on both offense and defense, so get your equipment and head to the lines. 57432, 19754, 62487, and 32741, you're the trackers, so take the field. 24612, you are at tosser, as usual, so go ahead and grab the ball and head to the base outline. We get to go first."

Coach Jenkins looked around at the remaining players and said, "You three are my trailers, so get ready to go in after our offensive series is done."

Coach Jenkins had a solid team overall, no thanks to his leadership. He had placed Mark and Brett, two of the most experienced thirteen-year-old marksmen, into position to help guard and defend the tosser's passes. He had four very speedy trackers in Jim, Ty, Lynn, and Andy, who would be attempting to catch the tosser's throws. All four of them were in their last year in this division.

Connor had been placed at tosser and was the team captain. His size and strength made him the perfect tosser. He could throw a ball sixty yards on a dime and could avoid the rush of the disruptor as well as anyone in the league. Matthew was stuck with Jant and Que as the defensive trailers, not a glamour position, but an important one.

The game was about to begin when Coach Jenkins noticed that someone had sneaked up behind him on the sidelines. Her heels sank into the soft ground of the field and the wind struggled to remove the small bonnet perched atop her head. It was Superintendent Margaret Casey, and she was carrying a small black notebook with several pieces of paper in it.

Chapter 3

"Superintendent Casey, to what do I owe the pleasure?" asked Jenkins.

Ms. Casey responded, "I am just here to make sure that all of our kids are eligible to play, academically. It looks like 24612 and 25871 have had some discipline issues recently."

Coach Jenkins looked at the papers and said, "That's Connor and Matthew, superintendent. I can probably replace Matthew, but I need Connor; he's the best player we have. You see, he plays the tosser position, and if you don't have a good tosser, you may as well forfeit the game."

Superintendent Casey looked around the field at the players preparing for the game and turned back to Coach Jenkins. "Well, I don't want to hurt the team, coach, especially since I do not necessarily like my counterpart in Sector 39."

Coach Jenkins, a sincere look of relief on his face, replied, "Thank you, Ms. Casey. We won't let you down. We're going to pour it on those Sector 39 boys."

"I've never really watched any of these beamball games, coach. I would like to know what all the fuss is about." Superintendent Casey walked to the edge of the field and looked at Connor. "Can you tell me what he is trying to do?"

Considering Superintendent Casey held the success of his team in her hands, Coach Jenkins decided to take the time to explain the game to his boss.

"You see, Ms. Casey, that is our tosser, Connor. He is the captain of the team and he is leading our offense onto the field." Coach Jenkins picked up a ball made of a yellow-colored rubber compound, just a bit bigger than a cantaloupe. "The tosser is responsible for throwing a beamball, like this one, to one of our four trackers down the field. The goal is to get the ball caught as far down the field as possible. If we catch the ball twenty yards from his throwing location, that box called the beam-base, we get twenty points."

Ms. Casey asked, "That's all you have to do is throw and catch a ball? I thought it was more complicated than that."

Coach Jenkins replied, "Oh, it is much more difficult than that. Look down the sidelines along both sides of the field. Do you see those two boys with the equipment on their wrists?"

Ms. Casey looked down the near sideline and could see two boys, each with something that looked like a big wristwatch on their arms. "What are those things on their arms?" Coach Jenkins pulled a spare laser tracker from his bag and handed it to her.

"This is a laser tracker, superintendent. Each team has two marksmen trying to either deflect the passed ball away from a tracker or toward a tracker, depending on whether they are on offense or defense."

Ms. Casey, confused, asked, "So they try to blow up the ball with these laser cannons?"

The coach snickered and said, "No, ma'am. The lasers are tuned to only react with the ball, and they will only alter the ball's orientation, not blow it up. Basically, the lasers are a defensive or offensive weapon to keep one team from catching the beamball."

Ms. Casey started to get the idea, but she was still confused about the extra players on the field, so she asked, "What are those three boys from Sector 39 doing on the field with our team's trackers?"

The coach pointed to a line just outside of the beam-base and said, "This is where the defense will use trailers to try to catch passes thrown by the other team. Once Connor releases the ball, they will be able to leave that line and try to catch the ball themselves. If one of them does, they get the points. It doesn't happen very often, but it can change the whole game."

Ms. Casey looked around the field one more time before leaving and asked one final question of the coach: "Who is that very large young man on the field and what does he do?"

She pointed at Rocky 32451 as he flexed his biceps in an attempt to intimidate Sector 37. The coach responded, "That is the primary reason why we haven't beaten Sector 39 the last two years. His name is Rocky and he is Sector 39's disruptor. He is held behind the beam-base line for a random amount of time, anywhere from three to eight seconds. Once he sees the line vanish, he is allowed to go after our tosser. All he has to

Chapter 3

do is touch the tosser to end the play, but he has been known to be a bit rough when he does."

"Well, I will allow Connor and Matthew to play, but if we hear of any more problems coming from those two, I will remove them from the team. In my opinion, it just seems like a waste of time, but good luck anyway."

Coach Jenkins, wanting to focus on the field responded, "Thank you, Ms. Casey. We'll give it all we have." Superintendent Casey walked from the sideline up to the stands to watch the matchup, and the officials signaled the start of the game.

Sector 37 was on offense and Connor started the game off. "Ready, set, go!" Connor dropped five yards behind the box line as Rocky paced and waited to give chase. Connor didn't go for the short, easier pass, but held the ball right up to the point of the disruptor line, disappearing.

Matthew shouted, "Look out, Connor!"

The ball was released, and it was a long pass right down the center of the field. Sector 39's trailers were in pursuit of the trackers, but they were well behind them. Just then, a Sector 39 marksman fired on the beamball and missed. The ball was so high that it was difficult to get a beam on it, but the marksmen kept firing until they saw the yellow ball flashing from a hit. The ball popped off its course and headed down to the right sideline. Two of Sector 37's trackers gave chase and one of the trailers from Sector 39 got close to it.

Connor shouted to Mark and Brett, "Pop it back up! Pop it back up!"

Mark and Brett fired and tried their best, but the ball fell well short of its original target and hit the ground with no one catching it. Sector 39's fans cheered and both teams headed back to the line.

Matthew, still on the sideline with Que and Jant, yelled out to Connor, "Short and steady—we need some points!"

Connor popped back, "Plenty more chances—just need to get the ball higher, you wuss."

Sector 37's first offensive series lasted for seven plays, and they were able to accumulate fifty points. Rocky had not reached Connor, but there was plenty of game left. Matthew took the field as a defensive trailer and did not have a lot of luck. He dropped a ball that would have given his team twenty points and then fell down trying to catch up to a tracker.

Connor continued to give Matt a hard time "Half the girls in our class could have caught that ball. Maybe we should call April to see if she'll fill in for you."

Matthew took it in stride, but as the fourth and final round of the game approached, he started to worry about the outcome.

Coach Jenkins gave a final pep talk to the offense. "We're just a few plays from putting this away, boys. Just keep it in the medium zone and they won't be able to catch us."

Connor confidently led the team to the field for the final time on offense knowing that if they could put together a few points, it would be over. The first six plays of the final round went well, with Sector 37 putting up 120 points. They now held a 480 to 310 lead over Sector 39. Coach Jenkins wanted to retain the lead and play it conservatively, so he called a time-out.

"All right, Connor, just throw it short. Our defense will hold the lead, and we don't want them getting any cheap points."

Connor grunted, "Sure thing, coach."

Connor grew more confident with each stride to the home box and called his trackers over. "We're not going short; we're finishing with a bang. All four of you go deep down the right side."

Jim spoke up. "Coach told us to go short."

Connor grabbed Jim by the shirt, yanked him forward into his face, and barked, "Coach isn't going to be the one that kicks your butt tomorrow in school if you don't go long! Now break!"

Connor took the ball for the final offensive play, and the trackers took off deep down the right side. Coach Jenkins was jumping and yelling on the sidelines, "What are you doing?"

Connor, confidence boiling over, started to pull the ball back to heave it down the field. Just then, the extended right elbow of one Mr. Rocky 32451 crashed into Connor's left temple and the ball went flying wildly into the air. Connor was flat on his back as blood started to stream from his head. All of the Sector 37 trackers ran back to try to

Chapter 3

catch the ball but Sector 39's best marksman had already deflected the pass to his own trailers.

The official called out, "Trailer catch at forty yards; forty points to Sector 39."

Connor picked himself up from the ground as Matthew ran out to check on him. Matthew whispered sarcastically to Connor as he helped him up, "Nice play."

Connor realized that he was bleeding and took a straight line to Sector 39's disruptor and promptly hit him in the back. "That was a cheap shot; you coulda broke my jaw!"

Rocky, unfazed, responded, "If I wanted to break your jaw, I would have, sweetheart. Go cry to somebody else."

Connor's temper got the best of him and he lunged at Rocky. Both boys were on the ground punching at each other as the officials and coaches moved in.

Coach Jenkins yelled, "Break it up!"

The officials blew their whistles and pulled Connor from the clutches of Rocky. The head official said, "The tosser for Sector 37 is ejected from the game for poor sportsmanship and the team is docked fifty points."

Coach Jenkins, irate at the official, ran to him and pleaded, "They were both involved. We shouldn't get punished if they don't."

The official responded, "If you don't get your team to their side of the field in ten seconds, you will forfeit the game. Score is now 430 to 350."

The majority of the members of Sector 37's team began to berate their best player. "Damn, Connor, we're screwed now! What the hell were you thinkin'? We had a chance this time. You blew it!"

Matthew jumped in to defend Connor. "Look, we wouldn't have the lead if it wasn't for Connor, so stop your cryin' and let's go play some defense. We can still win this thing."

Matthew led his defense onto the field knowing that it would be difficult to hold Sector 39 to less than eighty points in the last round of the game.

Matthew shouted out, "Que, you get the right side. Jant, sprint to the middle at release. Tim, put some pressure on him, and keep your hands up."

It seemed like the prospect of losing to Sector 39 again lit a fire under the defense as they played their best round of the day. The entire defense stepped it up, and with only one play remaining, the game was tied at 430 points. Not a great position to be in, but better than trailing.

Coach Jenkins called one final time-out to talk with his team. "Boys, we've played them to a tie, but I don't want a tie. I want a win."

Jim and Andy chimed in, "Come on, guys! Somebody make a play!"

Even Connor was trying to rally the team in his own way. "We got you 430 points; it's your turn."

Coach Jenkins continued, "They have been killing us on the twenty-yard out all game, so look for that."

Matthew said, "I've been trying to cover it, coach, but I'm just too slow to get there in time."

"Then run faster."

"Great, wish I had thought of that," grumbled Matthew.

The boys were about to move back to the field when Matthew noticed a man walking up behind Coach Jenkins. He was partially blocked by the rest of the team, but Matthew could tell that he was bald. He was wearing dark black pants held up with blue suspenders and an old gray T-shirt. There was writing on the T-shirt, but it was faded out. The man walked past the coach and straight toward Matthew. Matthew tried to move back but ran into Que.

The man came closer to Matthew, patted him on the shoulder as he passed, and said, "Good luck."

Matthew looked back at Connor as the man walked away. Connor shouted, "What's wrong with you? Get out there and win this game for me. I mean us."

Matthew tried to focus on the game, but wondered if this was the mysterious man from the warehouse. He had never seen the man before, so why would he wish him luck or pat him on the shoulder? He

Chapter 3

determined that he was just being paranoid and cleared his mind of the questions.

Matthew returned to the home line for the last play of the game. Sector 39 lined up its team and the play began. The trackers took off down the field, and Matthew saw their best catcher break at about twenty yards. The tosser released the ball and Matthew was off toward that twenty-yard mark as fast as he could go. Sector 37's marksmen fired multiple shots at the beamball but came up empty; the ball was on its original trajectory to the tracker.

As Matthew ran toward the twenty-yard mark, he felt different—stronger, lighter, faster—and he was making up ground on the tracker. The ball was in the air, headed into the tracker's hands. The crowd was screaming. Both teams were jumping up and down. Matthew left his feet and dove toward the ball. There was a crash of bones and skin.

Both boys were lying on the field and as they started to get up, the entire crowd grew quiet. Coach Jenkins yelled to the field, "Where's the ball?"

Connor wanted to run onto the field, but he didn't want his team to get disqualified. The officials huddled over the two boys and blocked the crowd's view.

Suddenly, Matthew jumped into the air with the ball safely in his hands, and the head official called out, "Twenty points to Sector 37. Game over!"

The crowds went into a frenzy, and all of Matthew's teammates rushed the field and began to hug and pat Matthew on the back. Coach Jenkins grabbed the ball from Matthew's hand and said, "This is going in our trophy room at the school. How in the world did you get to that ball?"

"I don't know, coach, I just had a rush of energy, I guess."

Connor gave Matthew a hug and whispered in his ear, "Thanks for covering for me. I owe you one."

Matthew couldn't believe what he had done, but he responded as any good brother would. With exaggerated confidence, he said, "I told you I would kick some butt today."

But something wasn't quite right to Matthew. How did he catch up to that ball and what did that old man have to do with it—if anything? Matthew looked around to see if he could find the man who had patted him on the shoulder, but he couldn't see him.

"Come on, Matt!" yelled Connor as he began to make his way with the team to the park's snack benches. "The team's gonna to get some cold cream and the coach is using his credits."

Matthew shouted back, "I'll be there in a minute! I'm just looking for something!"

Out of the corner of his eye, Matthew spotted the slow walk of a man wearing blue suspenders and heading out the front exit of the park. Matthew sprinted toward the exit and yelled at the man, "Hey, wait, mister! Wait a minute!" The man in the blue suspenders continued to walk, either ignoring or not hearing Matthew's calls.

Connor saw Matthew sprinting toward the exit and left the rest of the team at the snack tables. Coach Jenkins asked him, "Where you going, captain? We don't even have our cream yet."

"Sorry, coach. I've gotta go. You can get me some cold cream next week when we beat Sector 42."

Matthew was at the transport station and continued to look for the mysterious man in the blue suspenders. Connor ran up and asked, "Have you lost your mind? What are you doing?"

"He was here, the man from last night, the man from the warehouse window."

Connor shook his head and wondered why he gave up cold cream for Matthew. "There is no way the guy from the warehouse was at our game! Why would he be?"

Both boys heard a knock coming from behind them. The boys turned and saw the bald man in the blue suspenders sitting in the transport. He tapped on the window and waved at them, like he was playing with them. The transport took off and the boys watched as it vanished from sight.

Matthew looked back at Connor and said, "Now you believe me?"

"Yeah, I believe you. Now what do we do?"

Chapter 3

Matthew looked at the large outgoing board at the transport terminal and said, "We go home and we figure out how to get into that warehouse. I think we need to talk to this guy."

Connor dug in his pockets to pull out his credits for the ride. "I have a feeling that if we get in trouble for this, I'm going to kick your butt! So let's go."

Chapter 4

MEET MR. KELLINGTON

"What in the world's goin' on here?" asked Matthew as he and Connor walked up to the end of their street. The euphoria from their victory was still fresh in their minds, but a rush of adrenaline filled their bodies as they got closer to the old warehouse next to their apartment. They approached their building and noticed a different kind of flashing light bouncing off the walls and pavement around their home. These were the lights of a dozen security vehicles staked around the perimeter of the neighborhood.

Connor said, "Have you ever seen so many security teams in one place?"

"Not even when we locked Ms. Carlson in the broom closet in second grade."

Connor laughed and said, "Yeah, that was great. Let's see if we can hear what they're sayin'."

The boys made their way around the apartment complex and sneaked up behind a short brick wall that separated their building from the warehouse. The wall was only three feet tall, so the boys crawled their way to a point where they couldn't be seen by any security personnel but could hear what was being discussed. They were able to distinguish one of the voices as that of Sam, their own building's security lead. Even with the throngs of security team members moving about, they were well hidden.

"Where's your supervisor, boy?" asked a man in a gray suit with very short trouser legs. You could see his white socks between his brown

Chapter 4

boots and the bottom of his pants leg. He was in his mid to late thirties, wore a gold ring with a centered diamond stud, and had a small scar on his left cheek. He didn't look like the other security personnel. In earlier times, one might say he looked goofy.

Sam turned around and replied, "He's right over here, sir, but can I help you with something?"

"You one of the security leads from here?"

Sam replied, "Yes sir, I am lead over the housing complex behind us."

The man looked Sam over from shoes to head and said, "Well, I'll have to talk to you then. Call your supervisor over here."

Sam called out to his supervisor, Mr. Hugo Jackson, and he proceeded to Sam's location. Both Connor and Matthew noticed that the man in the gray suit had a strange slow accent to his speech. It was something that they had never heard before. All citizens were taught a specific way to speak and pronounce while in school. It had been a top priority of Minister Hathmec in the early 2100s. This man spoke with what would have once been described as a Southern twang.

As Hugo Jackson made his way over, Sam told him, "This gentleman wants to speak with you, sir."

Mr. Jackson looked at the man, grinned, and said, "This is no gentleman, Sam; this is Keith Kellington. What brings you down here?"

Mr. Kellington stretched his hand out and shook Mr. Jackson's hand, "Oh, I think y'all know why I'm here, Hugo. It's not every day we hear one of our security leads has been murdered on the job. In fact we don't ever hear of that happening, so Mr. Elliott thought it would be a good idea for me to come and find out what's goin' on."

The boys heard the word "murdered" and almost jumped out of their crouch behind the wall. A murder in Sector 37 was unheard of. Not only was someone murdered, but it was one of the security team members. They wondered if this had something to do with the strange man from the warehouse last night or the man who had found them at their game earlier in the day.

The boys wanted to talk to each other, but the fear of being caught eavesdropping was enough to keep their mouths shut.

"It looks like you've done a good job clearing the area, Hugo. Do y'all have clearers posted around the building?"

"Of course," said Hugo. "If anyone gets too close to the building, our security directs them away, per regulation."

Mr. Kellington continued, "So, was the young man who was murdered your partner?"

Mr. Jackson stepped in. "Now wait a minute, Keith. We don't know for sure he was murdered; it could have been an accident."

"That's why I'm here. We just wanna make sure we don't have any problems growin' here in Sector 37 that may require our helpful hands."

Hugo Jackson responded, "We have the best-trained security personnel in the world here, Keith. How could someone purposely take down one of them? The only people who could have murdered him would be one of his superiors or someone like you from Sector 1."

"I don't think that's the case, my friend."

Hugo Jackson walked up close to Mr. Kellington and whispered in his ear, "It couldn't be the old resistance movement again, could it? We haven't had problems with them for more than thirty years."

Mr. Kellington simply gave a quick glance to Hugo Jackson and prodded Sam to answer his question.

"Yes, sir, we have worked at this building together for the last year and a half."

Mr. Kellington pulled out a piece of paper. "This incomin' log report from last night says you called in for backup around eleven."

Sam responded, "Yes, sir."

"So, were you part of the team that entered the warehouse last night?"

Sam responded, "No, sir. I was going to be, but someone has to stay at post at all times, and Brett wanted to go with the search team, so I let him."

Mr. Kellington dropped the papers to his side. "I see. You didn't have the nerve to go lurkin' 'round in an abandoned warehouse."

Sam, appalled that his courage was being questioned, responded, "I was not afraid, sir! It was just that Brett can be very persuasive."

Chapter 4

"He's just messing with you, Sam. Keith knows what it's like out here for you guys."

"That's true, Sam; I'm just messin' with you, tryin' to ease the tension a bit." Keith Kellington put his arm around Sam and quietly asked, "Was he persuasive enough to talk you into a trip back to the warehouse this morning?"

Sam was disturbed at the tone of Keith's question and confused by the sudden change in his accent. He dropped his head and shook it up and down to signal that he had allowed Brett to reenter the warehouse earlier in the morning.

"Well, I don't wanna discuss this around all these other security teams, so you and Hugo come with me and we'll discuss this at Sector Headquarters. We've got plenty of surveillance video to go through to tell us if anyone was 'round the area to see anythin' else."

Mr. Kellington led Sam and his supervisor, Hugo Jackson, to a four-wheeled transport and left the area. Both Connor and Matthew peeked from behind the wall to see them driving away and crawled back to the safety of the rear of the building.

"Can you believe what we just heard?" asked Connor. Matthew, concerned, turned his back to Connor and began to breathe heavily. Connor put his hand on Matthew's shoulder. "You OK? What's the matter?"

Matthew shot back up, eyes wide, "Are you serious? That guy is from Sector 1."

"Yeah, so what?"

Matthew shook his head and walked around in circles. "He's looking for anyone who might have information about what happened last night."

"Yeah, so what?"

Matthew grabbed Connor's shirt and said, "He might come looking for two kids that were looking through their windows last night and saw a strange man staring back at them."

Connor pushed Matthew away. "You're out of your mind; there's no way anyone knew we were watching that building last night. How could they?"

Matthew pointed to a walkway light. "Don't you remember what April told us? There are sensors and surveillance equipment hidden in things all over the sector."

Connor looked up toward their window. "Do you think they could have seen us all the way up there?"

Matthew looked up and said, "I don't know, but we need to get home and tell April what's happening."

The boys ran back to their complex and made their way up to their apartment. They were careful to avoid security team members and made sure not to bring any attention to themselves. April stood in the living room, waiting on them.

"Where have you two been? I've been worried sick."

Matthew responded first. "We got back from the park and saw all the commotion in front of the building, so we wanted to see what was going on."

April looked worried. "You shouldn't be down there involved in those things. It can only lead to trouble."

Connor walked over to the window. "Not as much trouble as that security guard, Brett, ran into last night."

April looked confused, but curious, and asked, "You mean the Brett that works security for our building? What kind of trouble is he in?"

Matthew, hands shaking, proceeded to tell April what he and Connor heard while hiding behind the wall. "We just wanted to see what was going on, since we knew something had happened at the warehouse last night."

When the initial shock of someone actually being killed next door to their home wore off, a new fear took hold of April. "How do you know something happened at the warehouse last night?"

"It was Matt's fault; he got me out of bed to look at it."

April asked again. "He got you out of bed to look at what?"

Matthew grabbed April by the hand and walked her to his bedroom window and explained, "It was right over there; this blinding light coming from that window. How could me and Connor sleep with all that light shining in our window?"

"What else did you see?"

Chapter 4

Matthew continued, "We saw a security team go in; we saw the light die down, and we saw a man standing in the window looking back at us. I didn't think he saw us, but he was staring back at us from that same window."

April tried to keep the boys from seeing the concern in her face and brought both boys to the center of the room. "What did he look like?"

Connor attempted to explain. "He was an older bald guy."

April pulled back. "That's it? That's all you know? He was an older bald guy?" She started to laugh and walked back to the window. "Well, boys, if that's all you know, I think we'll be fine."

Matthew said, "He was wearing blue suspenders and a gray shirt when we saw him at the game this morning."

April paused for a moment, as if turned to stone, and slowly asked, "Did you say he was wearing blue suspenders?"

Matthew replied, "I'm not sure it was the same guy, but he was bald too and had on blue suspenders and his shirt had some writing on it, but it was all faded out."

April paused again to collect her thoughts. "Do you think the shirt had numbers on it, like eight and four?"

Matthew searched his memory banks and said, "Now that you mention it, yeah, it may have been numbers."

April ran back to the living room and began to grab her bag. "I'll be back in a little while. You two stay here and don't leave until I get back."

Connor ran behind her to the door. "Where are you going?"

She reached the door and turned back. "I need to see what I can find out from Sam."

"But Sam isn't down there. Some guy from Sector 1—I think his name was Keith Kellington—took him and his supervisor away in a transport," said Connor.

A true look of panic engulfed April's face, and she reentered the living room. "Keith Kellington? Are you sure he said Keith Kellington?"

The boys nodded in unison and Connor replied, "Yeah, we're sure. Why?"

April walked back to her bedroom without saying a word and emerged a few minutes later with instructions. "I want both of you to go to your room and keep a lookout for Sam, and when you see him, let me know. I'll keep a watch for him from the front window."

The boys walked up to April and Connor asked, "Why are we looking out for Sam, and what's the deal with Keith Kellington?"

April responded with a calm voice, "Do what I say and go keep a look out for Sam; we need to find out what he told Keith Kellington."

Connor asked, "But April—"

Before he could finish, she barked back at them, "I said go!" The boys jumped back and made their way to their room. April wasn't one to raise her voice.

"April never yells at us like that." Matthew poked his head out the bedroom door and caught a glimpse of April sitting by the window, wiping sweat from her forehead.

Connor replied, "Did you see the look on her face when we said Keith Kellington's name? She really wants to know what Sam told him."

"Do you think Sam will tell April anything?" asked Matthew.

Connor poked his head out the window and looked at all the investigators on the street. "I don't know. If I had someone from Sector 1 down here asking me questions, I think I would keep my mouth shut."

The boys continued to watch for a couple of hours as various teams went in and out of the warehouse. Several hours passed with no communication between the boys and April. Each time either Matthew or Connor attempted to leave their room, a quick stare from April drove them back in.

Just as it seemed their building guard would not make it back from his visit with Keith Kellington, a transport pulled up and out popped Sam. He began to make his way to the building security checkpoint, and the boys relayed what they saw to April.

Matthew said, "April, he's back. Sam's back down at the checkpoint."

April ran into the boys' bedroom to catch a glimpse of him as he rounded the front of the building. She then ran back to the living room to see him as he passed the building's side.

"You boys stay here and don't answer the door if anyone knocks. Just stay in your room and pretend that no one is here."

Chapter 4

The boys, again perplexed, decided not to question April this time and responded simply, "OK."

April grabbed her things and made her way to the building elevator. She was determined to find out what Sam knew and what he had told Keith Kellington. As the numbers on the elevator panel slowly counted down from nine, she prepared a plan of how she would approach Sam. Should she come right at him and demand answers? Should she act scared of the situation and hope that he calmed her down with information? She pondered her move and concluded that there was only one surefire way to ensure success. Sadly, it was the one thing she didn't want to do.

April reached the bottom floor and made her way to the front of the building. Various security teams were still walking around the area, taking notes and pictures as they went. She saw Sam, alone, in the office. Sector 37 had not issued a replacement for his recently deceased partner. She took a couple of deep breaths and opened the door to the office. As their eyes met, she hurled herself toward him, grabbed him around the neck, and planted a huge kiss on his unsuspecting lips.

She slowly pulled away from him. "Thank god you're all right! I had heard that a security lead from our building had been killed and I just thought the worst."

Sam, shocked by the outpouring of emotion, but with a big smile on his face, responded, "I'm fine. It was Brett." A look of confusion overtook Sam. "I didn't know you cared so much about me."

April walked around the office and acted as if she was embarrassed. "What do you mean, you didn't know that I cared so much? I would think it would be obvious that I care about you. I've been giving you hints that I'm attracted to you for months now."

Sam, with an even bigger smile on his face, said, "I never thought you had any feelings for me, other than a passing acknowledgement of my existence. I mean, I've always thought you were great."

April moved in toward Sam again and gave him another kiss. "Well, now you know I think you're great, too."

Sam and April discussed their mutual feelings for each other for the next twenty minutes as April looked for an opportunity to find out what had happened.

"I just can't believe someone was murdered here last night. Do you know what happened?"

Sam ducked his head and moaned, "The investigation teams are still working on what actually happened."

April took Sam's hand. "Don't you know what happened? I mean you were here when it happened, right? I'm sure the investigators have given you an idea of what went on."

Sam pulled back from April and said, "Look, I can't go in to what I've been told or what I've heard. This is an ongoing investigation, and to be perfectly honest, they have people here from Sector 1 looking at it. I don't want to get in trouble with anyone from Sector 1."

April mulled over her next move carefully. She didn't want Sam to think she was pumping him for information, but she also determined that this was her best chance to find out what he knew. She went with the guilt approach. "Wow, I can't believe that I actually threw my emotions and my feelings on the table with you and now you just shut me out. If we are going to make something work with us, you have to trust me. I don't know what is going on in my own neighborhood, people are dying, and the one person that I thought would put my mind at rest doesn't even trust me enough to tell me what he knows."

April began to make her way to the door to leave and turned around one last time. "I guess I was wrong about you."

Sam jumped to his feet and pleaded, "Wait, don't go! I'm sorry. You're right. If I can't trust you, then who can I trust? Please, come back in."

April slowly turned toward Sam and walked back into the office. They both sat down at his desk, and he told her the details of his meeting with Mr. Kellington.

"This guy that my supervisor knows, Keith Kellington, shows up here while some sector investigators are going through the warehouse. He wants me to go with him to the primary security headquarters for questioning. I'm thinking that it won't be a big deal because I really don't know that much, beyond calling in for backup last night. Brett and I saw this bright light coming from one of the warehouse's windows about eleven, and it needed to be checked out."

Chapter 4

Sam took a sip of coffee from the cup on his desk, moved to the office window, and pointed to the warehouse. "We couldn't see anything but the light coming from that window. Since the building is supposed to be shut down at night, I wanted a security team to make sure someone wasn't in there that shouldn't be."

Sam moved back to the desk and sat down. "The team arrived within five minutes of the call and came by the office to let us know that they were going up. Brett wanted to go with them, so I told him that he could. I thought it would be some good on-the-job training."

April asked, "When did you know that Brett had been killed?"

"Well, that's just it; the entire security team came back down after a couple of hours of sweeping the building, and they didn't find anything out of the ordinary. The room that the light was coming from was empty. The problem was that Brett wanted to go back into the warehouse after the rest of the team left. He kept saying that he thought they missed something. I got tired of listening to him so I told him to go take another look if he wanted to, and he did."

Sam began to get emotional as he started to realize that his decision played a part in Brett's death. April caressed Sam's hand. "It's OK. You can tell me."

After Sam took another sip of his coffee, he continued, "He hadn't come back and had been gone for two hours, so I called up the sweep team again." Sam wiped his eyes. "This time, they found Brett, dead, in the same room that the light had come from."

"Do you know how he died?"

Sam got up from his seat again and looked out the window. "I really don't know. They won't show me his body and no one will tell me anything beyond he's dead. My own supervisor still thinks it may have been an accident, but I don't think people from Sector 1 show up to investigate accidents."

April got up from her seat and joined Sam at the window. "I'm so sorry that you had to go through all that." April paused for a minute and asked, "What happened at sector headquarters?"

"We get to headquarters and I go through the whole explanation that I just told you with that Mr. Kellington. He really didn't say much while I was going through it all, but he did the strangest thing once I got done."

April asked, "What did he do?"

"He asked me to hold this rock that was sitting on his office table, so I did. He just sat there for a minute, didn't say a word, and stared at me. All of a sudden, he gets up, tells me to put the rock back down on his desk, and that he appreciated my honesty. He directed me back to the transport to come back to the post. My supervisor was waiting for me, and we left a few minutes later."

Sam went on to tell April that there was more to the man from Sector 1 than met the eye. "I thought he was kind of strange to be honest. That crazy accent; I could barely understand what he was saying. Then he would say something as clear as me or you would say it. It's like he was doing it on purpose."

April hoped that Sam had told her everything and asked a final question. "So, you didn't hear any explanation of what might have happened?"

Sam paused for a moment. "I didn't hear any explanations about what may have happened, but I did overhear one of the investigators tell Mr. Kellington that they had some surveillance video that he needed to see."

April asked, "What kind of video was it?"

Sam took April's hand and began to hug her. "I'm not sure exactly, but it sounded like there was someone in your building last night that was watching the lights in the warehouse at the same time that we saw them. It must have been pretty good video because one of the investigators said that they should have a positive ID within the hour."

Panic gripped April as she determined that the investigators had surveillance of her boys watching the warehouse. She pulled away from Sam and asked, "What do you think they'll do next?"

Sam cocked his head to the side and explained, "I would imagine the person they saw in the video will be getting a visit from the investigation team pretty soon."

April began to make her way back to the door as Sam walked after her. "Look, Sam, I am so glad that you're OK and I'm so happy that

Chapter 4

we both know what we're feeling for each other, but I really need to go check on the boys. We'll have plenty of time to continue our talk tomorrow."

Sam rushed to April's side and asked, "Can I have one more kiss before you go?"

April responded, "Of course you can," and proceeded to give Sam a deep and passionate good-bye kiss. As she walked out of the office she turned and said, "I'll see you soon."

Sam responded, "Absolutely!"

Once April had cleared the security post and the investigators on the street, she ran back to the elevator, jumped in, and selected nine. The numbers couldn't light up fast enough as she tried to calm down and determine what she needed to do next. The daylight was gone from Sector 37 and she knew that it was now or never to save her boys.

Chapter 5

ROOM 1313

The door flew open to the apartment and April began to grab some old bags stored in her closet. Both Matthew and Connor came into her room with looks of dread. They had never seen April look so flustered.

"So what did you find out from Sam?" asked Matthew.

April stopped her mad dash of pulling bags from her closet. "I need both of you to take a bag and get some clothes together. We need to get out of here as fast as we can."

Connor asked, "Why do we have to leave? Are we in trouble?"

April, tears welling up in her eyes, pleaded, "Please, just do as I say. I'll explain everything later."

Before another word could be spoken, there was a knock on the door. April put her finger to her lips and signaled the boys to be quiet.

Another knock at the door, and this time they heard a voice demand, "Sector security! Please open the door or we will open it for you!"

April knew that the security team would be in the apartment in mere moments. "Wait just a second; I need to put some clothes on." April turned to the boys and ordered, "No matter what they ask, do not admit that you saw anything last night. Do you understand me?"

Both boys replied, "Yes, ma'am."

April told the boys to stay in her room until she called for them. Before she left, she pulled what looked like a keychain from her dresser drawer and tapped it with her finger. She slid the keychain into her pocket, dried the tears from her face, and made her way to the front door.

Chapter 5

April had her hand on the doorknob, composed herself, and cracked open the door. To her surprise, she recognized the face of Keith Kellington. Mr. Kellington was flanked by four security team members, all of whom were large, intimidating men.

As he panned down the length of her body, a wry grin appeared. "You April 14561?"

April backed away from the door and replied to the Sector 1 detective, "Yes, sir, I am."

"That's good." He breezed past April and made his way into the small living room of the apartment, Southern twang in full affect.

April asked, "Can I help you gentlemen with something?"

Mr. Kellington replied, "Yes, y'all can, ma'am." Keith Kellington pulled out a small slip of paper and read it. "Connor 24612 and Matthew 25871; I need to ask 'em a few questions about what they saw last night."

April positioned herself between Mr. Kellington and the door to her bedroom, "I don't think the boys know anything about what happened last night. I'm not even sure what happened."

Mr. Kellington smirked. "Now, ma'am, you can either go get those two boys yourself, or I'll make you get 'em. It's your choice."

April cowered back and flashed a quick smile to the detective as she turned her head to her bedroom door and called out, "Boys, please come out here."

Both of the boys emerged from the bedroom, as they tried to avoid eye contact with the team of security personnel that looked them over. April put her arms around both of the boys. "Boys, this nice detective needs to ask you a few questions, so make sure you tell him everything you know."

Mr. Kellington thanked April and made his first comments to the boys. "I want you to be honest with me, young men, and if you are, this'll be real simple for the both of y'all. You understand me?" The boys both replied, "Yes, sir."

"We have video that shows both of y'all lookin' out your bedroom winduh around eleven p.m. last night. There were reported light refractions occurring in the warehouse right across from your winduh. Did y'all see those light refractions?"

The boys tried not to make eye contact with Mr. Kellington and looked at each other. Connor motioned to Matthew to speak up. Matthew cleared his throat and answered, "Well, sir, I'm not sure who you saw on that surveillance tape, but it couldn't have been us."

Connor jumped in. "We were already asleep at ten, and we know the rules about being out of bed after hours."

Mr. Kellington walked closer to the boys, a foot from each of them, and confronted the obvious with a firm and adjusted voice, no accent. "You are not answering my question boys. I don't care when you went to sleep and I don't care that you know the rules of the sector. I care that you were both up at eleven p.m. last night and that you saw the occurrence of light from that window."

Mr. Kellington made his way into the boys' room and pointed at the exact warehouse window where the boys saw the mysterious bald man the night before.

"In fact, this is the perfect spot to see what occurred last night; not a tree in sight. The light must have been blinding coming through this window."

Connor sucked back some air and found some courage. "We didn't see anything, sir; honest."

Matthew shook his head in agreement. "That's right, sir. We must have just missed it. We are really heavy sleepers."

Mr. Kellington bopped his head up and down and began to lick his teeth with his mouth closed. His accent returned. "I tell y'all what boys, Why don't you go on back into the bedroom. I need to have a private talk with, Ms. April, right?"

"Yes, sir." The boys walked to April's room but looked back to her multiple times before they got there. Mr. Kellington instructed the rest of the team to leave him for a minute with April, and he closed the boys' bedroom door behind them.

April began to speak to the detective, but only got out, "Sir, I really think that my boys—"

"Stop talking and don't move a muscle." At that moment April became motionless, like an old statue. She stood prone to Mr. Kellington. She strained to move any muscle in her body—a finger, a toe, even blink

Chapter 5

her eyes—but she couldn't. The only muscle that was working in her entire body was her mind and it raced with fear and terror as the detective looked her over.

Mr. Kellington took his finger and placed it on April's forehead. "It is so frustrating, isn't it? You want to move, you want to push me away, but you can't."

A quick chuckle left Keith Kellington's mouth. "But I can." Mr. Kellington pushed on April's forehead and she fell backward onto one of the boys' beds. The bed broke her fall, but she was still in a stonelike state as she stared up at Mr. Kellington. He stood over her and spoke in the same sadistic tone she had heard after the boys had lied to him.

"It's strange, but you remind me of someone I used to know quite well. Funny how a look can jog an old memory." Mr. Kellington walked to the side of the bed and went down to one knee; his mouth was just clear of April's ear. He spoke in a volume just louder than a whisper. It was unnerving to April.

"I have thousands and thousands of memories in my head. I take them as I need them and never have a second thought about it. I could take your memories and those of your boys and make them mine in a matter of seconds if I wanted to. In fact, I could take a lot more than memories."

A small tear began to develop in the right eye of April 14561, and it slowly made its way down the side of her cheek. Mr. Kellington rose from his knee and spoke, as if to the air. "You may move."

April regained control of her body. She could move her arms, legs, and fingers. She blinked and wiped the tear from her face. She began to stand when Mr. Kellington stopped her progress.

"Now, we do not condone using these types of controls on our younger population. The Supreme Leader has decided that it's not good to introduce young people to these types of realities until they have been properly taught to respect authority. We will only use them in the case of security or as a last resort."

April peered into the eyes of Mr. Kellington and a rush of anger flooded her system. She wondered, *Is he making a threat against my boys? Is there any way I can stop him from hurting them?*

Mr. Kellington continued, "I did not read your mind because I don't think you really know what happened here last night. If you don't get what I need from your boys, believe me, I will."

Mr. Kellington walked to the door of the bedroom, pointed to it, and made one final command, back to his Southern drawl. "You have one last chance, Ms. April. Now, you go into the other room and convince them boys to tell me everything they know."

At that point, Mr. Kellington's tone deepened and his voice rose to an alarming pitch.

"Or I will take both of those boys with me, run them through the ringer in Sector 1, and you will never see either one of them again!" Mr. Kellington walked back to the bed and calmly said, "I'm sure they would fit right in with the other inhabitants of the Mercury Camps."

April was able to stand and with a lowered head said, "I'll get them to tell you everything. If you promise not to take them away or put them through this, I'll get them to tell you everything they know."

Mr. Kellington stood toe to toe with April and raised his hand to her chin. He raised her head with his hand.

"Does a cat make a deal with a gutter rat? You'll do it and then I'll decide what happens next."

April knew she had no other choice and replied, "Yes, sir."

"By the way, how did you like that accent I was playing with? I found that one years and years ago. I like to bring it back up every so often. The rube that had it didn't require it anymore." April composed herself as Mr. Kellington looked at her with a menacing grin.

Matthew and Connor were alone in April's bedroom. The security team waited just outside of the door, so the boys had to be quiet. Matthew, worried for April, asked Connor, "What do you think that man is going to do to her?"

"I don't know, but she told us not to tell these guys anything, and that's what we're gonna do. Just keep our mouths shut."

Matthew asked, "What if they do something to her? We'll have to say something. Maybe we can make something up?"

Connor pondered for a minute. "Nothing is going to happen to us; stop being so dramatic. They won't do anything to us or April as long as

Chapter 5

we stay consistent." Connor walked to the bedroom window and stared out, "This whole idea that we are being controlled and that the government can just do anything to you that they want, it's just talk, you'll see."

Matthew curled up in a ball on the bed. "I hope you're right."

Mr. Kellington had April in the living room and commanded one of his security team leaders to get the boys. The boys emerged and made their way toward April. Mr. Kellington announced to the room that April had something to say to Matthew and Connor. April approached the boys and leaned in between their two heads, so each boy had one ear to her mouth. She slowly rotated her head, in order to see all of her surroundings and whispered to both of the boys, "Run."

April pulled away from the boys and lunged at the one security team member blocking the door and knocked him to the ground. She yelled, "Run!"

The boys took off toward the door and heard Mr. Kellington, in a loud, strong, monotone voice, "Stop at the door and do not move!"

For a moment, the boys did stop, but only for a moment. Matthew looked back through the open door and heard April scream, "Run, boys! Don't stop!"

Mr. Kellington, amazed, looked down at April being picked up from the floor. Mr. Kellington exclaimed, "What the hell is going on here?"

Seconds later, a loud explosion rocked the building like a sonic blast from the past. Everyone rushed to the living room window. A transport was on fire in front of the building. There were screams coming from all directions. Things like this just didn't happen in Sector 37.

Mr. Kellington ordered his men to go down to the street and help with the fire. "Take this woman to the holding location in Sector 37." He also told one of them to follow the boys and get them back.

They made their way to the apartment door and four more security team members showed up. They had something for Mr. Kellington.

A large man, six feet eight inches tall, led this particular team and said to Mr. Kellington, "Sir, we caught these two boys trying to run from the building."

Mr. Kellington looked into the hall and saw both Connor and Matthew standing there, no movement, just blank stares.

The large security team leader continued, "I'm a third-level team leader of Sector 37, so I forced them to tell me what they were running from."

Mr. Kellington, a smile on his face, told the boys, "There is no running from me, boys. I always get the information that I need."

"What is your name, third-level team leader from Sector 37?"

"My name is Johnson, sir."

"Good job, Mr. Johnson. Do you think you can handle one more request for me?"

"Of course, sir. It would be an honor to serve you in any way that you need."

Mr. Kellington told Johnson that his team needed to investigate the explosion, so he asked him and his team to lead the boys and their caretaker to the Sector 37 holding area.

"You have already done a wonderful job catching these boys. I can trust you to get them to the holding area, right?"

Johnson responded, "Absolutely, sir. I won't let you down."

Mr. Kellington signaled his men in the apartment to hand over April to Agent Johnson. "Now, Agent Johnson, I want you to be in complete control of these boys and their caretaker for the entire time you are transporting them. You can release them at the holding area and I can do my job from there."

Agent Johnson replied, "I was thinking the same thing, sir. I currently have the boys under my control." Agent Johnson broke a wry smile and gave a stern command to April. "Do as I tell you and nothing more, except breathe." April stood perfectly still as she awaited instruction from the young security agent.

Agent Johnson then commanded, "Everyone follow me to the elevator and enter it once the doors open."

The two boys, April, and the three security guards made their way to the elevator and awaited the doors to open per command. Mr. Kellington continued barking orders to the other guards.

"I want you to coordinate with local security to make sure that the fire is put out quickly. I want you to coordinate with the local housing authority to keep the Sector 37 civilians away from the blaze."

Chapter 5

Mr. Kellington paused and took a peek back down the hallway as the doors to the elevator began to open. The security guards were leading the boys into the elevator when Connor turned his head and stared at Mr. Kellington. Mr. Kellington was taken aback. He shouldn't have been able to do that, unless Agent Johnson had released control of him.

Mr. Kellington scanned the room again to see which of his men were still available. "You there; it's Quigley, isn't it?"

The older guard responded, "Yes, sir."

"I need you to go downstairs quickly and catch up with Agent Johnson and his team. I'm not sure what's going on, but I want to make sure he gets our assets into that transport."

"Yes, sir. I will call you once they are loaded and secured."

Mr. Quigley made his way from the apartment to the stairwell. A jaunt down nine flights of stairs for a security team member was no problem at all.

Back in the elevator, Agent Johnson gave orders to his team and his prisoners. "We are currently in a government-controlled housing elevator with cameras and surveillance in every corner to see what we are doing. I would suggest that the young people and lady in the elevator stay perfectly still until I tell them that they can move."

Agent Johnson told his team to exit the elevator first, followed by the two boys, and then he and April. "I want to make sure that we are clear of any official personnel and then we are to make our way toward the abandoned warehouse on the right of the building."

The elevator doors opened to the lowest level of the apartment and the security team moved out as directed. The area was covered with first responders dealing with the fire on the other side of the apartments. Sirens sounded in the background, and the air was filled with smoke and the remnants of the vehicle.

The team began to make its way toward the old warehouse when Mr. Kellington's man came running up behind them. He waved his hands and tried to get Agent Johnson's attention. He yelled, "Agent Johnson! Agent Johnson!"

Johnson turned around and ordered his men to continue moving forward. "I'll see what this officer needs."

"Can I do something for you?"

Mr. Quigley responded, "Mr. Kellington wanted to make sure that you don't have any problems. I am to report your progress once these assets are loaded onto a transport."

Quigley looked around and asked, "Why are you going this direction? The transports are back the other way."

Agent Johnson popped a smile and put his arm around the veteran guard. "We are simply trying to avoid the commotion from the explosion response. It wouldn't be good for other citizens to see us removing a couple of boys and their mother from this complex; it would look bad."

Mr. Quigley looked over Agent Johnson's team and asked a simple question. "Do you think seeing a *mother* being arrested with her sons would look bad?"

Johnson realized his mistake and had to make a quick decision. His cover was blown.

Before he made a move, Quigley reached for his communicator and declared, "Code 10! Code 10! I have a Code 10 at this mark." A Code 10 indicated that assistance was needed for terrorism against the state; every security team member within twenty miles was now aware of it.

Quigley reached for his chest, as Johnson, clearly not an agent, reached for something in his pocket. He hit Quigley with it before his hand reached his chest. Quigley went down to the ground and began to twitch, but it was too late; there were now dozens of guards running over from the fire toward Johnson and his team.

Johnson grabbed April by the hand as she grabbed Matthew and Connor and yelled, "Run to the warehouse! Follow me and stay out of range of those guards!"

Johnson led the group to the side door of the warehouse. The sector guards began to catch up to their position. Johnson couldn't believe that he was stupid enough to say the boys and their *mother*. No one said "mother" anymore, certainly not an agent of the state. His mistake could lead to all of them getting caught.

Mr. Kellington exited the apartment building and asked what had happened. He saw Quigley on the ground and grabbed one of the guards who had rushed over to him.

Chapter 5

"What's going on? What happened to that man?"

The guard responded, "It's an attack, sir. We saw some men dressed in security uniforms with a woman and some kids. I bet they had something to do with the explosion, too!"

Kellington threw his communicator on the ground and howled, "Damn it! I knew something was wrong with those boys. Where are they now?"

A sector guard came up behind Mr. Kellington and explained, "We have them cornered in that old warehouse, and we're moving in on them from the top and bottom of the complex."

Johnson continued to encourage the group. "We have to get up these stairs and get to the thirteenth floor. It's the only way out!"

Matthew yelled to April, "What's going on? Where are we going?"

April, sweat pouring from her head, replied, "Just keep up with Johnson. He'll get us out of here."

The clanking footsteps of security guards could be heard behind Johnson's team, catching up to his group. They were on the tenth floor and needed to keep moving as quickly as possible. "Climb boys! Faster, faster! We're gonna make it!"

Bang, bang, bang! The guards made more noise and were getting closer. Matthew and Connor could hear them yelling out threats. "Stop or we will be forced to put you down! I order you to stop! This is Sector Security!"

As Johnson's team reached the thirteenth floor, they looked down the hall at the final twenty yards needed to reach their destination. Three of Sector 37's finest blocked the way to room 1313. Johnson gave one last order to his team: "Boys, you know what to do. It's been an honor."

His three teammates, three crewmen, three friends, made a rushed dash toward the three security personnel blocking their path to room 1313.

"I order you to stop!" All of the guards rubbed their chests as they were tackled to the ground by Johnson's team. A struggle began and Johnson led April, Matthew, and Connor into room 1313.

Johnson took one last look at his friends as they held off the three guards and shut the door on them. You could still hear the pounding of boots on the staircases. The reinforcements were getting closer.

Johnson yelled to April and the boys, "Get to that door in the corner, quickly!"

The boys heard the other three members of the team as they screamed, "You can't control us, you bastards! It's not fun when we fight back, is it?"

They heard the throngs of reinforcements as they reached the scuffle. "We order you to stop or we will put you down!"

Johnson, April, and the boys reached the door in the corner and Johnson said, "Everyone in! Quick!" The door opened and April pulled in Connor and Matthew.

Matthew stopped. "What about the others? Are we just going to leave them here?"

Johnson replied, "You three are more important than any of us. Now get in there!"

Johnson pushed Matthew through the doorway and grabbed the door. He took one final peek and saw that the main door to the room was being opened. He closed the door in the corner with himself, April, and the boys squeezed together within it.

Connor asked, "So now what? Are we just going to hide in here?"

Matthew agreed. "They'll find us in no time."

Johnson reached behind April, who was crunched into the corner of the room, no bigger than a closet, and told them all to hold on. He pressed on three separate panels, and the wall that had made up the small closet suddenly turned into a wall of light. It was bright enough that it should have blinded them all, but it didn't. They all looked into the light and could feel subtle warmth.

Matthew looked up at Johnson. "What is this?"

Johnson grabbed Matthew, Connor, and April. "No time to explain; let's go!"

He pulled all four of them into the light and they were gone.

Back in room 1313, the security teams were doing a sweep, but found nothing. Mr. Kellington arrived and demanded answers. "Where are they? Who here is in charge?"

A young captain made his way over. "We have three of the terrorists, sir, but the other four have not been apprehended yet."

Chapter 5

Mr. Kellington, red-faced, asked, "Where the hell did they go? They didn't just vanish into thin air. I want this room completely checked, and I want answers."

Keith Kellington continued to berate the security teams in room 1313 as Captain Hugo Jackson walked in and motioned for him. "I think you need to see something, Kellington."

Mr. Kellington responded, "Your boys have really screwed this one up, Jackson. Thomas is going to be pissed!"

Hugo Jackson held up three chains, each with a small blue stone located in a pendant. Mr. Kellington looked at the pendants. "Whose are these?"

"They were removed from the terrorists, sir."

Mr. Kellington looked around the room and pulled Hugo Jackson close to him. "That's impossible. They must be fake."

Hugo responded, "We had to put them down with stunners; we couldn't control them."

Kellington barked an order to Hugo. "I want all three of them at the holding station in ten minutes. I'll find out what's going on here."

Hugo Jackson shook his head. "All three are dead. Once we had them physically under our control, my men said they just smiled at them and five seconds later, they were gone."

Mr. Kellington grabbed the three chains and pendants and gave two final orders. "Tell no one else about this, and get me Thomas Elliott on the communicator. It looks like the PROs are back."

"PROs, sir?"

Kellington leaned in and said in a hushed voice, "Persons Resisting Order."

Chapter 6

THE HATHMEC

The bright light faded away as Matthew, Connor, April, and Johnson discerned the shapes and objects that came into view. Matthew saw a long tunnel with random lights and distinct corners creating a path. He looked behind Connor and realized that the door, which had once led to room 1313, had vanished into the darkness.

Johnson was breathing heavily, and April hugged Connor. She began to reach for Matthew when he pulled away and exclaimed, "What's going on, and where are we?"

Johnson stood upright and motioned to the tunnel. "We just need to follow this path and all of your questions will be answered."

Connor moved to Matthew's side. "I'm with Matthew; we're not going anywhere else with you until we get some answers. Isn't that right, April?"

April took Connor and Matthew by the hand. "We need to trust Mr. Johnson. He'll make sure we get where we need to go."

The boys, perplexed, pulled their hands away from April and backed away from their caretaker. Matthew asked, "Do you two know each other?"

Johnson stepped in before April had a chance to answer and said, "Listen, you boys trusted me enough back at that complex to go along with my plan to save your mother. All I'm asking is to trust me a little more."

Matthew looked to April, as she nodded her head in agreement, but he wasn't convinced. He walked toward the tunnel, turned back to

Chapter 6

Johnson, and said, "Yeah, you seem real trustworthy. Did those three guys you left back at the warehouse trust you, too?"

Johnson's demeanor turned from one that was trying to reassure to one that was simply annoyed and pissed. Johnson leaned down into Matthew's face and pleaded his case. "Those three men back there are great friends of mine, you little twerp. You think because you want to go back and help them, that makes you some sort of hero? All that would have made you is a dead kid, or worse."

Matthew hung his head as Connor came back to his side. "Back off, man. We just don't understand why we had to run from those guys. Why didn't we just give up? We would have been fine."

April pulled the boys away from Johnson, and with her arms around both of them, told them the truth. "I am going to be completely honest with you boys, so I want you to listen to me and listen good."

The boys gave April their full attention as she continued. "Those guards wanted to get information out of you by any means necessary, and they would've used those means to hurt you both. They would've taken you away from me."

Matthew asked, "Why would they do that? We didn't see anything but some old guy in a window. Why didn't we just tell them what we saw?"

Johnson, quite frustrated, said with authority, "The government doesn't have to do the right thing, young man; all they have to do is get what they need from you and then dispose of you. I would have thought you two had read enough of those history books by now to understand that we are all slaves. We're all just too ignorant of the truth to know it."

Matthew grabbed April by the shoulder and asked, "Is this the person who brings us the books?"

Johnson replied, "I was only delivering them. You're about to meet the man who actually gets them for you; unless you would rather just stand here for the rest of your lives."

April continued with her explanation to the boys. "I have known Mr. Johnson here for quite some time, and I trust him without question. You two will just have to trust me on this."

Connor questioned April again. "We trust you, but we still don't know why we have to be afraid of that Mr. Kellington."

April moved to Connor's side and gave him a big hug. "I have known Mr. Kellington since before you were born, and all he knows how to do is hurt people."

Matthew asked, "Did he ever hurt you?"

"It was a long time ago. I'm not about to let him hurt either of you boys."

Johnson got between April and her boys and asked, "Do you think he recognized you?"

"No, but he did say that I reminded him of someone from his past."

Johnson took a deep breath and moaned, "Hopefully he won't put two and two together for a while."

While Johnson and April spoke with each other, Matthew and Connor moved to the other side of the tunnel and discussed their options. Connor gave his opinion. "I don't think we have much of a choice here. We can't go back the way we came, and it sounds like we'll get some answers if we follow this guy."

Matthew looked around the area again and replied, "I don't know if I trust this Johnson guy, but I trust April. Let's go with him and see what this is all about."

Johnson and April walked back over to the boys and April asked, "So, are we going to follow Johnson down the tunnel or do you have some other brilliant idea?"

Connor walked a ways down the tunnel and turned back. "Well, let's go. I want to meet this guy who has all of the answers."

Matthew followed suit and stepped his way down the tunnel. He looked at Johnson and asked, "There aren't any more secret doors we have to go through down here, are there?"

Johnson raised his hand and pointed. "Just keep going straight; you can't miss it."

Thirty minutes passed and the boys started to wonder if they had made a wrong turn. They were only going straight, so that didn't seem likely. It was very disorienting along the tunnel. For every few steps, another light would pop up ahead of them and another light behind them would go out. It was as if the tunnel could sense their location.

Chapter 6

Connor turned back to Johnson and April, who were walking behind the boys, and asked, "Exactly how far do we have to go down this corridor? We've been walking forever!"

Johnson didn't reply, so Connor asked again. "Is anyone listening back there? How much farther do we have to go?"

Suddenly, Johnson sprinted past Connor and Matthew and moved ahead a few steps. "No farther, boys. We're here."

The boys came to a stop in front of a small metal door with a latch on it. Johnson told Connor to go ahead and open it, so he reached for the latch handle to raise it, but he couldn't. Johnson sniped, "Too weak to lift a little latch, son? Here, Matthew, you try it."

Matthew stepped up and attempted to raise the handle but couldn't budge it a bit. Matthew glared up at Johnson. "What's the deal with this door? Does it have a lock on it we can't see?"

Johnson cracked a grin. "Out of the way ladies and let me give it a try." With little to no effort, he raised the latch and the door opened for the weary group. Johnson laughed and said, "See, that wasn't so hard; now go on in."

April gave Johnson a glance of disbelief and said, "As if this day hasn't been bad enough, you have to make fun of them, too."

Matthew, Connor, April, and Johnson walked into a room the size of a school gymnasium, without the basketball court and bleachers, and began to look around. The walls were covered in drop cloths and wires. The floor was an obstacle course of paths that wound between tables of electronics and books. The room had a cold aura about it that reminded the boys of a cave they had been in at the park. A light glaze of dust covered the tables and its contents, giving the room the odor of an old library.

Nothing in the room looked familiar to the boys or to April until Connor stumbled upon a table with a square box on it. He yelled over to Matthew, "Come here and look at this thing. It looks just like the one that we saw in our book the other night. There's the fruit symbol."

Matthew approached the small computer and explained to April, "Yeah, this is a home computer system from back in the 1990s." He turned to see another relic from the past. "Is that a real motorcycle?"

Connor heard Matthew utter the word "motorcycle" and was immediately pulled from the computer. "Just like from the 1950s! Can I ride it, April?"

April shook her head in a motherly, not-on-your-life kind of way, and tried to bring everyone back to the moment. "Where are we, Mr. Johnson, and when are we going to get some answers?"

From the darkened corner came a faint response to April's question in the form of a question. "Are you sure you're ready to accept the answers that you may get?"

The entire group turned toward the voice, and from the darkness walked a man wearing dark black pants held up with blue suspenders and an old gray T-shirt. Matthew paid particular attention to the T-shirt. He could clearly see the faded number on it that read "1984."

Matthew uttered, "You're the man from the park."

The man walked closer to the group and removed an old baseball cap that covered the few lonely hairs on his head. "I was also the one in the window the other night. I saw you boys staring at me."

Connor punched Matthew in the arm. "I told you he could see us."

Johnson walked over and put his arm around the man from the warehouse window and introduced him. "Boys, I would like you to meet Mr. Walter Wainright." Matthew looked to April and she gave a nod, as if signaling to Matthew that she approved.

Matthew extended his hand, and Mr. Wainright returned the gesture. "My name is Matthew 25871," said Matthew with a shaky voice.

Mr. Wainright pulled his hand away from Matthew and replied, "A number for a last name just won't do. That will be one of the first things that we take care of here; you deserve a last name."

Connor was still looking around at the room full of electronics, gadgets, and relics but finally spoke. "Wait a minute, Mr. Wainright. Who exactly are you and what are we doing here? Best I can tell, you live in some kind of old sewer and surround yourself with a bunch of old junk."

April snapped at Connor. "Be nice! Mr. Wainright is here to help us. He sent Mr. Johnson to get us away from those security teams."

Chapter 6

Connor replied, "You keep saying that he saved us from those guards, but they've never done anything to us; so what did he save us from?"

April began to speak, but Mr. Wainright intervened before she could. "Young man, have you learned nothing from the history books that I have sent to you?"

Matthew, excited to know where the books had been coming from, asked, "You were the one sending us those books? Why would you do that?"

"You can just call me Walter; no need to be formal from here on out. The reason that I have been sending you those books is because the truth about our world must be preserved; at any cost."

Connor replied, "What truth? That some crazy old guy wrote some fake history books to confuse kids?"

April grabbed Connor by the sleeve. "That's enough! Let Mr. Wainright continue."

"Remember, it's just Walter, but thank you. The truth is, the world as it is now should not be. This world has been altered by one man for his own benefit. The world we live in is based on his own warped idea of a utopia."

Walter walked over to a table that was loaded with pictures and books. He pulled a large page from an old plotter paper book and showed it to the group. "Do you boys recognize this skyline?"

Connor and Matthew walked closer to the picture and saw a large white stick jammed in the ground with a round white building on one side of it and a large rectangular white building on the other side.

Connor asked, "Where is this? I don't recognize it."

Walter replied, "This is Sector 1 boys, about two hundred years ago. Of course, back then it was called Washington, DC."

Walter grabbed another picture from the table and showed it to the boys. "See, this is what Sector 1 looks like now." The boys looked at the second picture and recognized the memorials to Supreme Leader Hathmec.

"Look, it's the Great Hall and the Hathmec Memorial, right where those other buildings used to sit."

Connor replied, "It seems to be missing that round building."

Walter explained, "That particular building was a symbol of democracy and how its people would elect citizens to represent them in their government."

Walter put the pictures away and led the boys, April, and Johnson into another room. "Have you ever wondered why the security teams and government personnel are able to subdue anyone just by telling them to do something?"

Connor looked to April. "April told us all about it. She told us that the government had come up with some sort of control device that they wear around their necks that can control anyone when activated."

Matthew added, "She said they couldn't control us with them because when we were born, the doctors forgot to inject us with something that made it work."

Walter reached into his shirt and pulled out a round pendant and showed it to the boys. The pendant had six symbols wrapped around a center, each with a distinct shape. Matthew traced his finger around the shapes and felt that one of them was filled with a hard stone of some type.

He asked, "Walter, what exactly is this?"

Connor chimed in before Walter could reply. "It looks like an ugly piece of jewelry."

Walter scoffed at Connor's remark and said, "This is no ordinary piece of jewelry, young man. This is a Power Pendant of Hathmec."

Connor asked, "So it is named after the Supreme Leader?"

Walter pulled the pendant out of Connor's hand. "Absolutely not! He has named himself after the pendant."

April took both of the boys by the hand and said, "Boys, this man has the answers that you've both been looking for. You need to let him explain what all of this is about."

Connor pulled his hand away from April's, shook his head, and paced around the small room. "Wait a minute! How do you know about all of this? Do you know this crazy old man?"

April responded, "He is not a crazy old man, and yes, I have known him for quite a while."

Chapter 6

Walter walked over to April and grabbed her hand. "She has been a part of the movement for many years."

Matthew asked, "What movement? April goes to work every day like everyone else."

"Boys, I want to tell you the story of a freedom movement that has been fighting back against Supreme Leader Hathmec for close to two hundred years. In order for you to understand why this movement exists, you must first understand where the Supreme Leader actually comes from."

Walter took a seat by one of his workbenches and asked, "Are you willing to listen to this story with an open mind and really search your own minds and hearts to determine its truth?"

Matthew responded, "Yes, I want to know the truth."

Connor rolled his eyes before he responded, "Yeah, let's hear it."

Walter began, "In order to understand where the Supreme Leader comes from, you must first understand that the Hathmec is not of earthly design. The Hathmec is made up of both alien technology and alien physiology. In order to understand it, you must first know how it arrived here and how it got into the hands of the self-appointed Supreme Leader." Walter Wainright spent the next hour telling the boys and April the story of Liam Liot.

Liam Liot was an alien traveler from the planet TERAH who was tasked with the job of scouting Earth for intelligent life and determining whether Earth could be used as a planet to inhabit should something ever happen to TERAH. The flight from planet TERAH to Earth took approximately two years to complete, so Liam and his partner-wife, Saras, were placed into a cryogenic sleep for the trip.

The technology gap between the planet TERAH and Earth was extensive, so this trip was expected to go off without a hitch, but that was not the case. Liam awoke from his cryogenic sleep to discover that his ship had crash-landed in the western portion of North America. Liam checked the ship to discover that his wife, Saras, was killed in the wreck. Her Hathmec pendant had become separated from her during the crash and she had no way to heal from her injuries. Liam was distraught and contemplated ending his life right then and there, but he decided that a good soldier would attempt to complete his mission.

Liam determined that the ship was beyond repair, so he took what he could from the vessel and made his trek across the country to the nearest inhabited area. Liam had landed in the early 1700s, and there were few people living in the western half of North America at that time. Liam looked like any other person on the planet, but he had the intelligence and technology of a master race of aliens in the Hathmec. The Hathmec gave its wearer a special set of skills, depending on the charms that were linked to it.

Matthew jumped in with an obvious question. "What do you mean, special set of skills?"

Walter responded, "I'm glad you asked. Let's use my Hathmec and charm as an example."

Walter held his pendant in his hand and pointed to a charm that looked like a snake suspended in midcoil. "This is the health charm of the Hathmec. It gives the wearer the ability to quickly heal from wounds, keep illness at bay, and reduce aging to a crawl."

Connor chimed in, "Reduce aging? How is that possible?"

Walter pulled out a piece of paper and handed it to Connor. "What is on that paper?"

Connor looked it over and said, "It says it's a birth certificate for Walter Wainright."

April asked, "What year does it say Walter was born?"

"It says 1955, but that's impossible. You would be over two hundred years old."

Walter replied, "I'm actually 230, but with the Hathmec health charm, I only age one year for every fifty years."

Matthew asked another question. "Then why do you look like you're in your fifties? Did you not start using the health charm until later in life?"

Walter chuckled and said, "We'll get to that as I go through the rest of the story."

"Liam made his way to the American colonies and learned as much as he could about the humans that inhabited this planet. With the use of his attribute and memory charms, he was able to quickly learn skills of the day and determined what the people of that time were thinking.

Chapter 6

Liam never had problems getting his way due to the power of the control charm. The control charm is used by security teams today to control the citizens of the planet.

"In fact, Liam became particularly involved during the time of the American Revolution. There were stories from British soldiers about a creature in the forests of the colonies that would torment their soldiers but could not be stopped by their bullets. It was actually Liam using his element charm and transport charm to confuse them. They thought they were seeing ghosts. He never actually killed anyone himself, but he was growing more compassionate for the American revolutionaries and wanted to help."

Matthew interrupted the story again and asked, "OK, so now there's an element charm and a transport charm. What do those do?"

Walter responded, "We'll get to all of that in a bit, but let's finish the story first."

Connor raised his hand and Walter said, "This isn't school, my boy. You can ask without raising your hand."

Connor grinned and asked, "I don't understand the control charm thing; do you just look at someone and they do what you say?"

Walter regained his train of thought. "No, Connor, the only way that you can control someone with a control charm or use any of the other charms is to place a carrier stone on that person or animal." Walter opened his hand and showed the boys a very small polished stone, similar to a small piece of marble, and said, "This is a carrier stone."

Walter sat the stone on the adjoining table and explained its use. "For someone who possesses a Hathmec pendant, the carrier stone allows him to either take or receive the powers of the charm. For example, Matthew, at the game when you felt that rush of energy and all of your aches and pains went away, I had shared my health charm with you."

"When did you put a stone on me?"

"I slipped it on you when I patted you on the back. It was a much smaller stone, more like a speck of dust."

April said, "So anyone who has a Hathmec can create their own carriers just by thinking about it?"

"The wearer of the Hathmec has their very DNA interwoven with the power of the pendant. It rushes through their blood and skin. This combination of physiology and technology allows the wearer to accomplish amazing things. This includes the creation of carrier stones."

Walter asked the group, "Now, can I continue with the story of Liam Liot?"

Johnson replied, "Yes, please continue."

"Liam Liot muddled around the colonies, was around for several wars, and even helped put in the first railroad systems around the country, but he was lonely. He determined that he was never going to be rescued by his native planet and had no way of repairing his own spaceship, so he decided to let time run its course naturally and simply pass away when it was time.

"Before he could do that, he wanted to make sure that Saras's Hathmec was never found by humans. Since a Hathmec charm is almost impossible to destroy, he decided to remove the charms from the pendant and give some of them to families he had met during his time on Earth. He would hide the others. This would keep them away from anyone who might determine a use for them.

"Liam's plan to fade as any other human took a sharp turn when he met a woman named Lana around the turn of the nineteenth century. Lana was a breath of fresh air for Liam and reminded him of why he had loved Saras so much. He took a different name, William Elliott, and wed Lana in the early 1900s. He wasn't sure if a human could have children with an alien until it was discovered that Lana was pregnant in 1902. She would go on to have two sons by the names of Evan and Daniel.

"Liam lived and aged with Lana. He was content raising his two sons and growing old with this new love. He had removed his own Hathmec before they were married and placed it at their home around Washington, DC. He acquired a job as a city engineer and life was good. All was well until 1920, when his oldest son, Evan, was struck with a disease that could take his life. Doctors couldn't help Evan, so Liam had to make a decision that would alter all of our lives forever.

"Liam decided to pull out his Hathmec pendant and create a new pendant for Evan. He then copied his own health charm and gave it to

Chapter 6

Evan for his pendant. Within minutes, Evan felt better, and within the day, he was completely healed. Liam made the decision that he wanted to give both of his sons the ability to heal from illness, so he also gave a Hathmec to his younger son, Daniel.

"Liam refused to use his Hathmec several years later as he watched his wife pass away in 1959. As Liam began to grow ill in early 1960, he brought his two sons together. Both were still young, as they had used the power of their Hathmec charms for years. Liam decided to tell his sons of his true origin and gave them the option to use the power of the Hathmec to help this world. He turned over his own Hathmec to Evan, who then gave a full copy to his brother, Daniel. Liam's pendant contained all of the charms needed for each skill. Liam Liot passed away early on a Saturday morning at his home in Washington, DC.

"His sons, Evan and Daniel, decided to use the full powers of their Hathmec pendants to change the world. The brothers worked together for over twenty years until the younger of the brothers, Daniel, saw that he and his brother weren't working toward the same goal. He wasn't happy with the methods Evan had used to get things done, so he confronted him. Since Liam had given his original charms to Evan, he had the full control over any copies of them that were produced, even Daniel's. Evan took Daniel's charms from him and had him killed."

"Wait a minute, Mr. Wainright," interrupted Matthew. "Are you telling us that this Evan Elliott is the Supreme Leader?"

Walter cleared his throat. "Yes, Evan Elliott is the Supreme Leader and he killed his own brother, a very good friend of mine, Daniel Elliot."

April told her boys, "Walter was close enough with Daniel that he told him this story before he was killed. He was concerned about what his brother might do when he confronted him. Walter has been leading the fight against the Supreme Leader ever since."

Connor asked, "Where did you get your Hathmec pendant?"

Walter looked at the pendant and said, "Daniel copied his own and gave it to me a few weeks before he was killed. He only copied the health charm because he was worried about the effects that the other charms might have on true humans."

Matthew asked, "True humans?"

"Yes, you have to remember that Daniel and Evan are half human and half alien, so they weren't sure if the full power of the pendant could be used by someone that didn't have some alien in them. It turns out that humans can handle the power, but they have a lessened ability to use it."

Connor asked another question. "I've never seen a security guard throw a carrier stone at anyone, so how do they control people?"

Walter put his head down, as if he was ashamed to answer Connor's question, but he eventually looked up and said, "The reason that guards or anyone else with a Hathmec can control anyone, without using a carrier stone, is due to something that still haunts me."

"Evan Elliott didn't think it was good enough to only have control over someone when he could place a carrier stone on them. He orchestrated a plan so that every baby, after they were born, would be injected with serum that carries faint traces of carrier stones from his Hathmec."

Matthew interjected, "So, you're saying that all humans are injected with these carriers during a child's vaccination shots?"

Johnson added, "He started using the shots in the year 2020, and by 2050, he could control the vast majority of the world."

Walter continued, "Since every Hathmec copy that has ever been made, besides the one that I have, came from Evan Elliott, he has total control over every man, woman, and child on this planet. The health charm on my pendant protects me from the copies he has made for his security teams and governors, but it is no match for his, one on one."

Matthew walked over to April and Connor and tried to figure out what to say next. "If that's the case, what can anyone do to stop him?"

Walter showed a small grin on the left side of his face and slyly responded to Matthew, "I'm so glad you asked me that, because we do have a plan to stop him, but we will need your help."

Matthew, confused by the comment, responded, "Our help? What in the world can we do to fight the Supreme Leader?"

Johnson took a quick peek to a door at the far side of the room and asked Mr. Wainright, "Should we go ahead and take them to room 3?"

Walter shook his head no and said, "It's already been a long day for these young men and April. How about we let them get some rest and we can show them room 3 in the morning."

Chapter 6

Matthew and Connor both showed their displeasure. Connor demanded, "We don't need any sleep; we need more answers."

"Yeah, go ahead and show us this room 3 now."

Walter turned to April. "What do you think?"

April took one look at the boys and said, "They won't be able to sleep anyway. Let's go ahead and see what's behind door 3."

"Mr. Johnson, please lead the way."

Johnson led the two boys, April, and Walter to the door labeled room 3 and put his hand on the doorknob. He turned to April and the boys. "Now, when you go in here, keep to the side walls and don't get too close to the...well, you'll know it when you see it."

As Johnson turned the knob on the door, the boys' hearts raced with anticipation and dread as to what they would see on the other side. The door opened and Matthew could see inside the room. Only one thing came from his lips: "Oh my god!"

Chapter 7

THE RORIMITE TUNNEL

"What is it?" uttered Matthew, as he looked at the stray images flashing through a wall in the center of the room.

Matthew walked closer to the wall when Johnson put his arm up in front of him. "I told you not to get too close. Get back here with the rest of us."

April grabbed both Connor and Matthew's hands. The boys were mesmerized by the images as they flashed back and forth across the opening. It was the size of a doorway but had no boundaries of structure, like a doorframe. A person's face flared in and out, along with scenes of buildings and animals. The images were blinding at times, but were also soft, as if looking at a cloudy sky or an insect as it ran along the grass. There for an instant and then gone; moments in time preserved by this strange mirror.

April asked, "Walter, what are we looking at? It's like a movie suspended in air or a storm contained in a bottle."

Walter Wainright walked to the far side of the room and pulled a lever attached to a small console secured to the wall. The doorway to the images vanished in the blink of an eye. The other side of the room had replaced the exciting views of the doorway. Connor exclaimed, "What did you do that for?"

Walter moved back to the front of the room and said, "There's no sense in using any more power than we have to. You've seen what you need to see."

Chapter 7

Matthew strolled into the area previously occupied by the bizarre images and asked, "What exactly have we seen, Mr. Wainright?" Walter crossed his arms and raised his brow. "I mean Walter. What exactly have we seen, Walter?"

"What you have before you is a technological marvel that was originally part of Liam Liot's spacecraft. The problem was that Liam Liot couldn't use this wonder due to an extreme lack of a power source. He had no way to run it."

Connor asked, "Run it? Is it some kind of movie projector or something?"

Walter scoffed at Connor's statement. "No, it's not a fancy movie projector."

Walter placed his hand on the control module. It was clear that he was still impressed by the magnitude of what it could do. "It's the only known time machine in existence."

Matthew and Connor's eyes grew to the size of tennis balls as they stared at each other in disbelief. Connor replied, "A time machine? You're out of your mind, old man." April shot Connor a stone-cold stare and reminded him about his manners.

Walter removed his hand from the console with the lever and said, "I don't blame the boys for not believing me, April; this is a hard one to swallow. You see, this time machine can only be powered by the sector power crystals that were installed in all the districts about twenty years ago."

Matthew asked, "How does it work?"

"Glad you asked."

"The minute that Liam Liot's spacecraft crashed on Earth, it began recording history and storing it inside this panel. The power required to record was next to nothing; it actually used reserves from a type of alien battery internal to it."

April said, "So it's some type of recorder. Something you can use to see what actually happened from the time Liam landed to present day."

Walter replied, "That is one use for it, but the truly extraordinary use is that you can actually go back to those times through this powered portal. It is called a rorimite tunnel. Loosely translated, it's a time mirror tunnel."

With the rorimite tunnel shut down and the lights to the room powered up, April noticed all of the control systems and panels that lined the room's walls. The control boards lit up like Christmas lights and the panels illustrated pulsating graphs and power readings from throughout the room. The balance of the room was similar to a doctor's office from the twentieth century: white walls, clean smell, but no personal touches of style at all.

Connor revealed a wry grin and chuckled to Johnson. "You actually believe this junk? If Liam Liot could time travel, why didn't he just go back and save his wife from the crash?"

Johnson tapped Connor on the head with his index finger and said, "You're not listening, little man. The tunnel didn't start recording until after they crashed. Even if it did, there was no power source to run this thing until a few years ago."

Walter added, "Yes, the main power drivers from the spacecraft were damaged beyond repair. Earth just didn't have the technology or structure at the time to help Liam. Besides, Liam eventually came to terms with living on Earth and the life that he could have here."

April reviewed the control panel. "What makes you an expert on this machine, Walter?"

There was a large wall full of books that Walter leaned against as he replied, "Daniel Elliot trusted me with things that he didn't even trust his own brother with. For quite some time, Daniel knew of his father's library of technical specifications for the spacecraft and all the equipment that was within it."

Matthew asked, "Is that stuff in the other room from the craft, too?"

Johnson said, "Some of it is, but a lot of it is just artifacts from the early 2000s."

Connor picked up one of the books and joked, "I guess everything in the alien specifications are written in English to make it easy on you, right?"

Walter snickered at the boy's wit but explained that one of the first pieces of alien equipment that did work was a translator box. He used the translator over several decades to decode all of the alien specifications.

Chapter 7

"I am the world's only expert in alien time travel," revealed Mr. Wainright. "This is the only weapon we have against the Supreme Leader and his followers, and I need your help to use it against him."

"I still don't get it Walter," said Matthew. "What can we do that you couldn't do yourself in the past?"

Walter pondered the question and presented his response in three distinct validations. "Number one, you cannot time travel within your own lifetime. That pretty well takes me and Johnson here out as far back as 1950. Number two, the goal of this trip is very specific to both of your ages."

Walter paused for a moment, and Matthew asked, "What's the last reason?"

Walter scratched his head and turned to April. "I just think that you and your family are meant to do this."

Connor picked up an old cell phone from one of the tables and said, "Well, that's reassuring; he has a good feeling about not killing us in the alien time machine."

April asked, "What is it exactly that you want us to do for you?"

Walter grabbed a small notebook and reviewed it before answering April's question. He explained, "If you remember, I told you that Liam Liot had separated his alien wife's Hathmec and presented some of the charms to people or families that he had run across during his early time on Earth. One of the families that Liam gave a charm to was the Curry family. This was back in the early 1800s."

Walter removed a photo from one of his folders and passed it around. "You see the young lady in the center of this photo?"

Connor and Matthew started to grin and in a muted volume said, "She's really cute."

Walter rolled his eyes and took the photo from the boys. "Yes, she is a very cute young lady, but she is also the owner of Saras's attribute charm for the Hathmec pendant."

Walter saw that April and the boys were befuddled, so he clarified, "You see, this is Amanda Curry. She was sixteen years old in 1984 and had been the owner of this alien treasure since her birthday of that year."

Connor started counting on his fingers and asked, "You said the Currys got the charm in 1800; doesn't that make her 184 years old?"

Walter shook his head no and explained, "The Curry family was given the charm in 1800, and it was passed from family member to family member over those 184 years. In fact, Amanda's grandmother had planned on giving her the charm when she was born, but Amanda's mother kept it until she thought Amanda was mature enough to take care of it."

Connor strutted over and put his hand on Walter's shoulder. "So, we just need to go back to 1984 and take the charm from this girl and bring it back to you?"

Walter removed Connor's hand and said, "I wish it were that easy, but it will take a bit more skill than that. A Hathmec charm cannot be taken from someone by physical force and then be used by that person. It is linked to the owner, and only the owner of the charm can relinquish that power to someone else. It must be of their own free will."

Matthew asked, "So, if we take the charm from her, it's just a useless decoration?"

Johnson replied, "That's right; you need to find a way to get Amanda Curry to give you the charm of her own free will."

Walter pulled the Hathmec from his shirt and stared at it. "The charms from Saras's Hathmec are the only objects on Earth that compare to the power of Evan Elliott's Hathmec. We must find all of them before he does."

April found it difficult to take her eyes from Walter's Hathmec and asked, "Are you saying that the Supreme Leader is looking for these missing charms as well?"

"No, April, he has already found them. He found them over the last two centuries, with his first find coming in 1984. It was Amanda Curry."

Matthew utilized his logical mind and asked, "Wait a minute...won't we change history if the Supreme Leader isn't the one who finds the charm?"

Walter replied, "Another good question, my boy; that's why we are going to let him think that he found the charm with a decoy."

Walter reached into the drawer of one of his many workbenches and pulled out a small, square, shiny yellow charm. "This replica of the

Chapter 7

attribute charm should do the trick. I've worked on it for years to make sure that it is identical to the real thing, beyond having alien powers. This is what you will use to trick Evan Elliott into thinking that he was successful in retrieving the attribute charm."

Connor grabbed the fake charm. "This is never gonna work. The Supreme Leader is all knowing; he'll see right through this, April."

Walter cringed for the first time and started to reveal his own frustrations. "Stop calling your mother by her first name!"

Connor was stunned and backed away from the table. He watched as Walter's face grew red. "She is your mother, or your mom, or mommy; I don't care what you call her, but not April. No one in 1984 called their parents by their first name. If they did, they were smacked in the mouth or grounded, so you might as well get used to calling her Mom."

Johnson added, "Another thing—you two are brothers, plain and simple."

Walter continued his tirade. "The Supreme Leader is no god; he's just a man who has too much power. This will succeed if you will work together to make it happen. You three are our only chance."

April concurred and asked Johnson and Walter to give her a minute alone with her boys. They agreed and left them alone to talk.

"I'm sorry I wasn't able to tell you boys everything about me. I thought you were too young to understand all of this."

Connor's body shook with nervous energy, and he couldn't look his mother in the eyes. "I still don't think we really know everything we need to know about your past, April—or Mom, whoever you are."

April replied, "I am your mother and I am Matthew's mother, and I care about you boys more than anything in this world."

Matthew asked, "How did you meet this guy? Did you always know he was gonna ask us to do this?"

April shuddered as she prepared herself to answer that difficult question. "I met Mr. Wainright just before Connor was born, and he helped me through some tough times. He taught me, just as he has been teaching you, about the true history of the world and what the Supreme Leader has done to control it and us."

Matthew tried to wrap his head around all of it. "Do you really believe all the things Walter's telling us? I mean, do you really trust him?"

April responded without hesitation. "I trust Walter with my life and I would trust him with yours. Walter has been putting these plans together for a very long time. He knew he would need a young man to do the job, and when I had Connor, he saw his chance to recruit me. He knew it would just be a matter of time before you boys were old enough to help."

Connor pounded his fist on the table. "So I'm just here to do his dirty work for him?"

"Of course not, but I knew once you and Matthew learned the truth, you would want to do everything you could to help Walter's cause. I promise both of you that I am as passionate about this as anyone. It just happened a bit earlier than I had hoped."

Matthew responded, "What do you mean it's happening earlier than you'd hoped."

April described the conversation that she had with Walter Wainright fourteen years earlier, while holding Connor in her arms as a newborn baby. "Walter Wainright helped me and I promised to help him. We had planned on introducing you to all of this when you turned sixteen, but plans can change at the drop of a hat."

Matthew placed his hand near the rorimite tunnel where the images had been earlier and said, "So Connor's being asked to help save the world, but what about me? How do I fit into this?"

April put her arms around Matthew. "You were the blessing that I never expected. You were added to my little family just days after Connor was born. From that point on, I decided that you would be raised as brothers and we would all work for the common goal of helping Walter and his followers."

Connor approached April and Matthew. "You know, this is a lot to take in all at once."

April responded, "I know it is, but we have to decide, as a family, whether we are going to help Walter and this cause or turn our backs on the truth. My vote is to help."

Chapter 7

"Can you give Connor and me a minute alone?" April agreed and went out the adjoining door.

Connor rubbed the top of his head with ever-increasing speed. "This is freakin' crazy, man! Time travel and resistance movements; April's like a spy or something, and we've been brought to the land of the lost down here."

Matthew asked, "Do you believe April loves us?"

"Yes, I know she loves us."

"Do you think she would ever ask us to do something that she wasn't sure was the right thing to do?"

Connor paced around the room and replied, "I know what you're trying to do, but I'm just not sure about this. I still think they're keeping something from us."

Matthew said, "Well, the only way that we can ever find out for sure is to go along with this and see what happens."

Connor sauntered over to the rorimite tunnel and punched his hands into its empty void. "It would be cool to see what things were like a couple of hundred years ago." He stopped punching and stared at Matthew. "You realize we'll probably walk into this thing and just explode or something."

Matthew joined his brother at the tunnel and with a smirk of his own said, "If I'm going to explode, I wouldn't want to do it with anyone but my brother."

Connor pushed Matthew away, laughed, and said, "Don't get all mushy on me. I'll still kick your butt all the way back to Sector 37."

Matthew scanned the room one final time and asked, "So, are we going to do this or not?"

Connor grabbed Matthew around the neck and playfully rubbed his head. "Yeah, let's do it."

As Matthew and Connor entered the adjoining room, they saw April, Walter, and Johnson standing around a large circular table. Like in the room they had just left, there were various gadgets and junk sitting all around. April, confident in her boys, asked, "Well, what do you two think?"

Connor blurted out, "Let's fire this time thing up and get going. I have a cute chick in 1984 waiting for me."

April ran to the boys and gave them both a loving embrace. "I am so proud of you two."

Matthew paused for a moment and gave April a surprise that she had waited for the majority of her adult life. It was a simple gesture but meant so much to her. Matthew simply told her, "We're proud of you too, Mom." Tears filled the eyes of the thirty-two-year-old mother of two as she realized the effect that she had had on the two young men standing before her. She wiped her eyes and heard Walter in the background.

"Let's not get ahead of ourselves just yet, boy. We still have some preparations to make before you all head off to 1984."

Connor asked, "What kind of prep work?"

Johnson grabbed some old magazines from one of the tables and passed them out. "We need to make sure you know what you're heading into. These magazines are reprints from originals that came out around 1984."

Walter emphasized, "Yes, please pay close attention to the words in the articles and how people are dressed. It is very important that you don't stick out; you need to blend in with the people of the time."

Johnson reiterated, "The 1980s were nothing like today, so you need to prepare yourselves."

"When you get there, pay close attention to how everyone talks. You'll be in the South and if you don't sound a little like everyone else, they'll think something is wrong with you."

Walter took out a set of plans, a checklist of all the things that must be completed before April and the boys left. The first action was the most important. "Come over to the desk; I have something very important to give each of you."

They saw three pendants lying side by side; each of them had a blue health charm inserted into it. Walter told them, "I have three copies of my own Hathmec pendant for you to take on your trip. Go ahead and put them around your neck."

Chapter 7

A warm rush overwhelmed each of their bodies and any aches or pains that had been present were gone. Connor noted, "I can see better."

Matthew added, "My leg isn't hurting anymore."

April was shocked. "Nothing hurts anymore."

Walter explained that they were now a part of the Hathmec legacy and no one, except Walter himself, could ever take the pendants away from them. He asked each of them to create a carrier stone in their left hands.

Each of them accomplished this task with no problem. Connor said, "It's like I've always known how to do this."

Walter explained that the Hathmec itself furnishes the knowledge that is needed to create the stones. "The moment you placed those on your neck, you were given the knowledge of the pendant and how to use it. Over time, you will master what can be done with it."

As the boys continued to practice their newfound skills creating carrier stones, Walter looked over the checklist and inquired about the second action. "In order to get things set up properly for you in 1984, we need to figure out what you will all be called."

Connor asked, "What do you mean? Why can't I just be Connor?"

Walter understood the boy's confusion and explained, "Everyone deserves a last name, not some random number, so I want you to tell me what your last name is going to be."

April suggested, "We could go simple like White or Black, perhaps Smith."

Connor wanted to go with something flashy. "How about Encarnacion or Thunderlion?"

April rolled her eyes and asked Matthew what he thought.

Matthew quietly contemplated his response and suggested. "Well, Walter said that we were his best chance for stopping the Supreme Leader, so how about we use that for a last name?"

Connor asked, "You wanna be called Matthew Supreme Leader?"

Matthew said with a chuckle, "No, I wanna be called Matthew Chance."

Walter said, "I like it." He shook all three members of the family's hands and said, "I would like to introduce April Chance, Connor Chance, and Matthew Chance."

Matthew looked to his mother and brother with a wide-eyed smile. "I've never had a last name before; this is pretty cool."

Connor borrowed a pen from the desk and wrote his name out to see what it looked like. "It's not too bad, but I still think Thunderlion would be better."

April reviewed the signature and gave her seal of approval. "I think the Chance family will do just fine."

Matthew sidled up to Walter and looked over the checklist. "What does 'calibrate R tunnel' mean?"

Walter hadn't noticed Matthew standing beside him and was startled. "That is the most important task left to complete, my boy. I have to make sure that the tunnel is calibrated to the proper time and place to ensure that I don't send you to the wrong place or accidentally land you in a pond or lake."

Matthew asked, "How long will it take to get that done?"

Walter looked at his watch and replied, "I should have it ready in the next six to eight hours. I suggest you boys and your mother look over your magazines and get some rest before I send you on your way."

April saw an envelope with her name on it lying on a nearby table and picked it up. She was stopped by Walter. April saw intensity in Walter's eyes as he grabbed her hand. "Is something wrong? I thought this was for me."

Walter released her hand, a smile returning to his face, and said, "No, this will be for you, but not until you get back to 1984. These are very detailed instructions and directions for you to follow while there."

April asked, "Wouldn't it be better for me to go ahead and review these, just to prepare?"

Walter replied, "No, I think it would be better for you to wait and look at these once you get there." Walter leaned in close and whispered, "Another thing—don't let the boys see anything in this packet." April was surprised by the request, but told Walter that she understood.

Chapter 7

Connor made an astute observation as he read through one of the magazines. "Why do we have to leave so quickly for this mission? I mean, we have a time machine here, so why the rush?" Walter, surprised that Connor developed such a question, responded with both a logical answer and an explanation of the R tunnel.

"You make a very good point, Connor, and I wish we had the time to prepare all of you better, but we don't. When you saw the light coming from the warehouse window, I was actually doing two things." He clarified that he was harvesting the energy that would be needed to run the time tunnel and he was also moving his base of operations from that building to their current location.

"You see, boys, our operation is constantly avoiding Sector 1's sweeps and scans of the planet; we have to keep moving or they'll discover what we're up to." He explained that the power grids for each sector could power the tunnel. He also explained that he could only harness enough of that power to keep the tunnel active for two weeks.

Matthew asked, "Are you saying that we only have two weeks to convince this girl that she should give us that charm?"

Walter responded, "Of course not." The boys felt relieved until Walter finished his response. "You will probably only have about a week and a half by the time you get to her town, find her, and actually introduce yourselves to her."

Connor threw his hands up in the air and started to berate Walter. "This is just great; we have a freakin' time machine here, but we don't have any time to get ready to go two hundred years in the past. Then when we get there, we have a whole two weeks to get the job done!"

"That's right," responded Walter.

Matthew interjected, "I just don't understand. When we go back in time and then come back, won't it be instantaneous to you here? We can just come back a couple of seconds after we leave."

Johnson disagreed and asked Walter to explain "the whole time travel thing" to the boys. Walter walked over to the desk and drew a line on it. He explained that time travel is a bit different from what the boys may have seen in the movies.

"The tunnel must remain open the entire time that you are gone, and I must monitor it to make sure nothing comes through it that shouldn't come through it. The entire two weeks that you are gone, two weeks will pass here as well."

April asked, "So the tunnel only works in one direction; is that what you are saying?"

Walter responded, "In simple terms, you're correct. One of the reasons I chose this location for this trip is based on its location. None of this was here in 1984." Walter went on to explain that the current base of operation was part of a national park and the location would be well hidden when they arrived in the Atlanta area in the year 1984.

"I can only keep the tunnel open for two weeks. The power we'll be pulling from the sector power supplies will lead G1 right to our door if we pull for any longer."

Matthew asked, "What is G1?"

Johnson explained, "G1 stands for Government 1; that's what we call sector leaders and Sector 1's hit men who continually search for us. Our goal is to avoid anyone associated with G1."

Walter told the boys and April to get some sleep and rest up for the trip. "Time travel is going to take a bit out of you, even with the health charm around your neck. It will keep you from completely passing out, but it will probably take a couple of hours to really get to feeling good again. You may even have some hallucinations, so don't freak out if you see tiny pink elephants dancing around when you come to."

Walter led them to a side room. "Rest up and I'll come and get you when the tunnel is ready." The boys and April entered the room with little talk and all three lay down on the bed in the corner of the otherwise empty room.

Matthew pondered a question as he was lying between his brother and mother that everyone seemed to have forgotten about. He still didn't know who killed Brett back at the old warehouse. He began to bring it up to his mother and brother, but before he could, April said, "Let's just get some sleep, boys."

Connor replied, "I agree, let's just get a little shut-eye."

Chapter 7

Matthew didn't want to be the one to ruin the excitement of the moment and decided to keep quiet about the warehouse incident. For all he knew, Brett just had an accident. Maybe Keith Kellington had something to do with it. The worry drained from Matthew as he tried to close his eyes and get some sleep. The excitement of the pending trip was just too much to bear for the new Chance family, and they simply lay there in silence until a knock was heard at the door a few hours later.

Walter Wainright poked his head into the room and asked, "Are you ready to go?"

They had all daydreamed about what they were about to do. Each of them had their own ideas of what 1984 would be like. April worried about their mission and how the boys would handle themselves. Connor fantasized about Amanda Curry. He was her hero and she rewarded him with a kiss and the attribute charm. Matthew thought of nothing but the three men from Johnson's team who had sacrificed themselves for him and his family. He wondered where that fire and passion came from.

April and the boys were given clothes that accurately matched the style of the time. The boys were both in stonewashed jeans and T-shirts, while April was put into a kind of cloth jumpsuit. The jumpsuit was pink with white sneakers to go with it. She refused to put on the matching headband.

Connor commented, "You know, this isn't so bad; I kind of like the jeans."

April replied, "I look ridiculous. Is this really what women wore back then?"

Walter said, "I've been around for a long time. You'll just have to trust me."

Walter and Johnson led the boys and April back into the R tunnel room. The Chance family could see that the tunnel was fired up, and it looked ready to go. Johnson pulled out three backpacks and gave one to each member of the family.

Connor asked, "What are these for?"

"These are important items that you'll need for the trip. There are some gadgets that could come in handy in Matthew's bag."

Matthew asked, "What kind of gadgets?"

"Alien gadgets, my boy. Don't worry about them right now; I'm sending instructions along so you know what they're for."

Walter reached into his pocket and pulled out one last item. "I almost forgot to give you this watch." Walter placed a fairly large watch on Matthew's wrist. It was silver with a shiny, almost glistening look to it.

Matthew asked, "Is this some type of special time watch that helps us know how much time we have to get back to the tunnel?"

Walter, astonished, replied, "Actually, that's exactly what it is, and more. You see the four buttons on the side; each has a special trait that you will learn about later. I want you to pay close attention to this button on the top of the watch."

Walter pointed to a triangular button that had a small flap covering it. "This button should only be pushed in an emergency situation, and it can only be pressed once."

Connor motioned to Matthew and said, "Maybe I should hold on to it for you?"

Walter shook his head and said, "No, the watch is for Matthew." Matthew looked down at the face of the watch and saw a counter regressing from 336. Walter grabbed Matthew's wrist and said, "That is 336 hours from the time you go through the tunnel to when you need to be coming home. If you're down to zero, you'll be stuck in the past and the future will be as it is now—ruined."

April asked a final question. "Anything else we need to know before we leave?"

Walter pulled his hand up to his goatee and said, "Yes, one last thing. Remember what you're there to do. Get the pendant and get home. We want to make sure that things stay as close to actual events of the time as possible. Any major changes could be a disaster to current time."

Walter hugged April. The two boys got a hearty handshake. "All I can do is wish you luck and safety." Walter moved back to the control

Chapter 7

panel, pushed a couple of buttons, and the R tunnel wall lit up as bright as the youngest star in the sky. "It's time."

April took one hand of each of the boys, and they slowly made their way to the light of the tunnel. Connor yelled to Walter, "Is this going to hurt?"

Walter screamed back, "Probably!" In the blink of an eye, the Chance family was gone.

Chapter 8

WILL WORK FOR FOOD

The kaleidoscope of colors and images overpowered the senses as Matthew, Connor, and April entered the R tunnel. Matthew looked to his right and saw April grasping his hand. The flow of light and sound surrounded Matthew as if trapped inside of a rolling disco ball. Matthew looked to his left and observed random images of time as they passed all around him.

Bright illumination intermixed with the reflections of people and places that had long since passed away. Matthew found it difficult to know whether he or the tunnel was moving. It was hard to tell how much time passed while in the vortex. The three members of the Chance family looked at one another and wondered when the psychedelic slide show would end.

Suddenly, as if someone had flicked the power off to a television set, all three of them were lying on their backs, surrounded by the sweet smell of fresh flowers and grass. Matthew looked up and noticed the bushy overgrowth of tall maple trees as the sun peeked through gaps in the leaves. The awkward shape of a cactus tree caught his attention, and he tried to pick himself up from the ground.

April got up from the ground first and said, "OK, that was weird. You boys all right?"

Connor popped up and replied, "I feel like an alien charm is filling me up with goodness and feelings of the supernatural kind."

April replied, "I'll take that as a yes. How about you Matthew?"

Chapter 8

Matthew pushed himself up from a seated position and wandered around the area. He spotted a small cave covered up just behind him. The cave hid the flashing lights and images that made up the tunnel. He took a deep breath and said, "The tunnel should be hidden well in that cave." Matthew looked down at his watch. "We have just over 335 hours to do what we need to do."

April opened up her backpack, full of papers and notebooks sent by Mr. Wainright. She leaned back against the stump of an old tree and opened a notebook titled, "OPEN ME FIRST." April read through the first few paragraphs and chuckled.

Connor asked, "What's so funny?"

April looked up from the page and explained, "Nothing really—it's just that the first sentence on this page says that if we are reading this first sentence, that means we didn't blow up on the trip through the tunnel."

Connor replied, "Nice to know his confidence was so high."

Matthew asked, "OK, so what are we supposed to do now, Mom?"

April thought, *Mom! Hearing that will never get old.* The boys noticed her grin and knew the significance of a "mom" comment.

"Based on what Walter gave us, it looks like we're in the middle of a state park called Spicewater." She explained that there should be a creek and small lake located just north of their location. They needed to find the creek and follow it east until they arrived at the park's main office.

They all stood still and concentrated on the sound of running water. Matthew and Connor both exclaimed, "I hear it!" Matthew pointed in a direction that could only be described as down a hill and to the east of the tunnel.

Connor said, "But I actually heard it first."

April replied, "It doesn't matter who heard it first; it only matters that we find it."

The family took off down the hill. They were almost to the bottom when Matthew asked, "How are we gonna find the tunnel again when it's time to go home?" April opened her notebook again and stopped the boys' progress.

"You're right; I should have read farther down the page. Walter says that your watch has a locator function that can be used to mark the position of the tunnel. It says that you can point the watch at the location you want to find later and just push this button and it stores it for later."

April showed Matthew the button and Matthew turned his wrist toward the opening of the small cave. The watch emitted a small red beam. It hit the face of the cave opening and then disappeared. A small icon blinked on the face of the watch that stated "Store 1." He looked over at Connor. "I guess it worked."

April added, "Based on Walter's description, all we have to do is hit that icon when it's time to get to the tunnel, and the watch will lead us there."

Matthew replied, "We'll just look for the area close to the cactus tree."

Connor asked, "What cactus tree?"

The Chances continued their trek to the creek. They jumped over logs, dodged mud holes, and listened for the sounds of rushing water. Birds rattled the tree limbs and took off and landed in unison with the family's steps. Matthew and Connor helped their mother maneuver through the thick woods.

They reached the creek in a short time and Connor asked, "Does anyone know which way is east?"

Matthew's watch had a compass, so he tried to navigate. "Yeah, we need to follow the creek downstream, per the watch."

Connor grabbed Matthew's wrist and exclaimed, "Dang! I should have gotten a watch, too. I get dibs on the first gadget thing that Walter said is in your bag."

April walked in between the two boys and put her arms around them. "Let's get going; I'm not sure how far we are from this office, and I don't want to get caught out here in the dark."

The family walked alongside the park's creek and were amazed at all they saw. The wonderful colors of the changing leaves on the trees were all around them. The slight noises, cracks, and pops of the woods around them kept their senses awake and in tune with their

Chapter 8

surroundings. April said, "It's so beautiful here; it's even nicer than the park back home." It was a perfect fall day in the state of Georgia.

They followed the creek until they ran into a large, sparkling lake. There were hundreds of people on the water in boats, and ducks landed with little effort along the edges of the banks. In all, the Chances had completed their walk in less than thirty minutes. They were only a few minutes away from the park office, as Connor pointed out.

"That must be it!" he exclaimed.

Matthew asked, "How do you know?"

Connor pointed to a sign just a few feet ahead that read "Park Office" and had an arrow pointing to the building. "I can read, you moron."

Before they left the lakeshore, Matthew asked, "What are those people in the boats doing with those long sticks?"

Connor didn't know, so they both looked to April for an explanation. April opened her notebook and hoped to find an answer. Instead of answering, she changed the subject. "We need to get up to that office and see if we can get a ride into town. It looks like we're going to Atlanta."

Connor asked, "Is that the name of a town or are we looking for someone named Atlanta?"

Matthew took the opportunity and repaid the moron comment. "Now who's the stupid one? Don't you remember anything we read?" Connor shrugged his shoulders.

"Atlanta was a really big city back then. There were no districts, just cities. I think the smaller areas are called towns."

April chimed in. "That's right; I think our district is really close to where Atlanta was located back then."

Connor rolled his eyes. "Fine, it's a city then; let's just figure out how to get there."

April led the boys up a narrow path to the park office. She saw a park ranger loading up some gear into the back of an old red-and-white pickup truck. April approached the ranger and asked, "Excuse me, sir, can you tell me if there is any way to get a ride into Atlanta from here?"

The ranger turned around and the family was flashed by a name tag that read "Joe." He had a comforting smile that ran from ear to ear.

"Well, yes, ma'am, there's a bus that runs from here to the city every couple of hours you can catch a ride on."

The southern accent of the ranger was startling but endearing to the Chance family. "Only two bucks apiece for the ride."

April replied, "Two bucks, you say. Well, that's not bad at all. Do you happen to know when the next bus arrives?"

Joe took a look out over the lake. "Most of the fishermen have finished up for the day and there are only a few boats on the water, so it's about five. There should be another bus in about fifteen minutes."

Matthew took Connor by the shirt sleeve and whispered, "Fishing… of course…I read about that."

Joe pointed to a bench at the front of the office and said, "Just wait over by the bench and take bus number 2212. It'll get you back to civilization. If you need anything else, just ask for Ranger Joe Walley." April thanked the young ranger and motioned for the boys to follow her.

April said, "OK, boys, I'm pretty sure I saw some numbers on some green pieces of paper in my bag. That's probably the two bucks that the ranger was talking about for the bus, but I have one question."

Matthew interrupted his mother. "Let me guess? What's a bus?"

April furled her brow and glared back at Matthew. "I know what a bus is; it's like a transport with no rails. What I wanted to ask was if you noticed anything strange about that man, Ranger Joe?"

Connor asked his mother, "Did *you* notice anything strange?"

"Just that he was so nice and helpful. He had on a uniform and everything, just like one of the security team members back home."

Matthew looked to his mother as they reached the bench and said, "Maybe men in uniform are just nicer in 1984."

There were others waiting by the benches when the Chances arrived. There was an older couple with a child, probably no more than six or seven years old, looking through a pamphlet about the park. The young girl sat on the older gentleman's lap as he pointed out things on the map they had seen earlier in the day.

The young girl wore a bright yellow-and-white sundress with white, strapped sandals. She giggled as she recognized pictures of animals and

Chapter 8

sites in the park. April noticed that the bottom of the dress was wet. "She just got a little too close to the edge of the lake."

April was startled. "I'm sorry, were you talking to me?"

The older woman replied, "Yes, I couldn't help but notice you staring at my granddaughter's dress; she accidently dipped it in the water a little earlier. She can be a handful sometimes."

April smiled as she asked, "So, this is your granddaughter and you made a day of it at the park?"

The older woman moved close to April and said, "Yes, this is my granddaughter, Cassie, and my husband, Glen."

"My name is Nancy." She leaned into April and said, "Cassie's parents, my daughter and son-in-law, were killed in a car wreck a few months ago, so Cassie lives with us now."

April replied, "That's awful. I'm so sorry for your loss."

Nancy's face frowned and her wrinkled skin drooped to the corners of her mouth. "Yes, it has been difficult on all of us, so we try to take some weekend trips, just to try to enjoy the day with Cassie."

Connor listened in on April's conversation and interrupted. "So, they just let you have Cassie, even though you're so old?"

April snapped at Connor. "Don't be rude to this nice woman!"

Connor stepped back and said, "I didn't mean any disrespect, ma'am. I just figured she would be better off with younger guardians, that's all."

Nancy, perplexed by the young boy's comment, replied, "Well, young man, I think Cassie belongs with her family, not some strangers who don't even know her. We'll be OK; we raised our daughter and we can raise our granddaughter."

Matthew eased over to Cassie and her grandfather and asked the little girl, "Did you have a good time at the park today?"

The little girl looked up from the pamphlet and shyly nodded yes. Glen asked Matthew what he thought of the park. Matthew smirked and said, "I wish we could've stayed longer and done some fishing, but we need to be getting home."

"I'm sorry to have been so rude. My name is April and these are my sons, Matthew and Connor." April continued to get a sense of satisfaction from calling them her sons.

Glen extended his hand to Matthew and said, "Well, it's nice to meet you folks. So, where are you from? You sure don't sound like you're from around these parts. If I had to guess, I would say you're from up North."

April looked confused, and she almost blurted out Sector 37. Her mind raced as she struggled to remember the name of the town that they were supposed to be from. All of a sudden, a bus pulled into the parking lot across from the benches. April said, "Oh, look, I see the number 2212 on the side of the, um, the um..."

Matthew intervened, "Bus?"

Glen said, "It sure is, but that isn't ours. We're taking the 2213."

The bus pulled to the curb and opened its doors. April noticed the paper money that two other passengers used to pay for the trip and she started to dig into her bag. Nancy tapped her on the arm and said, "I hope you and your boys get home safely; it was very nice to meet you." April returned the comment and motioned the boys to get on the bus.

As they loaded on, the driver said, "That'll be six dollars for Atlanta, station 2."

April pulled out a stash of money and counted out six singles to give to the large, sweaty driver. The bills included several tens, twenties, and hundreds.

The driver looked at April, astonished by what he saw. "Good grief, lady! You shouldn't be pulling out that kind of cash when you get into the city; you'll get your throat slit."

April, startled by the comment, thanked the driver and moved to the rear of the bus, where Connor and Matthew had already found seats.

Matthew waited for April to sit down before stating the obvious. "Can you believe what we just saw?"

April responded, "Yeah, it's amazing that those two older adults are going to raise their own granddaughter. No government to say they are too old to care for her and no one telling them they can or can't go to the park for the day; it's just wonderful."

Both of the boys looked at each other and grinned. Connor explained, "Yeah, that's great and all, but we were talking about those two girls who got on the bus before us."

Chapter 8

April turned to the front of the bus and saw two younger ladies wearing cutoff blue jean shorts, flip-flops, and bikini tops. Both had deep suntans and laughed as they discussed something from a magazine they couldn't put down.

"Oh, I see—yes, that is way too revealing for a young lady."

Matthew whispered to Connor, "Do you think all girls that age dress like that here?"

"I hope so."

April responded, "I heard that."

The bus pulled away from the park office, and the Chance family began to discuss their next moves. April removed her binder and passed out pages to the boys. She told them, "Each of you read these and then we'll swap. We should be able to get everything read before we get to Atlanta. We'll know exactly what we need to do from there."

Matthew asked if they could do some sightseeing during the ride, but April was insistent on getting all of Walter Wainright's instructions read before they arrived in Atlanta.

Walter was thorough in his preparations. He had sent hundreds of pages of documents, instructions, and suggestions for the Chance family. He wanted the family to get to Atlanta and take another bus to Memphis, Tennessee. The bus that they were currently on would get them within one mile of a main bus terminal in Atlanta, so it was easy walking distance.

Once in Memphis, the family needed to buy a car and drive approximately two hours into the extreme northwestern part of the state to a town called Travis. Once in Travis, they were to go to a mobile home park called Horizons and rent a home to live in. As April dug through her bag, she found a fake driver's license for her and fake birth certificates for the boys.

Walter had sent along well over $20,000 in cash to make their needed purchases. Walter had been putting this plan together for years, and he spared no details that he felt would help April and the boys.

April focused her attention on the tasks that needed to be done while in 1984 while the boys were more focused on the descriptions and explanations of the times. Walter described, in great detail, the attitudes of the people at the end of the twentieth century. He described that the thinking of this area of the country was considered conservative for the time and a person's pride was his biggest weakness.

In 1984, the people of the South loved their country, their faith, their guns, and their football. Everything else was just there for decoration. For the boys, it was important that they understood the minds and attitudes of the young people of the time.

Walter gave details of the music of the time, the advent of cable television, and the pecking order of the normal American high school. It would be important to get in good with the kids that were in Amanda's clique, as he called it.

The trip from the park to Atlanta was broken into two segments. The first segment was down small two-lane roads. There wasn't much to see and the vicious bouncing of the bus was enough to make anyone sick. The second leg of the trip would be much more interesting.

Matthew said to Connor, as they read through Walter's instructions, "So we need to learn as much as we can about things called football, pop music, and video games. That shouldn't be too hard."

Connor responded, "He says that we should get a teen magazine when we get to Memphis and make sure we learn everything in it."

Matthew pointed to a picture of a football player and asked, "Do you think football is anything like beamball? It looks like this guy is throwing a ball similar to a beamball."

Connor's eyes lit up. "Yeah, I bet it's a lot like beamball. Where are the lasers?"

Matthew was captivated by the views of the city as the second part of the trip began. "Connor, look; those buildings are so tall."

Connor knocked Matthew out of the way and said, "Yeah, they all look different, too. They're made to different heights, and look, that one's round." April began to tell the boys to get back to the studying, but she was also drawn to the window.

She turned her head from side to side in excitement. There were so many sights, buildings, and people walking on the sidewalk. They were wearing different clothes and hats. April even spotted someone with art painted on his arm. April was taking it all in when she said, "This

Chapter 8

isn't what I expected, boys; it's even better. Everyone looks so different here."

A loud grinding noise encompassed the bus and the boys and April almost jumped from their seats. Matthew looked up into the sky and saw an airplane coming down toward the bus. Connor yelled out, "What is that!"

The bus driver activated the intercom and said, "Sorry about the noise everyone; the airport is just over that ridge and it can get loud when they come in for a landing. There are hundreds of flights going out every day."

Matthew said, "I thought flight was deemed too dangerous."

Connor chimed in, "Yeah, only the leaders are allowed to fly in their special planes."

Matthew yelled to the bus driver, "Excuse me, sir, but can anyone fly on these planes?"

The driver, confused by the question, responded, "If you have enough money; anyone can buy an airplane ticket, son." He went on to let the passengers know that they were just a few minutes from the bus terminal, so they needed to be collecting their things.

"What a load of crap!"

Connor asked his brother, "What are you talking about?"

"We live over two hundred years in the future, but we aren't allowed to fly in airplanes, but back in 1984, people could just buy a ticket and fly wherever they wanted? It's a bunch of crap!" Matthew's face turned a mild shade of red as Walter Wainright's truth became clearer.

Connor pondered his brother's comments for a moment. "Well, I'm sure there's a logical explanation for it. We shouldn't jump to any conclusions yet." Matthew wanted to reply to his brother's lazy comment but felt the bus come to an abrupt stop.

The bus driver's loud voice reverberated over the intercom as he announced they had arrived at their destination. The Chance family collected their backpacks and made their way to the front exit of the bus. April quietly told the boys to stay close to each other; she didn't want them to get separated. The boys told her that it wouldn't be a problem.

They then proceeded to run to the front of the bus and offered their assistance to the two young ladies in the bikini tops. "We'll help you with your bags!" They were politely denied their request, but the boys still felt a sense of accomplishment that they had garnered the nerve to ask.

April proceeded to the nearest terminal employee. She needed to determine the best way to go about purchasing tickets for the bus ride to Memphis. The boys explored the surrounding area. They wanted to investigate the busy terminal and find out what else was different about the past.

The boys were astounded at what they saw. In one corner, they saw men dressed in suits carrying briefcases. In another corner, a family of four wore T-shirts, tennis shoes, and baseball caps. In another corner, a couple of friends smoked cigarettes and pointed out some "prime meat," as they called it. They yucked it up while they waited for the bus. In the last corner, an older man sat on the floor, clothes torn and stained, with a sign sitting in front of him that read "Veteran, please help—Will Work for Food."

Matthew imagined what would happen if this same scene were to be played out in his sector, but it seemed impossible to fathom. Connor pointed to the older gentleman with the sign and said, "See, that would never happen back home. He wouldn't have to beg for food."

Matthew wanted to learn more about the man's situation, so he started to make his way over to him. He had to dodge all of the people who moved about the terminal. It was nothing like waiting for the bus at the park bench. He was getting a taste of the big city. He was just a few feet from the veteran when April came up behind him and grabbed his shirt. "I told you two to stay close. Now come on, our bus is leaving in ten minutes; we need to get loaded up."

As the family loaded back onto another bus for the trip to Memphis, Matthew asked, "Any trouble getting the tickets?"

She replied, "I'm getting good with the money thing; it's really just basic math."

The family sat down and noticed that this bus was packed to capacity. Connor asked if they should continue their studying. April knew

Chapter 8

that there wasn't enough room on the bus to pull out a bunch of papers, so she told the boys to get some rest.

Connor wanted to look through the gadget bag, but April wouldn't allow it. "Absolutely not! Who knows what's in there. We'll look at it when we get to Travis."

The family decided to relax during this ride and took in all that they could see on the bus and outside the windows. This would be a twelve-hour ride for the family, and it was a good time to reflect on what they had seen thus far.

April thought about the family they had met at the lake and how good it felt to tell someone that Matthew and Connor were her sons. She had already seen so many differences in people in just the first few hours in the past that she was overwhelmed. Commonality was the norm in April's time.

While everyone still had his or her own personality in the future, you were pressured to conform to a set way of thinking. Over time, that caused everyone to think the same about everything. April needed to know what people wanted out of their lives in this time and how they planned to reach those goals. She thought about her family's mission and reminded herself that it was her responsibility to make sure that they didn't fail. They *couldn't* fail.

Connor slumped into his seat and observed the rest of the bus. It was strange for him to see people dressed so differently and acting so differently from each other. It wasn't that he didn't like other styles. He was big on the rolled-up jeans of the 1950s. He just didn't feel comfortable here.

He looked to his left and saw a young military man with a crew-cut and then looked a few rows farther to see a man with purple, spiked hair. That hair would put someone's eye out if they got close enough. Connor didn't quite have the same attitude as his brother about the things they had seen. He also couldn't seem to stop going back to those two girls in the bikini tops. He was a fourteen-year-old boy, after all.

Matthew watched the time count down on his watch. He and his family had been in 1984 for only over half a day and he was already feeling the pressure of the short amount of time that they had. His thoughts drifted to the old man in the bus terminal and how he begged for help. He just couldn't understand how someone could get to a point of begging for food. Connor was right—that wouldn't happen back home.

Matthew thought about his brother and mother and how family meant something here. He also got a little angry thinking about his own life. He wasn't sure about the past, but he decided, on that bus, that meeting Walter Wainright was fate and that helping Connor get that Hathmec charm was meant to be. He knew that Walter Wainright would lead him to the truth, and he would do whatever he could to get to the truth. He relaxed for a few minutes and then spent a little time thinking about those two ladies in the bikinis. April couldn't figure out why both of her boys had such big smiles on their faces. Boys will be boys.

Chapter 9

I'M A SOPHOMORE

Matthew stood on the steps of the Hathmec Memorial and looked across the throngs of people. They all chanted his name and cheered as they jumped up and waved their hands. Matthew saw his mother and brother in the front row of the crowd clapping their hands. He felt the excitement in the air. He stepped up to a microphone and addressed the crowd. "Sector 1 and the rest of the world: you are free!" The crowd erupted. He saw young girls and old men weep into their hands. The chants of "Thank you" and "Matt Chance" filled the air as Matthew stood back and enjoyed the moment.

The cold air filled with the breath of the cheering crowds and an echo of jubilation that had never been heard before. Matthew motioned for his family to join him, but they were gone. They had to be close. They would want to celebrate such an awesome achievement. Matthew called out, "Connor! Mom!" There was no reply, only the continued chants of the crowd. Matthew panicked. Where were they? Why weren't they here?

"Matthew, Matthew, wake up! We're gonna be late!"

Matthew's eyes slowly began to come into focus as the outline of Connor stood over him. Connor thumped Matthew on the forehead with his finger and said, "Come on, man! I'm not heading into the jungle of high school without you." Matthew knocked Connor's hand away and rolled out of bed.

Connor asked, "What were you dreamin' about? You had a stupid grin on your face."

Chapter 9

Matthew told him that it was none of his business. He was embarrassed to tell Connor the truth.

April poked her head into the boys' room and said, "We're leaving in ten minutes; I have to get you to the school and enrolled by eight."

April and the boys had arrived at their small mobile home just a day before. They had spent the majority of the last day studying their new home, Travis. So far, everything that Walter had wanted them to do had gone off without a hitch. April purchased a small car, jet black, with leather seats and something called a seat belt already equipped.

Their short time in Memphis proved that April's fake ID was prepared to perfection. She had quite a time learning the rules of the road. She did quite well for someone who had never driven a car in their life. Following traffic signs and maps and keeping the car at a certain speed were all challenges. It took them six hours to make the two-hour trip from Memphis to Travis. She needed to work on her navigation and map-reading skills.

They found the address of their new home, and April set up a contract with the mobile home park's owner. April had learned that by adding just a little more cash to a deal, it closed out faster. A quick smile from the lovely blonde didn't hurt either.

The family's new home was furnished with a refrigerator, a stove, and a television set. The set picked up only three stations, and the boys had already learned the ancient sibling fighting style known as channel battles. One liked station three and the other five, so it had been a battle for supremacy for most of the night before. Connor won the majority of the battles, but Matthew held his own a couple of times. The time in front of the television was useful for the boys. They practiced their pronunciation and tried to copy the mannerisms they saw on the various shows.

The home was exactly what the family needed. A decent-size living room was right next to the kitchen, still decked out in seventies swag. Two small bedrooms and a small bathroom divided the house between the boys and April. There was a nice shed located just behind the home, back in a wooded area of the lot. The owner of the property told April that she could use the lawn equipment stored there anytime she wanted. He gave her a key to it. The home was secluded enough to keep nosey neighbors at bay but close enough to town that the Chance family could execute their plans.

Connor asked, "Is there anything we should take with us to school, April?" April frowned at Connor. He cleared his throat and said. "I mean Mom."

April replied, "You'll probably need a pen and some paper. Back home, the school already had all of the things you needed."

Matthew said, "I saw some pencils and paper in one of the drawers in the kitchen." He went to fetch some supplies. Connor walked to the corner of the kitchen and grabbed one of the three backpacks.

He made it to the front door before April grabbed the bag. "What do you think you're doing?"

Connor replied, "We may need some of this stuff. You never know what we may run into."

April took the bag from him. "These gadgets of Walter's are only to be used in emergency situations, and to be perfectly honest, I don't think we should use them at all." She took the bag into her bedroom and threw it under her bed.

On her way back to the door she snatched the two empty bags. "Here, take these to hold whatever books or supplies they give you at school."

Matthew took the bag and asked, "Don't you think Walter would want us to keep the gadgets with us at all times? What if someone breaks in and steals them?"

April replied, "Who would break in?"

Matthew pointed to the television. "I don't know, but it seems to happen a lot on TV."

April chuckled and said, "I'll keep an eye on them. I promise."

The family loaded into the car, but April didn't start the engine. She turned to the boys and said, "I know that I've put a lot of pressure on both of you, but I'm only doing it to keep us safe, so you must do as I tell you. Walter has trusted us to do a job, and we're going to do it and get home as fast as we can. This school is nothing like what you're used to. These kids will be nothing like you're used to."

Chapter 9

April started the car and pulled onto the street. Matthew asked his mother, "What will you be doing while we're at school?"

"I'm gonna check out the town and see what I can find out about the Curry family, especially Amanda."

Connor patted April on the shoulder. "Great idea! We need all the help that we can get." He leaned back. "Of course, I figure she'll be putty in my hands once she meets me. I'll probably have the Hathmec charm before the end of the day."

Matthew rolled his eyes and asked, "Do you think we look OK? I mean, are we dressed right for this?"

April based her answer on what she had learned from her reading. "I think you both look great. Based on what Walter said, blue jeans and T-shirts are the way to go. I'll go out and get you some more clothes while you're at school." Both of the boys wore T-shirts depicting various hair bands of the day, as well as a certain style of tennis shoe with no laces.

The family pulled into the local high school's parking lot. Connor read the sign hanging over the top of the front entrance: "Eastview High School." Matthew noticed the glass windows that greeted them and spotted paintings of a man on a horse. He carried a javelin and shield. He read the captions under them: "The Fighting Chargers."

He asked, "What the heck is a Charger?"

Connor pointed at the painting on the window and said, "I guess that is."

April motioned to the boys and said, "Come on, we have to go to the main office to register you two."

As the boys entered in the main lobby, they were bombarded with the extreme visuals of the time. On one side, they saw large boys huddled in a corner pushing each other back and forth and growling about the hit they saw last week. Each of them wore a jacket with an *E* sewn onto the front of it. Connor quipped, "Some sort of gang maybe?"

On another side of the lobby, a group of smaller statured boys looked through books and held calculators. Matthew heard one of them say, "You have to use the Pythagorean theorem, stupid." They wore buttoned-up shirts and tan slacks.

I'm A Sophomore

Matthew looked to Connor. "Those must be the brains of the school."

The Chance family had entered a strange domain that seemed devoid of purpose or clarity. The lobby reeked of dirty sweat socks and overused aftershave. The sanitary regulations of 2185 were nowhere to be seen and no magazine or instruction manual could prepare the boys for what they were about to embark on.

April opened the door to the main office, and the boys filed in behind her. There sat a rather aged woman, perhaps in her sixties or seventies. April stood silent for a moment and expected the secretary to acknowledge her existence, but it wasn't working. April cleared her throat to see if she could force a response. Still nothing; it was as if the woman was in another dimension.

"Excuse me, is this where I need to register my boys for classes?"

The secretary picked her head up from her work and said, "Yes, sweetie, this is the place."

She studied the boys. "Let me guess—a freshman and a senior?"

April knew that her boys had to pull off sixteen so she blurted out, "No, ma'am, my boys are both sixteen and should be sophomores. See, I have paperwork to prove it."

The old secretary said with a chuckle, "OK, I believe you; that one just looks younger than sixteen to me. Let's see those transcripts."

Matthew leaned into his mother's ear and whispered, "Real subtle there, Mom."

The paperwork that Walter had sent was working perfectly. No one had a clue that Matthew and Connor wouldn't be born for another two hundred years. The boys watched the kids in the lobby while April finished up. They were focused on what the boys in the hall were doing until they looked over to a door that was labeled "Girl's Restroom." As if a gateway of angels had been released, the door opened and a sea of pretty young ladies poured out of it.

Both Matthew and Connor were mesmerized by the big hair, short skirts, and jeweled bodies that skipped out. Matthew asked, "Why would anyone want to stop girls from dressing like that?"

Chapter 9

Connor replied, "How is it possible that every girl in this school looks better than any girl we've ever met?"

Connor and Matthew hadn't realized that they were ogling the majority of the school's cheerleading squad. That wasn't a fair representation of the school's overall cuteness factor. The boys were about to drool on the door to the office, but they were interrupted by the entrance of an older gentleman wearing a gray suit and tie.

"It's not polite to stare, boys." The older gentleman spoke with a deep baritone and in a militaristic style.

Connor divulged his true feelings. "Can you blame us? Those are some really good-looking girls over there."

The gentleman responded, "I do not like to think of them like that boys, especially since that one there is my granddaughter."

Matthew took his hand and put it over his face in embarrassment. Connor stuck with the honest approach and said, "Congratulations, sir. You should be proud."

"Who exactly are you boys? I don't believe I have ever seen you at my school before."

Matthew asked, "Your school, sir?"

"Yes, my name is Phillip Baxter, or Principal Baxter, as my students call me."

April darted over to the door. "Oh, Principal Baxter, it is so nice to meet you. My name is April Chance and these are my sons Connor and Matthew." She extended her hand and said, "They're starting classes today."

Principal Baxter reached his hand toward April's and said, "Well, we are glad to have you here, and I am sure the boys are going to do just fine, as long as they spend their time on their work and not staring at my granddaughter and her friends all day."

April giggled and responded, "Oh, don't you worry; my boys are very serious about the work they need to get done. You won't have any problems out of them."

Principal Baxter popped both of the boys on the back and began to walk away. "See that I don't. I won't tolerate troublemakers at my school." He disappeared into an office behind the front desk and closed his door.

April glared a hole into each of the boys. They both mouthed the word "sorry." The secretary held up a couple of pieces of paper and called for the boys. "These are your schedules, boys. It's pretty strange that you both have the exact same schedules, but that's how they came out of the computer, so it must be OK." The elderly secretary pulled out a small map of the school and started to point out the important locations within the school.

The layout of the school was pretty simple. All of the classrooms were in the outside loop of a big circular building, with a library in the center of it. A large gymnasium was on the far north side of the structure, and the building held about six hundred students. This building was much smaller than the district school the boys had gone to back home, so getting around was not going to be an issue.

The secretary went on describing every nook and cranny of the school. The boys were ready to move on when Matthew picked up the intoxicating scent of strawberries and cinnamon. It overpowered all other smells in the office, but it was wonderful.

Matthew turned his head and saw a gorgeous young lady walking to the desk just to the side of him. She wore a short blue jean skirt, a pink flowing top, and white tennis shoes. She accessorized with hoop earrings and several bracelets on her wrists. Her beautiful blond hair was teased out all over her head. She was wearing makeup, but not so much that you couldn't tell she was beautiful without it. Connor turned to see the girl and then copied Matthew's stupid grin from earlier in the morning.

The secretary continued to explain the layout of the school, correcting herself more than once. She didn't notice that the boys were not paying any attention to her. April punched Matthew in the arm. "What?"

April whispered, "That's her, that's Amanda." The girl was talking to another secretary in the office about seeing Principal Baxter later in the day. She was about to leave the office when April cried out, "Wait!"

Chapter 9

The girl turned around with curious eyes. "Yeah, can I help you with somethin'?"

April didn't know what to say and looked to her boys. They were both incapable of speech, so April said, "My boys here are new to the school and starting classes today. It looks like you have been here for a while."

The girl responded, "Yeah, this is my second year, so I kinda know my way around." The boys were drawn in by the girl's country twang. It was quirky, but hypnotizing.

The secretary looked up from her map and said, "That's a wonderful idea, Ms. Chance. I'm sure that Amanda can show your boys to their first class."

April asked, "Your name is Amanda?"

"Yes, ma'am, Amanda Curry."

April exclaimed, "That's great! You can show the boys to their first class."

Amanda didn't look thrilled to get stuck with two new guys, so she tried to make up an excuse to get out of it. "Well, actually I'm *really* late for English with Mrs. Greir, so I'm not sure if I've got time to show these fellas around."

Matthew reviewed his schedule and saw that he and Connor also had English with Mrs. Greir for first period. "That's perfect! We have English with Mrs. Greir first this morning, too."

Amanda shook her head and said, "I guess it makes sense for me to walk with you to class then. Grab your stuff and let's go."

Connor looked to April. "See you this afternoon."

The boys followed Amanda out the door, and April thanked the secretary for her help. She watched the boys disappear down the hall and said a quick prayer to herself. "Please, god, help them."

"So, you guys are both sophomores?" Matthew started to answer Amanda, but a sudden wave of fear engulfed him. He didn't want to say the wrong thing. Maybe he just didn't want to sound stupid.

Connor stepped in. "Yeah, we're both sixteen, so we're sophomores."

Amanda looked at both of them as they started to round the library and said, "You look sixteen, but I'm not so sure about your brother." She looked at Matthew and said, "You don't look much bigger than my little brother."

Matthew replied, "Well, I'm just as old as my brother here and a whole lot smarter."

"Where are you guys from?"

Matthew replied, "Georgia—we're from Georgia."

Amanda squinted her eyes and said, "Really? You don't sound like you're from Georgia. Where's your accent?"

Matthew explained that Georgia was full of many different accents. Their accent was just muted compared to a Tennessee accent.

She replied, "I've never heard that before, but if you say so."

Amanda stopped at a locker. "I need to grab a book out of here; did you get locker numbers when you registered?"

Connor rummaged through some papers and asked, "Is this it, 102B?"

Amanda looked at his sheet and said, "Well, that's right here next to mine."

Connor smiled. "Well, I guess we'll be seeing a lot of each other then."

"You better get a lock before you put anything in there. The guys around here will take anything that isn't locked down."

Matthew found the number on his sheets and said, "My number is 509B."

Amanda took the sheet from Matthew and said, "That's on the other side of the building. You can go find it after class."

Connor finished up a little happy dance by his locker, as it seemed that he would have the most access to Amanda going forward.

Amanda glanced at Matthew's schedule and said, "This is really weird. You guys have all of the same classes that I have."

Matthew took the schedule back and replied, "Wow, that *is* weird. I guess we'll just have to become good friends taking all these classes together."

Amanda pursed her lips and said, "Kind of jumping the gun there, aren't you? Besides, who says that either one of you is even worth my time." She walked into a classroom and motioned for the boys. As they

Chapter 9

entered the room she whispered to both of them, "I already have a lot of friends."

"Where have you been, Ms. Curry? I thought I was going to have to send out a search party."

"Sorry, Mrs. Greir. I was asked to bring you these two new fresh minds to mold."

Mrs. Greir looked over the boys and said, "Well, let's see your schedules." Mrs. Greir was a younger teacher, but she had no style to speak of. She hobbled over to the boys due to a damaged heel on her right shoe. Her thickly rimmed glasses took nothing away from the wreck of a hairdo she modeled.

"It looks like we have brothers joining our journey to learn the proper use of the English language. Class, please welcome Matthew and Connor."

The class didn't seem overly enthused to meet Matthew or Connor. The boys in the class looked like they wanted to throw something at them. Mrs. Greir motioned the boys to two empty seats and said, "Go ahead and take a seat, boys; we have a lot of work to do."

The boys listened as Mrs. Greir reviewed the use of capitalization for the names of people, cities, states, etc. The boys tried to pay attention to the teacher, but they were busier looking around the room at the different types of kids who stared back at them. Some kids were wearing shorts, some jeans, some skirts, some boots, and some tennis shoes.

The girls in the room ranged from Amanda, who was just possibly the most gorgeous person either of the boys had ever seen, to girls who looked like they didn't own a mirror. There was girl in the corner with stringy hair, big glasses, and shabby sneakers. This was similar to what the boys had seen in the city. Such differences from person to person!

"Mr. Chance, Mr. Chance, are you paying attention to me?" Both Connor and Matthew snapped back to the present and saw Mrs. Greir staring at them.

Connor answered first, "Yes, ma'am, I'm paying attention."

She formed a sarcastic smirk and said, "Good, then you can give me an example of a city name to finish out this sentence that is both a city name and a person's name."

Connor looked to Matthew first and then blurted out the first thing that came to his mind: "Hathmec."

Mrs. Greir looked to her new student and asked, "Hathmec? Who or what is a Hathmec?"

Matthew looked to Connor with worried eyes. Connor realized that Supreme Leader Hathmec, Hathmec Hall, and all the other things named after him didn't exist in 1984. Mrs. Greir asked again, "Well, Mr. Chance, what are you talking about?" Matthew sensed that Connor had no idea what to say.

"Mrs. Greir, Hathmec is a town in Georgia, where we're from, and it was named after its founder many years ago. Probably a better example would be Travis, where we live now."

"I don't know of any Hathmec, Georgia. Oh well, you are correct—Travis is a good example, so let's work with that."

Connor patted Matthew on the hand. "Thanks, bro. I'll do better next time."

The boys survived their first class and were startled by the ringing of a bell that seemed to come out of nowhere. They watched their classmates jump up from their seats and head for the door. Matthew noticed a younger looking girl staring at him. She seemed a bit awkward, with her glasses sagging on her nose. Her coveralls seemed a size too big for her.

Matthew asked, "So are we done for the day?"

She giggled and said, "We are for this class, but we have five more to go. Where are you headed next?"

Matthew pulled out his schedule and said, "Looks like I have Chemistry 1 with Mr. Knott."

The girl frowned and grabbed her bag. "That's too bad. I have Advanced Chemistry next period."

Matthew shook his head in disbelief and asked, "You're old enough to be in Advanced Chemistry, as a sophomore?"

"I'm not a sophomore; I'm a freshman. I just get to take upper-level classes."

"Come on, Cassie, we're gonna be late, and you know I like to get the best seat in the lab."

Chapter 9

Matthew asked, "Who is that?"

"That's my brother, Jack. We're twins, but I'm the smart one." It was clear that Jack was Cassie's twin. Besides the scar on his nose and the hair on his face, they looked quite similar.

The boy walked over and said, "Yeah, she got the brains and the looks. So, are you and your brother twins, too?"

Matthew replied, "Not exactly, but we might as well be. Isn't that right, Connor?"

Matthew turned to see that Connor wasn't there and began to look around the room. Jack asked, "Did you lose something there, Matt?"

Matthew grabbed his backpack and stumbled past the desks in the room. "Sorry, I need to go. Maybe we can talk more later." He took off out the door and almost knocked over Mrs. Greir.

Cassie grinned at Jack and said, "He's kind of cute."

Jack replied, "He seems a little strange to me. Come on, we're gonna be late."

Matthew walked around the corridor of the school and searched for Connor. He made his last turn and saw his brother standing with Amanda Curry at her locker, along with three rather large boys. They looked upset with Connor. Matthew got to the locker in mid-conversation and interrupted. "Is everything OK here?"

The boy at the front of the pack turned to Matthew and snapped, "Who the hell are you?"

Matthew quietly replied, "I'm Matthew and this is my brother, Connor."

Amanda grabbed the large boy by the arm and pulled him toward her. "Trey, get a grip! These are a couple of new guys that I showed around this morning, that's all. Connor was just asking me about the classes."

Matthew noticed that the other two large boys with Trey had created a cone around him and Connor. Matthew assumed that this would make it easier to pounce on both of them when the time came. Trey explained how things worked at the school, at least in his mind. "You two losers stay away from my girl or you're gonna get pounded. That means no talking to her, looking at her, or even thinking about her."

Connor wasn't one to back down from a fight. He furled his brow and responded, "Oh really? Well, I'm thinking about her right now. In fact, we're having a great time hanging out together in my mind." He looked to Amanda and said, "How about we make it a reality?" Trey told his buddies to hold Connor and he prepared to pound him.

"All of you boys OK?"

Trey turned around to see Principal Baxter and backed off from the brothers. "Yes, sir, we were just introducing ourselves to the new guys here."

Principal Baxter motioned down the hall and said, "Yes, I met them this morning as well. I think all of you need to head on to class now. The last bell will ring in exactly two minutes. I wouldn't want our star quarterback being late for class."

Trey grabbed Amanda's hand, and they began to move toward their next class. The boys heard Amanda mumble, "You are such a jerk."

Principal Baxter turned his attention to Connor and Matthew. "It looks like you two are making a quick impression here at the school. Just remember, I know all and see all here, so keep your noses clean."

Once Principal Baxter was out of earshot, Matthew turned his attention to Connor and gave him a shove. "What the hell was that all about? You're gonna get us killed before the end of the first day."

Connor shoved Matthew back and said, "Look, I just made an impression on the girl that we are trying to woo here, and now she knows that I won't take any crap from anybody."

Matthew replied, "Oh yeah, I'm sure she'll be impressed when you're lying in a bloody heap in the middle of the hall. We've got to figure out how to get to this girl. Just pissing off her boyfriend isn't going to do it."

The boys continued to go to class through the morning, with no more incidents until they reached their lunch period. Both boys were sitting alone at a cafeteria table trying to decipher what they were about to eat. Connor threw something onto Matthew's tray.

Matthew just stared at it and asked, "Why did you do that?"

Connor responded, "I'm not sure if that is some kind of meat or fruit or what it is, but I'm not eating it."

Chapter 9

Matthew heard a familiar voice. "Wow, you two sure didn't waste any time getting in the doghouse." Matthew turned to see Cassie and her brother, along with another friend, moving toward them with their trays. "Do you mind if we join you?"

Matthew motioned for the small group to join them and asked Cassie what she meant. Before she could answer, the third in their group spoke up. "You stood up to Trey and his pack of goons and basically told them all to stick it, and that was before second period had even started."

Connor asked, "Who exactly are you?"

The small-statured boy replied, "Sorry, I'm Pete, or Pete the Meat, as most around here call me."

Matthew asked, "Why do they call you Pete the Meat?"

"It's in reference to dead meat. I get picked on a lot. I'm small, they're huge, and it's just the law of the jungle." Matthew attempted to force down a french fry and told Pete that he shouldn't get picked on for being small.

Pete explained that Trey and his buddies were stars on the school football team and it was just natural for Amanda, a lead cheerleader, to date the starting quarterback, whether he was a jerk or not. "It's just the way things are. The cheerleaders date the ballplayers and the rest of us get what's left over."

Cassie jumped in. "I am *not* a leftover! Isn't that right, Matthew?"

Matthew looked to the girl in the black-and-white striped glasses and wanted to be diplomatic about his answer. He shook his head. "Of course you're not a leftover."

Pete sensed the tension and said, "Regardless, the hottest girls in school are cheerleaders and Amanda is at the top of that list, so unless you're planning to join the football team anytime soon, I would just cut my losses and avoid the big three."

Connor asked, "The big three?"

"Yeah—Trey and his two goon offensive linemen, Rick and Austin."

One of the goons came by the boys' table and grabbed the tray in front of Pete and dumped it in his lap. He cackled, "Nice one! Looks like Pete the Meat has some cleanup to do!" Connor began to get up from his seat to confront the boy, but Matthew pulled him back down.

Cassie and Jack helped Pete clean himself off and Connor asked, "How exactly would someone get on the football team?"

Jack replied, "The season just started, but I know that walk-ons are allowed up to the fourth game, so you would just have to convince Coach Dane to give you a tryout."

Pete asked, "You aren't really considering joining those Neanderthals, are you?"

Connor responded, "Don't worry about that. I'm planning on taking your dear friend Trey's job."

Pete and the others laughed and flexed their muscles. Cassie said, "You guys are crazy! You're just gonna get hurt."

Matthew put his hand to his chest and looked at Connor. "I think we'll be OK. We just need to get a tryout."

Chapter 10

PITY DATE

"I guarantee it; you won't regret givin' us a look. I know we don't look as big as most of the guys on the team, but we're really strong for our size."

Connor responded, "Speak for yourself. I'm plenty big enough to handle your guys."

"We're both quick and tougher than we look."

Matthew and Connor had the head football coach for the Eastview Chargers cornered for over ten minutes and were trying everything to convince Coach Dane to let them go out for the football team. He didn't seem impressed. "Boys, I'm telling you, I just don't think you'll be cut out for the team. We take football real serious around these parts and you don't have any background in the sport. I don't even see where you played back in Georgia. Not that we have much respect for football coming out of Georgia around these parts."

Coach Dane's bright red trousers cut into the overhung belly of the seasoned high school football coach. He had seen it all in his twenty years and his gut told him that two walk-on sophomores weren't worth his time. The tobacco stuffed into his jaw was problematic for the boys, as they struggled to understand the words coming from his mouth.

"But coach, we found out that you still have four open spots that freshmen are filling. I promise we are worth more than some fifteen-year-olds."

The coach looked the boys over again, impressed by Connor's build, and asked, "So what positions are you trying out for?"

Connor responded, "My brother here is a trailer and I'm a tosser."

Chapter 10

Matthew's eyes grew to the size of grapefruits. "He means that I would like to try out as a cornerback and he's a quarterback."

Coach grabbed a clipboard and chuckled "Let me get this straight; you think you can cover and tackle my boys in the open field, and you think you're better than Trey Wilson."

Both shook their heads in the affirmative and said, "Yes, sir."

The coach pointed to the locker room and said, "Just for pure curiosity's sake, I'll give you a shot. There are extra uniforms, pads, and helmets in the locker room. Go find some that fit and be on the practice field at four and we'll see what you got. Don't blame me if you both have to go to the nurse's station when we're done."

The boys only had an hour to get their gear on and figure out a way to impress the coach. Luckily, there was a picture of a football player hanging up in the locker room, so the boys positioned all of their pads in the correct orientation. For someone who had never suited up for a football game it could be a confusing proposition.

Matthew and Connor discussed their strategy. "Connor, we have to make you look good, so let's try to set it up so you throw to me as much as possible. The guys on the team will probably drop passes on purpose just to make you look bad."

Connor responded, "I'm a little worried about the plays these guys run. I don't know any of them."

Matthew stood up from the bench and ran through some things that he had picked up on Sunday. "Remember what we saw on the television. You take the snap from the player in front of you, drop back four or five steps, find the open receiver, and throw it."

Connor looked at the clock on the wall of the locker room. "It's 3:55, we better get to the field." They grabbed the helmets that they found in a locker that could best be described as disgusting and walked to the practice field behind the school.

The rest of the team had already practiced for over an hour, and the first-team offense was running plays. The boys walked up to the coach and noticed a small crowd gathered around the fence surrounding the field. On the other side of the fence resided the majority of the school's cheerleaders, including Amanda Curry. There were also faces not normally interested in the football team, Cassie, Jack, and Pete among them. They were as interested as anyone to see if the two new guys could survive an audition with Coach Dane.

The boys sneaked up behind the coach and said, "We're ready, coach. What do you want us to do?"

Before Coach Dane could answer, a shout came from the field from none other than Trey Wilson himself. "You gotta be kidding me, coach! What are those two losers doing out here?"

Coach snapped back, "You didn't hear, Trey? These boys wanna be on the football team, so we're gonna give 'em a tryout."

Coach Dane looked to the shorter of the brothers and asked, "Matthew, right? I want you to cover that receiver, number eighty-one. Don't let him catch any passes. I'll give you five chances to stop him." Matthew ran out to the field while the coach lumbered out to the offensive huddle. Matthew and Connor couldn't hear what he was saying.

"Look, boys, we have to let some of these kids try out every once in a while just to keep the parents and principal off my ass, so just run our plays, catch the ball, and run over this kid a few times and we'll be done with it."

Trey added to the coach's comments. "Let's run a couple of picks on this little prick. He won't make it five plays."

Matthew was still wearing his health Hathmec and took a position covering number eighty-one. Trey Wilson walked up to the line and barked out the plays. "Thirty-two, thirty-two, set, hut...hut." All the players were in movement, along with number eighty-one, and Matthew tracked him closely. Number eighty-one was moving laterally across the field when Matthew felt a thunderous blow to his chest.

He had just run into another offensive player who had set an illegal pick on him to clear him out of the way. Number eighty-one easily caught the pass that Trey Wilson had thrown. Connor saw what happened and began to open his mouth, but the coach stopped him, "You have to deal with what's thrown at you in this game." He yelled to the field, "So, Mr. Chance, do you wanna try this four more times?"

Matthew bounced right up, looked to the sidelines, and said, "Let's try it again." The coach was surprised that the boy had gotten up so fast,

Chapter 10

but he was confident that another shot or two like that would get him off the field.

"Go ahead, run another one." Again, Matthew was lured into an illegal block and knocked down, only to pop up again. This went on for four plays. The coach looked to Connor and said, "Well, he may not be a good ballplayer, but he can sure take a shot." He yelled back to the field, "This is your last shot kid; make it count."

Trey Wilson yelled out the final hut on Matthew's last chance to make the team, and his receivers all started on their predetermined routes. This time, as Matthew tracked number eighty-one, he made a split-second decision to dodge the player who tried to block him. In doing so, he got farther behind the receiver than he anticipated so he had to make up the gap.

Trey Wilson threw the ball high into the air and it headed straight for number eighty-one. It looked as though he would make the catch in stride. Matthew saw the ball in the air, and his mind replayed the catch that he had made to save the beamball game just a few days earlier. He remembered the power that he felt in his legs and the speed that he had gained through the health charm, so he called upon it once again.

Within an instant, Matthew had made up the ground on the receiver and he leaped toward the ball with extended hands and caught it before it ever got to number eighty-one. He was lying on the ground with the ball, and as he got up, he extended it into the air for all to see. As if a firecracker had been detonated, the few students behind the fence started to cheer. Even the lovely Amanda Curry smiled in appreciation of the accomplishment.

On the sidelines, Connor peered up at Coach Dane and saw the look of astonishment on his face. The coach told his offense to run another play. Trey Wilson objected and said that it was just luck. "Then run another play and prove me wrong," yelled the coach.

The offense ran ten more plays, and Matthew Chance either intercepted or knocked down every ball that was thrown his way. The crowd around the fence started to grow as they watched something that they had never seen before: Trey Wilson getting shown up.

"Ten out of ten isn't luck. Connor, are you as good as your brother?"

A small glint pierced through Connor's eyes as he overflowed with confidence and said, "I'm better."

The coach turned his attention back to the field and called Trey and Matthew to the sideline. "Trey, you're out. I want to see what the other brother can do."

A look of panic and pure anger gripped Trey Wilson as he tensed up and verbalized his frustration. "You're gonna let this little twerp take snaps from my team!"

Coach Dane was not deterred. "I make the decisions on who steps on that field, son, and don't you forget it!"

Trey threw his helmet to the ground and stared a hole through Connor as he made his way to the bench. "Can I work with Connor at wide receiver, coach?" asked Matthew. Coach agreed and pulled one of the other players off the field. Connor and Matthew hustled to an unpleasant huddle.

The boys in the huddle looked grudgingly at the sophomore who now ran their practice. "OK, guys, I don't really know any of the plays that you run here, so let's just run the same play Matthew's been whippin' you on." Connor pointed to Matthew. "You run straight down the field and cut in at about thirty yards."

The rest of the guys in the huddle started to laugh and Connor asked what the problem was. One of Trey's best buddies, Austin, said, "That would be like a fifty-yard out pattern. There is no way you got the arm for that."

Connor replied, "You just block for me." As the boys broke the huddle, Connor walked with Matthew to his spot on the line and said, "Don't you dare drop this ball." Matthew grinned at his brother and flashed him a thumbs up.

Connor leaned down and placed his hands between the center's legs to receive the oddly shaped football. He barked out the same calls that he had heard Trey use a few minutes before. Connor pulled back from the offensive line and squeezed the oblong football in his right hand. The football was easier to hold than a beamball, so it should be easier to throw.

Chapter 10

Three rather large upper classmen were bearing down on him. It seemed the offensive line hadn't done a very good job blocking for Connor. Now half of the defensive line was about to pile-drive him into the ground.

Connor wasn't fazed, as he spun out of the clutches of the first defender, darted to the right to avoid the second, and stiff-armed the third to the ground. He dashed to the right side of the field and spotted his brother. Matthew had reached the point in his route where he broke off to the center of the field. Connor reared back and unleashed the football. Coach Dane marveled at the young boy's arm strength as he watched Matthew coral the ball into his arms, right in stride. "Run it again," yelled the coach.

The team ran back to the line and started another play. This time a few of the offensive linemen actually blocked for Connor. Connor dropped back and saw an opening to number eighty-one and fired the ball on a rope right into his hands. Coach Dane yelled out, "Run it again!" Again, the team ran to the line and Connor fired another strike, this time to the tight end.

This played out ten more cycles, with a similar result each time. Coach Dane called the boys back over to the sideline. "Well, boys, that was one the best displays of football skill that I have seen on this field in quite some time."

Connor thanked the coach and asked the obvious question. "So, are we on the team?"

"On the team? You want to know if you made the team? Of course you made the team!"

He went on to explain that if Connor and Matthew knew the playbook, they would both be starting next week. "You can't officially start joining us for practices until next week, so just start learning the playbook for the rest of the week and we'll see you on the practice field starting next Monday."

The news of the coach's excitement didn't sit well with Trey Wilson.

"Coach, are you out of your mind? You wanna start these two sophomores over me?" Trey continued his tirade as the coach made his way to the locker room. "I'm a third-year starter and I made the All District team last year."

Coach put his arm around his star quarterback and explained, "Look, son, you're a good quarterback, but that boy has the best arm I have ever seen on a high school kid. You'll be the starting quarterback until we can get Connor up to speed on our playbook and then I'll move you to linebacker. It's about the team, son, and no one player is bigger than the team."

The coach left the practice field and headed back to his office. Trey made his way back to the field where he ran into his cohorts Austin and Rick. "Come here, guys, I need to talk to you about something."

On the other end of the field, Matthew and Connor headed to the fence to see how Amanda had reacted to their amazing play. Before they made it there, Matthew was stopped by Cassie and Jack. "That was unbelievable. How did you guys do that?"

Jack added, "Yeah, you took some pretty bad shots and got up like it was nothing."

Matthew responded, "Well, Connor and I have played back home for a while, so we're used to the pressure of the game."

Connor was already making his way toward the group of cheerleaders at the end of the fence line and Matthew attempted to do the same, but Cassie had other plans.

"So Matthew, you know there is a back-to-school dance on Friday night, right?"

Matthew had never heard of a dance, so he replied, "A dance—really? I didn't know that."

Cassie continued, "Yeah, I mean, I don't mean it like a date, but since you are new and all."

Matthew looked to Jack for assistance. Jack was no help. In fact, he just made fun of the whole thing. "Good grief, Cassie, you sound like one of those desperate girls from Advanced Chemistry."

Matthew wasn't sure how he should handle himself and replied, "Well, I think a dance would be a lot of fun, but I should probably see what Connor's planning on doing first. I may end up going with him."

Chapter 10

Jack snickered and said, "You're going to the dance with your brother? That's worse than me going with my sister, which it looks like I'll be doing again this year."

Matthew was embarrassed and looked past Cassie to see that Connor had once again run off. He didn't see Amanda either. Jack saw that Matthew was searching around and offered his help. "Are you looking for your brother?"

Matthew said, "Yeah, do you know where he went?"

Cassie was disappointed in the response from Matthew and moved her line of sight from Matthew's feet to his eyes. For some reason his eyes made her feel all warm and tingly inside.

She hid her disappointment and disclosed that Connor had walked around the side of the building with Amanda and her friend. "I think her name is Beth," added Jack.

Cassie poked Jack in the side and said, "Yeah, Jack has a crush on Beth; she is sooooo cute."

Jack fired back, "I don't think you of all people should be making fun of me for enjoying the looks of someone of the opposite sex."

Jack went on to explain that it was simple biology and pheromones. "We learned it in Biology. Even the two of us, with our obvious mental gifts and keen insight into the vast knowledge of the universe, can turn into piles of mush when confronted with a tight sweater or excesses of perfectly placed makeup."

Matthew backed up and pondered what he had just heard. "I have to say, Jack, you don't sound like a freshman when you talk."

Jack replied, "I know; I'm gifted."

Cassie added, "Yeah, our mom had us tested."

Matthew turned his attention back to tracking down Connor. Before he left, Cassie asked him, "You're not going to become one of those jerks are you? I mean you seem like a nice guy, so don't let those guys turn you into a jerk."

Matthew smiled at the awkward girl and replied, "I promise that I won't become a jerk if you promise to help me with my Chemistry homework."

She grabbed Matthew's hand and shook it. "You've got a deal." He pulled his hand away and ran off toward the side of the building.

Out of the corner of his eye he saw a truck pull out of the parking lot. On the steps that led to the side door of the gymnasium, he saw Amanda Curry and her friend leaned over and huddled around something. Matthew attempted to be clever and walked up behind the girls. "So, what's so interesting? Can I see too?"

The girls parted and revealed what they were so concerned about on the step. There was Connor, cut, bleeding, and curled up on the steps of the school. Matthew bent down to check on his brother and asked, "What happened? Who did this?"

Amanda Curry started to speak up and was stopped by her friend. "You don't want to get him in trouble. He might get kicked off the team."

Amanda stepped up and said, "That ass *should* get kicked off of the team."

Matthew's face began to turn red and his fists clenched. He turned to Amanda Curry and asked, "It was Trey and his band of idiots, wasn't it?"

Amanda was embarrassed by the actions of her boyfriend and lowered her head. She admitted that it was Trey. "I was just talking to Connor and they came up from behind him and knocked him down. Rick and Austin held him while Trey kicked and punched him."

Beth added, "We tried to stop them, but they're just too big and we didn't want to get them into any trouble."

"Did I get hit by a car or somethin'?" Connor was coming to and could recognize the shape of his brother standing over him.

"Are you OK?" Connor stood up with the help of Matthew and told the group that it would take more than three morons to keep him down.

Matthew saw that Connor's cuts were beginning to heal and his bruises were already lightening up. Luckily for Connor, the health charm of the Hathmec was quickly healing him of his wounds, but unluckily for the boys, they didn't want Amanda or Beth to see it.

"I really need to get Connor home. I'm sure our mom can clean him up."

Chapter 10

April Chance walked around the corner of the building, looking for the football field. "There you are! I've been looking everywhere for you." April caught the first glimpse of Connor's swollen face and the blood that had stained his football uniform. "Oh my goodness, what happened? Did he get hurt at practice?"

The boys had told their mother the night before that they would attempt to make the football team. April had no idea that Connor had been beaten up by Amanda Curry's boyfriend. Matthew responded to his mother, "He'll be all right, Mom; we just need to get him home."

Amanda rushed up to Connor and implored, "You need to go to the hospital. They probably broke your ribs or your nose." Connor started to regain his senses and his strength and reassured Amanda that he would be fine.

Matthew closed the door to the car and made a request of the two girls. "Don't let anyone know what happened here."

Connor rolled down the window and reminded the pretty cheerleader with the flowing blond hair, "So Amanda, you never answered me."

Amanda leaned into the window and said, "Yes, I'll go with you to the dance." A smile came to Connor's bruised, yet healing face.

Matthew, confused, asked, "He asked you to the dance? I thought you were with Trey."

"I was, but he's obviously not the kind of guy that I need to be dating, so I'm going with your brother."

"Come on, Matthew, we need to go!" exclaimed April. Matthew climbed into the front seat of the car and the Chance family rode off from the school's parking lot.

"You got a date with Amanda Curry; that's great!"

Connor replied, "Yeah, all it took was for me to get my butt kicked to convince her that Trey is a jerk and I am less of a jerk."

April was confused and said, "OK, so I'm assuming that you both made the team, but I'm still a little fuzzy on why Connor is getting blood all over the car."

Matthew went through the whole day's events, just as he had done the night before with his mother. It was going to become a ritual of the

Chance family to review all of the day's events and determine a strategy for the next. "We need to figure out a way to make Connor look like he's still bruised and battered. The health charm works fast." By the time the family made it to their mobile home, Connor was almost healed from the beating he had taken from Trey and his friends.

Connor asked, "So what do we do now?"

Matthew replied, "Well, since we are supposed to be going to a dance on Friday night, we may want to try to figure out what happens at a dance."

April interrupted, "Don't worry about the dance, boys. I will do some research here in town and I'll get you ready for it."

April had spent the last two days around the town, finding out as much as she could about the Curry family. So far, she had learned where they live and what business they were in, and she picked up some information on Amanda's normal routine. "Come straight home after school tomorrow and we'll work on the dance situation."

Matthew announced that they would walk home after school. "I think it's considered un-cool to have your mom pick you up in the afternoons." April agreed and the next day's plans were set. The boys would avoid Trey and his friends as much as possible. Connor would continue to get close to Amanda Curry, and Matthew would get the lowdown on school dances from their new friends, Cassie and Jack Jenkins.

As the boys walked home on Wednesday afternoon, they had determined one very important fact. Two freshman geniuses were not the proper resource to find out what happens at a school dance. Based on their description, you would sit in a corner all night, watch all the other kids dance and have fun, drink punch, and try to avoid awkward situations. While that all sounded less than appealing to the boys, the image of one of them pulled close to one Miss Amanda Curry while some slow sappy music played in the background had some definite appeal.

"Don't worry, Matthew, I got you a date too," confided Connor. "Do you remember Amanda's friend who was out back while I was getting my butt kicked yesterday?"

Matthew replied, "Her name is Beth, right?"

Chapter 10

"Yeah. I talked Amanda into getting you a pity date with her, since she's still mad at Austin. I think Amanda said, 'What's the worst that could happen?' Beth agreed."

Matthew rolled his eyes and said, "Gee, thanks, just what I need, a pity date. I could have gone with Cassie and had someone to talk to."

Connor stopped his brother on the side of the road and lectured him about student cliques at the school. "Look, I think Cassie and Jack are nice and all, but we have a job to do, and that means getting in good with the popular kids. We can be friends with the Jenkins, but we need to keep it quiet. Based on what I've seen, we are now football players and we date cheerleaders. Friday night, I get to spend the whole evening with Amanda Curry. Considering she's the one that has our charm around her neck, I think that's a good thing."

Matthew agreed but also threw in his own thoughts. "I agree that we have to get in with her group, but I think the only way that we are ever going to get her to give up her necklace is to find out who she really is. I just can't believe that all there is to this girl is a cheerleading uniform and a pretty face."

Connor replied, "Regardless of that, Amanda and Beth are going to meet us at the gym after the football game."

The boys walked into the house and saw that April had moved all of the furniture in their living room to the bedrooms. "What are you doing?"

April explained that she had spent all morning at a local record store, where they sold music. She talked to the shop owner and bought up several records that she could use to teach the boys how to dance. "Look, I even bought a nice record player from the store." She explained that she spent enough money on the records, so the player was a steal at fifteen dollars.

Connor interjected, "So you bought a bunch of music records and a record player. How does that teach us how to dance?"

April grinned and placed the first record on the player. It started up and a fast-paced, energetic song poured from the speakers.

"This nice young man at the record store introduced me to a television station where all they do is play music and show what they call music videos with people dancing in them. It's really a good idea; I bet that station can keep going on forever." She explained that she watched fifteen music videos in a row and was totally confident that she could show the boys what she learned.

"Now back up boys, this can get a bit crazy looking, but I guarantee that you'll fit right in at the dance." April bounced up and down and swayed her arms in the air. She stepped toward the boys and said, "One, two, one, two, three." She jumped to the left and jumped to the right.

The boys watched their mother careen all over the living room. She stopped and pivoted around one foot. She continued what some would describe as uncontrolled convulsions, and told the boys, "I must have been pretty good at the shop, because several people stopped by the window to see what I was doing."

"By the way, I called the school this morning to see what else I could find out about the dance, and I was offered a chaperoning job for Friday night."

The boys looked at each other with confused eyes and asked, "So you'll be at the dance, too?"

April replied, "I sure will. I may even have to hit the floor with these dance moves myself." She stopped for a moment and stared down her two sons. "Don't just stand there; get to dancing! We have to get you two into shape before Friday night."

For the next four hours, Matthew, Connor, and April jumped and sprayed themselves all over their home in the middle of Travis, Tennessee. An onlooker would have called the police or an ambulance based on their movements. It was a combination of fighting maneuvers and a seizure. Regardless of the outcome, it was still a night of fun, laughter, and, for the first time, family togetherness.

Chapter 11

GIRLS AND GADGETS

"I don't get these things. They look like the rings Amanda wears to school." Matthew read the instructions sent along by Walter while Connor asked more questions. "So, you're saying that these things will amplify anything?"

"Just shut up and listen to the instructions," replied Matthew.

The boys had discovered several "gadgets," as Walter had put it. They had sneaked into April's room and removed the bag, with the goodies, from under her bed. Any of the items could come in handy against an onslaught of football players. Both of the boys had been warned, earlier in the day, that Trey had shot his mouth off about them. He said, "Both of 'em are gonna get a butt kickin' if that Connor shows up to the dance with my Amanda."

Connor had convinced everyone that he was still hurt due to the beating he received from Trey on Tuesday. April used shoe polish to bruise Connor's face each morning, and he acted the part of a recovering patient quite well. He got a hug from Amanda after he struggled to lift his bag on Thursday.

Matthew continued pulling items from the backpack and started asking questions of his own. "Jack and Cassie told me that the only reason Trey hasn't ripped your head off already is because he's scared they might suspend him for the game tonight."

Connor spun two colored, round rings in his hand and asked, "So, is Cassie OK with you going to the dance with Beth?"

Chapter 11

Matthew removed what looked like hiking boots from the backpack and replied, "I don't think she knows I am. I sure didn't tell her."

"You didn't want to hurt her feelings?"

Matthew put the two brown hiking boots on his feet and shook his head. "I don't wanna hurt her feelings, but I also don't want her to get mad at me. Cassie and her brother are a wealth of information about the school and Travis." Matthew pressed the tongue of the boot and observed a small array of light shoot out from the front of them.

Connor asked, "Is it some kind of laser boot? Can they cut down trees or slice steel?"

Matthew jumped up on his bed and pointed his feet to the edge. "Based on what Mr. Wainright wrote, I should be able to walk right off the end of the bed and just keep going without hitting the floor."

Connor backed up from the end of the bed. "I've gotta see this; give it a try."

Matthew took two steps on the bed and extended his leg. He was hesitant about taking the full step.

"Come on man, take the step. The worst that can happen is you fall three feet and bust your butt."

Matthew took a deep breath and closed his eyes. He took a step of faith and then another. Connor, mouth wide open, clapped his hands. "You're floating; that's awesome!" Walter called them memory boots. The scanning ray that emitted from the boots allowed the wearer to continue along a path started on solid ground.

"Do you really think we'll need something like that tonight?"

Matthew replied, "Probably not. We'll leave these here, but we'll take the snap rings."

The boys heard the front door of the house open. "It's Mom; quick, take off the boots and hide the backpack." Matthew pressed the tongue of the boots and dropped the three feet to the floor of the boys' room. He threw the boots into the backpack and put it under his bed. Connor threw him one of the two snap rings to put in his pocket. April entered the room and, like any other mom, knew something was up.

"What are you guys working on in here?" April had already told the boys not to mess with Walter's gadget bag until she had gone through it herself. The boys determined that she was never going to go through the bag. If she did, she wouldn't let them use anything she found. So far, the boys had found the memory boots and the snap rings.

The rings were no bigger than a ring for your finger but they could pack quite a punch. When used properly, the ring could be used to amplify the smallest sound to that of a sonic blast. Something as simple as a handclap or a snap of the fingers could create a blast strong enough to knock down a door. Both boys had a ring stashed in their pockets.

"We're just trying to get ready for the dance. Where have you been?" asked Matthew.

April didn't believe her son, but she let it go because she was so excited about the clothes stuffed in the shopping bags she carried. "I found some things for both of you for the dance tonight and a lovely dress for myself." April was excited and chatted about all the different types of clothes she had found. "The colors, boys—you just wouldn't believe all of the beautiful colors of cloth that the stores have."

The boys pulled out their new shirts and pants and put them on the bed. "Matthew, I bought you some black dress pants and a classic white button-up shirt. I think you look good in black and white." She held the shirt up to Matthew and smiled.

"For you, Connor, I went with these tan pants and a bright blue shirt. The blue will bring out the color in your eyes." She held the shirt up to Connor and turned him to the long mirror located at the side of the bed. "Don't you look handsome!"

The boys both looked into a third bag lying on the bed and Connor asked, "What are these things?" He held up a long, but thin, leathery looking rope and April clapped her hands in excitement.

"That is the part that will bring both of your outfits together boys. That's what the lady at the store said." She walked over to Connor and placed the leathery strap over his neck and said, "They call it a bola tie." Matthew laughed at his brother, but stopped when he realized that his own bola tie was being pulled from the bag. April's eyes began to water and she turned to a fourth bag.

"These new socks and shoes will really finish off the look. You'll look just like the mannequins in the store window. Now go ahead and

Chapter 11

get ready. I need to do my hair and put my dress on." She walked from the boys' room and yelled back, "We leave in an hour."

Connor and Matthew changed clothes and discussed the strategy for the night. Matthew was the only one actually strategizing. "We have to remember to stay close to each other tonight. If we get separated, that's gonna be the perfect time for Trey and his buddies to pounce on one of us." Connor buttoned his bright blue shirt and his mind drifted into another world.

"Do you think Amanda will kiss me good-night? I would think after we dance for a while and I show her how much fun I am, she'll want to kiss me good-night."

Matthew realized that his brother wasn't paying attention to him and threw out a ridiculous thought. "Maybe you could run off and marry her right after the dance. That way, she'll almost be sure to give you the attribute charm."

Connor picked up on the sarcasm and replied, "I really don't think she'll be ready for marriage after just one date, do you?"

Matthew smacked his brother on the head and said, "No, you idiot, but I think if we aren't careful, Amanda's gonna think we're both stupid and we're never going to get that charm from her. You need to remember why we're here."

Connor poked his head out of their door and said, "I think April's getting sucked into this place. I don't think I've ever seen her so happy."

Matthew agreed, but got back to business. "Like I was saying, we need to stay close to each other tonight."

Connor shook his head. "I have one of the snap rings and you have the watch; we'll be fine."

Matthew looked at the second button from the top of his watch and said, "I've never even tried this thing. It may not even work."

Connor closed the bedroom door and stood in front of Matthew. "There's only one way to find out; let's try it." Connor pulled his hand back and said, "I'm gonna hit you square in the nose unless you use that watch to stop me."

Matthew begged his brother, "I don't think we should do this. We'll just try it out if we need it."

Connor began the countdown, "Three, two, one." Connor's fist came flying toward Matthew's face and Matthew reacted to it. He touched the second button from the top of his watch and placed the watch between Connor's fist and his own face.

A resounding thud resonated as Connor was flung back into the boys' closet. Books and papers fell onto Connor's head as Matthew rushed over. "Are you all right?"

Connor wobbled his head and stood up. "Well, that seems to work just fine."

That button was known as the reflector. Based on what Walter described, it would deflect or project back any force that it came into contact with. The force of Connor's punch was deflected by the watch, and that force propelled Connor back into the closet. "That's a really cool button."

Matthew responded, "The only bad thing is how long it lasts. Walter says that it can only stay activated for a couple of minutes, and when it dies, it takes half an hour to recharge."

The boys cleaned up what they could in their room and started to the car for the short trip to school. April heard on the radio that the football game was over, so the dance should be starting shortly. April called to the boys, "Load up!" The boys saw their mother for the first time in her new dress and were amazed.

April Chance emerged from her home wearing a blue silk dress that only came down to her knees, with a small slit up the side. Sparkly blue high-heeled shoes and a plethora of jewelry finished out the look. Connor was the first to speak. "Wow, I didn't know you could wear something like that, Mom."

Matthew asked, "What is that on your shoulders?"

April explained that they were shoulder pads. "This is popular in this time and I want to make sure I fit in."

Connor asked, "What about the shoes? Can you even walk in them?"

April looked down and explained, "I have been practicing for the last hour in my room. The lady at the store said that I needed them. She said that you have to make sacrifices for beauty."

Chapter 11

Matthew chuckled. "I guess your gigantic teased-up hair was the lady at the store's idea, too." April walked to the driver's-side door. She could feel the sarcasm that oozed from her boys.

"You both shut up and let's go." The boys climbed into the car and they were off. They only stopped on the way twice for April to readjust her shoulder pads. The boys made a joke about her using their football equipment next time.

They reached the school and several kids had already streamed into the gym. It was a gorgeous fall evening in West Tennessee. A full moon lit up the night sky and a slight nip of falling temperatures was felt on the tip of their noses.

April dropped the boys off and they strolled to the front door and waited on their dates. April parked the car and realized that her new shoes were not a good option for walking long distances. She made her way into the gym and staggered toward the chaperone corner at the far end of the building.

The boys studied their peers while they waited on their dates. They wanted to know how they were walking, talking, and acting with their dates. One of the juniors had his arm around his date. One of the seniors had his tongue down his date's throat. One of the freshmen looked scared to look his date in the eye. Matthew and Connor had never been to anything like this and they would have to learn on the fly.

Since both Amanda and Beth were cheerleaders, Matthew and Connor expected them to be two of the last to show up, but that turned out not to be the case. They got their first glimpse of the girls walking up the sidewalk and began to panic. "What do we say?" They both turned around and acted as if they hadn't seen them.

"So, are you two ready to tear up the dance floor?" asked Amanda. The boys turned to see Amanda Curry and Beth Perry standing in front of them, their cuteness on display.

Connor stumbled as he tried to reply. "Sure...we...can...tear the floor up...if you want."

Amanda looked to Matthew. "What about you? Excited for your first ever Eastview Fall Fling dance?"

The four of them looked odd standing with each other. Connor was eye to eye with his date, due to her high-heeled boots. Matthew was a good two inches shorter than his date, due to her high-heeled boots.

Matthew looked to Beth, who was wearing a tight white cotton dress, and replied, "Absolutely." To be honest, Matthew had a hard time taking his eyes off of Amanda as they walked through the front door of the gym. He couldn't believe that a girl could look that good in pink leg warmers. They shot out from under her neon miniskirt and baggy top.

Beth tapped Matthew on the shoulder and asked, "Are you not even listening to me?"

Matthew replied, "I'm sorry. Did you say something?"

She put her hands on her hips. "You didn't even bother to get me a corsage?"

Matthew panicked and asked himself, "What's a corsage?" Beth showed him the pretty ones on the other girls in the gym. "See, look at Brittany's corsage; it's beautiful." Matthew apologized for the error and asked if she wanted any punch.

"I bet Austin would have gotten me a corsage. His mom always remembers those things."

Speaking of moms, Matthew glanced over to April to see how she was doing with the rest of the chaperones. It seemed that April might have slightly overdressed for the occasion. The other parents and teachers wore blue jeans, track suits, and the occasional cotton dress. Her silk power dress and heels stuck out like a sore thumb with the rest of the adults. She stood to the side of a snack table and had not spoken to anyone. She was looking around the gym when she was startled by a wayward voice.

"Wow, I wish I woulda put on my tux." April spun to see a tall man wearing a police officer's uniform coming toward her. "I'm sorry, didn't mean to startle you. I was admirin' your dress there and just wanted to come over and introduce myself."

April reached her hand out to the young officer and said, "My name is April, April Chance."

The officer grabbed a small cheese and cracker from the table and asked, "You must be new to town cause I know just about everybody

Chapter 11

who lives here and I can't say that I've ever had the pleasure to meet an April Chance."

April was mystified by the officer's southern twang and ease of conversation. She was glad that someone had taken the time to talk to her. There was something about this man that seemed familiar to her, but she couldn't figure out what it was. April explained to the young police officer that she and her sons had just moved to Travis and she was looking to make a permanent home for her family.

"Well, my name's Danny Charles, or Officer Charles, if I ever pull you over for speedin'." He explained that he was asked to cover the local school dances, just to make sure there were no fights or altercations among the students.

"So April, is your husband here too or did he leave it up to you to cover the whole dance?"

April responded, "Oh, I'm not married. It's just me and the boys."

The young officer asked April if she would like to get some air. "It's kinda stuffy in here, maybe we could talk outside." April agreed and the two went out the side door of the gym.

Connor found Matthew and asked, "Did you see where Mom went?"

Matthew responded, "Not really. I've been a little more focused on the dance floor."

"What do you mean?"

Matthew pointed to the floor and said, "Haven't you noticed that no one on the floor is dancing like April showed us last night? They're barely moving out there."

Connor pointed to Amanda and Beth, who were talking by the punch table, and said, "I'm a little more worried about our dates. I'm running out of things to talk about. They keep talking about some music video with a zombie in it. Sounds like the zombie dances around and turns into a big cat or something stupid like that. I have no idea what they're talking about."

The boys backed away from the dance floor as one of the songs they had practiced dancing to with April came over the speakers. Amanda and Beth ran up to them and grabbed each of their hands. "We love this song; you have to dance with us." Connor and Matthew looked at each

Girls And Gadgets

other in terror as their dates dragged them to the center of the gymnasium floor.

The boys looked at the streamers tied to the crossbeams of the gym and the posters on the walls of all the popular music acts of the time. The beat was pounding, the rhythm of the music was intoxicating, and as Amanda and Beth looked to the boys to make the first move, it just began to flow through them.

Matthew and Connor gyrated to the music, arms thrashed, quick starts and stops, just as their mom had shown them. Both boys had their eyes closed as they prayed that they weren't making fools of themselves. They took a peek at their dates and realized that they were both laughing, but not necessarily at them.

Amanda grabbed Connor's hands and they began to move around the gym. "Wow, Trey would never let loose like that. You guys know how to have fun."

Beth grabbed Matthew's hands and said, "You guys look ridiculous, but at least you're trying. Here, put your hands on my waist."

The boys and their dates danced around to the next three songs and had a great time doing it. It wasn't the most impressive dancing in the world, but it got the job done. Matthew glanced over to his brother and Amanda as they jumped up and down on a number one tune. After one exaggerated jump, he noticed something pop out of the top of Amanda's shirt. It was a square charm, yellow in color, hanging on a small gold chain.

The music died down and Connor led his date toward the front door of the gym. Matthew began to follow, but Beth grabbed his hand. "Come on, I need a drink." Matthew reluctantly followed his date back to the punch table.

"That is so much fun. I can't believe you and your brother don't mind looking like complete idiots out there just so we can have a good time."

Matthew responded, "Anything to help you have a good time."

Beth looked to the punchbowl and asked, "So, do you have something to spike the punch with? That'll really get the dance going."

Matthew pulled his pockets out and replied, "No, must have left it in my other pants."

Chapter 11

The gym was packed with kids and the music was so loud that you could barely hear the thud of feet that slammed onto the basketball court. The DJ had started the strobe light and it covered the entire dance floor. Matthew listened as Beth went on and on about the difficulties of her hairdo. "Can you believe it takes my mom an hour every night to roll my hair?"

Matthew shrugged. "That must be a lot of rollers?"

Beth agreed and was about to explain her issues with cheerleading when she saw Cassie Jenkins running toward the punch table. She asked, "I wonder what the supergenius is up to?"

Cassie called out to Matthew, "Matthew, I need your help! Matthew!"

Matthew and Beth made their way toward her. Matthew asked, "What's wrong?"

Cassie stopped and caught her breath; she wasn't used to running. "You have to come with me. Jack and your brother are getting beaten up in the parking lot."

Beth rolled her eyes. "Those idiots are back at it. Go on with her. I'll try to find Officer Charles."

Matthew raced out of the gym with Cassie on his tail. As they exited the door, Matthew could hear Cassie asking, "So you came to the dance with her?"

Matthew responded, "Not now; we'll talk about it later." He rounded the far end of the building and there at the front row of parking spaces was Connor lying on the pavement. Trey reared back and kicked him in the stomach. Connor twitched in pain and rolled to his side.

Jack was pinned down by one of the football team's defensive linemen, and Amanda was held by another. Matthew arrived at the lot and called out to the pack, "One, two, three...seven guys to take down my brother. You must really be proud of yourselves."

Amanda tried to pull away from the large senior lineman and yelled to Matthew, "Just go get some help. I think Connor's really hurt."

Trey pointed his finger at his former girlfriend. "You shut up! This is your fault!" Trey walked over to Amanda and put his hand on her shoulder and said, "This wimp tries to steal my spot on the team, and then you reward him by coming to this dance with him." Connor tried to get up from the ground, but Trey moved back over and kicked him in the face.

"That's enough!" yelled Matthew.

Trey looked to Matthew, beer bottle in his left hand, and said, "I have to admit, your brother can sure take a beating."

Matthew saw a small object lying on the ground close to one of the cars in the parking lot. It was the snap ring he had given to Connor. Matthew looked to Jack and the boy that held him to the ground and said, "Why don't you let him up?" He looked to the boy holding Amanda and said, "You can go ahead and let her go, too." He walked within two feet of Trey and said, "I'm gonna take on all seven of you."

Trey laughed and taunted Matthew, "What are you gonna do? You're a little punk compared to your brother. I could kick your ass with one hand tied behind my back, blindfolded, and hopping on one leg."

Matthew reached down to his watch and pressed the second button from the top. He took another step toward Trey and said, "Come on, second string; let's see what you got."

At that, Trey Wilson dropped his bottle of beer and took his first swing at Matthew. Matthew raised his hand toward the star quarterback and proceeded to toss him ten feet back into a parked car. The windshield cracked from the force of the hit and Trey was knocked for a loop.

Austin and Rick made their move toward Matthew. He was trying to move Cassie away from the danger area. Austin got a shot in on Matthew's side, but Matthew was able to block the next punch headed toward his face. Austin was thrown fifteen feet into the air and landed flat on his back. You could hear the air leave his chest on impact.

Rick grabbed Matthew around the waist and threw him toward the parked cars. At that, the boys who were holding Amanda and Jack let them go and joined Rick. Amanda tried to jump onto one of the boys' backs, but he threw her to the ground.

The act of striking any young woman would have made Matthew Chance mad, but to do it to Amanda Curry was unacceptable. Rick shouted, "All right boy, now we're really gonna stomp your ass." All three boys jumped onto Matthew and began to throw punches. Amanda and

Chapter 11

Cassie screamed for help, but it wasn't needed. Matthew had picked up the snap ring that Connor dropped earlier and he had it positioned at the three boys over top of him.

"You had enough, wimp?" Matthew turned over with the ring in hand and snapped his fingers into it. All three boys were tossed like sacks of garbage at the dump and slammed into the side of the gym. The final two football players who were there made their way toward Matthew, but they stopped at the sound of an approaching voice.

"You boys stop right there! What's goin on here?" Beth had arrived with both Officer Charles and April. The two players who hadn't tangled with Matthew ran off into the darkness of the parking lot. Trey Wilson came to.

"What's goin' on here, Mr. Wilson?" the officer asked Trey. "You causin' problems for these three boys?"

Officer Charles looked around the area and saw four more of the largest football players on the team lying on the ground. He looked to Matthew and asked, "You took on seven players from the football team and you're the one still standing?"

Matthew placed the snap ring back into his pocket and said, "We just got lucky, officer. They've been drinking, so we must have been too quick for them."

Officer Charles called for some backup and a couple of police cars drove up into the lot. "Y'all can head back to the dance. We'll take care of these boys." Officer Charles walked over to April, who was tending to Connor, and said, "I'm sorry our discussion had to be abruptly ended like this Ms. April." Officer Charles extended his hand. April extended her hand, expecting a shake, but Officer Charles kissed it instead.

"Maybe we can continue our talk over dinner some night."

April held Connor, who was still hurt and bleeding from the altercation, and said, "I better get him home and clean him up." She smiled at Officer Charles. "It was nice meeting you." The family started toward the car, but Amanda blocked Matthew's path.

"How did you do that? That was one of the most amazing things I've ever seen."

Matthew looked to the gorgeous blonde and said, "I told you. I just got lucky."

Amanda shook her head. "You just took on and took out half of the seniors on the football team."

Cassie and Jack walked up behind Amanda and added, "Yeah, Matthew, I haven't even seen anything like that in the world of professional wrestling."

Matthew cleared his throat and replied, "Look, the important thing is that everyone's OK. I couldn't let them hurt any of you."

"Come on, Matthew, we need to go!" yelled April.

Matthew turned to Jack, Cassie, and Amanda and said, "I'll see you all on Monday. Just go back and enjoy the rest of the dance and tell Beth that I'm sorry for running out on her." Matthew headed to his mother's car and they sped off.

Beth found Amanda as she made her way back to the gym and asked, "Did Matthew leave?"

Amanda told Beth that he apologized for running out on her and asked, "Did you have a good time with Matthew?" Beth shook her head yes, but then went on to say that both Connor and Matthew seem a little too weird for her.

Amanda grinned and thought, *I need to find out more about those two brothers—especially Matthew!*

Cassie and Jack were walking well behind Amanda and Beth and discussed what they had just witnessed. "Can you believe how he tossed those guys? I've never seen anything like it. He's half their size and threw them around like they were dolls."

Cassie pondered some other items. "Can you believe he came here with Beth Perry? What does she have that I don't?"

Jack replied, "Besides a rocking body, curly hair, and some very short skirts, not much at all. And I think you are missing the point here. There is no way Matthew Chance could have done what he did without some help."

Cassie shrugged her shoulders and asked, "What kind of help?"

Jack replied, "I don't know, but I think something alien is going on here."

Chapter 11

Cassie laughed, and said, "I think you've been watching too many sci-fi movies."

Back at the Chance residence, Matthew and April were helping Connor into the house. "I'm already feeling better, guys. I can walk on my own."

April opened the front door and asked, "Will there be a day that you don't get beat up at that school?"

Connor looked to Matthew and said, "After the beating that Matthew put on those guys, I don't think we'll have to worry about them anymore."

April grabbed Matthew by the arm and looked at his watch. "You used this to stop those boys, didn't you?"

Connor replied, "Yeah, he used that and the snap rings that Walter sent with us."

April dropped Matthew's hand and said, "You used one of the things in the backpack that I told you not to mess with?"

Matthew began walking to his bedroom and replied, "We had to do something. We can't keep letting these guys push us around, and I certainly couldn't let anything happen to Amanda or our friends."

April walked into the kitchen and grabbed a drink. "This is all my fault. I haven't been doing what I should have been." April took off her sparkled heels and threw them into her room. "I am such a fool, worrying about new dresses and dances for you boys. We have been here a week already and we don't even know if this girl has the attribute charm."

Matthew came back out of his room, "That's not entirely true."

Connor asked, "Which part?"

Matthew explained that he saw the charm on Amanda's neck while they were dancing. "She's wearing it."

April grabbed both of the boys around the shoulders and added the obvious. "Now all we have to do is convince her to give that charm to one of you."

Matthew looked to a calendar that was hanging on the wall and said, "We have one more week to do it."

April looked at the calendar and said, "I let this place get the best of me. All the freedom, all the options, I just let it get to me. No more. We're not here to make friends. We're not here to win the big game. We're not here to join the community. We're here to get that charm from Amanda Curry, and that is what we're going to do."

The Chances headed to bed on the night of the Eastview Fall Fling and knew that a lot of work was still ahead, but they also knew that the attribute charm was within reach. Visions of Amanda Curry filled the thoughts of Matthew Chance on this night. He wanted to know what she was thinking and he wanted to know why he felt so strongly about her. Connor may have taken her to the dance, but he wasn't the one who protected her. If only Matthew knew what was to come.

Chapter 12

MIRROR MIRROR

"Matthew. Matthew, wake up!"

Matthew rubbed his eyes and looked at the clock in his bedroom. "Come on Mom, we were up until three a.m. Let me sleep until nine."

April pulled the cover from Matthew's bed and explained her rude sleep interruption. "Amanda Curry is waiting for you in our living room. She wants to take you to the morning parade downtown."

Matthew sat up in the bed and said, "I'm sure she asked for Connor, not me."

April rummaged through Matthew's clothes and corrected him. "No, she specifically asked for you. Now get dressed and get out there." She threw Matthew a T-shirt and a fairly clean pair of jeans. "I'll keep her busy while you get ready." Connor rolled over in his bed, oblivious to Matthew's actions.

"It's very nice to see you again, Amanda." Ms. Chance offered the young girl a drink and something for breakfast, but Amanda turned down both. April sat on the couch beside the lovely cheerleader and noticed the square charm on a chain around her neck.

Amanda observed the strange look and asked, "Is there something wrong, Ms. Chance?"

April averted her eyes and replied, "Oh no, I was just noticing the lovely necklace around your neck." April's voice had cracked while making the comment.

Amanda grasped the charm with her hand and said, "Yeah, this necklace has been in my family for years. I've had my eyes on it since I

Chapter 12

was a little girl and my mother finally gave it to me as a present for my sixteenth birthday."

April regrouped and complimented her young guest. "It's just lovely. You should be proud to wear it. I would think you would only give that up to someone very special."

Amanda replied, "They would have to be very special."

Matthew emerged from his room and saw his mother and Amanda chatting it up. Amanda heard him walk up and said, "So, are you ready to go?"

Matthew asked, "Where exactly do you want to go?"

Amanda explained that the town always threw a fall parade on the Saturday after one of the early football games and today was that day. Amanda said that she felt bad about what had happened last night, so she wanted to show Matthew that the entire town wasn't as bad as a few football players. "We really need to get going; it starts in about ten minutes."

Matthew looked back to his bedroom and asked, "What about Connor? I can get him up and he can go with us."

Amanda stood up from the couch, confused. "I figured he would barely be able to move after what Trey did to him last night, much less be able to stand up and watch a parade."

Matthew realized that Amanda was right. If Connor hadn't been wearing the Hathmec, he would be laid up for days. "Oh yeah, you're right; he needs his rest."

Amanda replied, "OK then. I have my parent's truck, so I can drive us."

Matthew and Amanda jumped into Mr. Curry's black pickup truck with rolling wave designs on the door. It was a perfect morning for a parade. No rain, no fog, and no football players were around to ruin it. You could smell the fall dew on the ground and see hazy footprints in the grass in the early morning hour.

April woke up Connor and argued with him about going to the parade. "You should be in the hospital after the beating you took last night. You have to lay low for a few days."

Connor was upset that Matthew had left with Amanda. "She went to the dance with *me*. I should be going to the parade with her."

She replied, "Matthew has it covered. I saw the attribute charm."

Connor pulled the fake charm that Walter had sent with them from his backpack and asked, "Did it look like this?"

April held the fake charm in her hand, studied it, and replied, "Exactly like this."

Connor asked, "What do we do now?"

"You're gonna stay here and I'm heading to the parade. I can keep an eye on Matthew." April grabbed her bag and made her way out the door. Connor fumed for a few minutes and headed back to his room.

"Wow, I didn't realize there were this many people in Travis." Matthew took in the crowds that lined the streets of downtown. He watched the local churches and community groups pull their floats of papier-mâché down the street. He also saw a stream of fire trucks, old cars, and school bands parading down the middle of the road.

Matthew asked, "Who are the people on that float?"

Amanda told him that those lovely ladies were the winners of the fall beauty pageant. "They're the winners in the sixteen-to-eighteen-year-old division. See, Beth was a runner-up."

Matthew looked to the lovely blonde and confidently announced, "Well, I don't see how they could have a beauty pageant without the prettiest girl in Travis." Amanda's cheeks turned red, but before she could respond, Matthew added, "Of course, you're a nice person, so you probably don't compete in all of them—just to give other girls a chance to win."

Amanda shook her head no and said, "Please, I am not the prettiest girl in town. I'm also not nice enough to let other people win."

Matthew and Amanda made their way around downtown for most of the morning and talked about school, family, and getting out of Travis. "I can't wait to graduate. I'm gonna get into college, somewhere out of state, like Florida."

Matthew wondered why she was so determined to leave Travis. "You'll be leaving your family and your friends; doesn't that bother you?"

Amanda explained that most of her friends would end up marrying someone way too soon after school, get stuck in a dead-end job, and the

Chapter 12

highlight of their year would be the local football games and parades. "I want more. I can be someone important." Matthew agreed that doing something important was a good goal, but he was also starting to figure out how important family could be.

"Don't get me wrong; I love my parents and my little brother. I mean, he can be a real pain in the butt, but I still love him." She went on to explain that just because she wanted to get out of Travis, it didn't mean she wouldn't miss her family. "I'm sure you can understand what I mean; it's the same as how you would feel leaving your mom and brother."

Matthew replied, "I don't think the dynamic at my house is quite the same as yours."

Amanda grabbed Matthew's hand and pulled him toward the sidewalk. "Let's test the theory then."

Matthew, puzzled by the request, asked, "How do you propose we do that?"

She replied, "Come over to my house tonight around five and eat dinner with me and my family. We're having homemade spaghetti and my mom's a great cook."

Amanda gave Matthew the directions to her house and asked if he wanted to go to a movie after dinner. She pointed to the movie complex located downtown and explained that she had wanted to see this movie for weeks. Matthew tried to hold back the huge grin that had already flooded his face, but he was unsuccessful. This would be a great opportunity to find out more about Amanda.

Downtown Travis was beginning to clear out as the parade ended. The town's main street emptied and the normal flow of traffic started to fill the streets. April had followed Matthew and Amanda for most of the morning, only stopping to admire the canopied shops along the parade route. It was the typical eighties small southern town. There was a library on the corner and a video rental place at the end of the block. April could smell the detergent being used at the local coin-op laundry, and she loved the mural on the exposed brick wall of the downtown electronics store.

She walked up behind the two kids as they passed the local pharmacy and asked, "Did you enjoy the parade?"

Amanda turned to see Matthew's mom and replied, "Yes, ma'am, it was even better than last year's."

Matthew told April that he was invited to Amanda's to eat with her family. She replied, "That sounds great. I'll be helping Connor tonight anyway. His face still hurts and he's all swollen, so I may have to fix soft food for a few days."

She glanced over to the library and noticed a familiar face in the crowd. Matthew could tell that his mother had lost her train of thought and tried to pull her back to the conversation. "Mom is something wrong?"

She hesitated for a moment and said, "That man standing by the library."

Matthew looked and saw the man. "Is that Keith Kellington?"

Amanda asked, "Who's Keith Kellington?"

Matthew played it cool. "He's just a guy that we know from Georgia. I'm sure that's not him though; just someone who looks like him." Matthew took Amanda by the hand and pulled her over to the side. "Why don't you head on home and let your mom and dad know that I'll be coming to dinner tonight. Since Mom's here, she can give me a ride back home."

April heard what Matthew had said and added, "We should get back and check on Connor." Amanda agreed and told April good-bye. She also checked one last time with Matthew to make sure he was coming to dinner.

He replied, "Absolutely! I'll be there around five."

Amanda walked off toward her truck, which was parked behind the line of downtown stores. Matthew and April watched to see what the man by the library did next. "He's going to the parking lot."

April and Matthew made their way around the backside of the pharmacy and saw the man make his way toward Amanda's truck. April told Matthew to stay behind the wall and left to cut off the man.

She waved her arms around and yelled to the man, "Excuse me! Excuse me!"

The man stopped his forward movement and turned to April. Obviously frustrated, the man asked her, "Yes, what do you want?"

Chapter 12

April kept a good distance and said, "I'm sorry to bother you sir, but I just know that we've met before." April wanted to distract the man and determine his name. She described a man that she had met a few years ago in Georgia that helped her with her groceries.

"You were so nice to me and I never got the chance to properly thank you for your help."

He replied, "I believe you are mistaken, ma'am. I've never been to Georgia."

April continued the charade. "Of course you have, Steve. Don't you remember the Quick Stop on Highway 70?" Amanda's truck pulled out of the parking lot and the man threw down a piece of paper in disgust.

He moved within inches of April and said, "Look, lady, my name is not Steve, it's Keith, and I've never met you before."

Matthew kept a close eye on what was happening and prepared himself to jump in if the man made any threatening moves toward his mother. He saw the man walk away, and April made her way back to the wall behind the pharmacy. "What happened? Do you know who it is?"

April shook her head. "Yeah, it's Keith Kellington."

Matthew walked around in a circle and asked, "Has he followed us into the past?"

Matthew paced around and April grabbed him by the arm. "This isn't the Keith Kellington that we met back home. I think this is the Keith Kellington from 1984, who doesn't have a clue we exist."

Matthew held his Hathmec and said, "Wow, he looks the same two hundred years later. This thing really works."

April gave the signal to head back to the car. "Let's get home and check on Connor. You've got a date to get ready for."

Matthew asked, "What do you think Keith's doin' here?" April assumed that he must be a part of Evan's team that took the charm from Amanda.

Matthew got into the car and reasoned, "Something must have changed; we still have six days before the charm's taken."

April started the car and said, "Maybe she didn't go to this parade the first time."

"What should we do?"

April replied, "We just have to be careful."

Matthew and his mother returned to their home to find that Connor had been busy. He had placed the remaining contents of the gadget bag on the living room floor. "What are you doing? I told you not to mess with that stuff until I had a chance to go through it."

Connor, a smug look on his face answered, "Since Matthew's busy with my girl, I thought I would go ahead and see what other goodies Walter sent with us."

April picked up what looked like a roll of duct tape and questioned its use. Connor took the roll of tape and peeled a small piece from it and placed it on the couch.

Matthew looked at the tape, unimpressed, and asked, "So that's it?" Connor sat down on the couch and placed his hand on the tape.

"Where did he go?" asked April. She and Matthew could no longer see Connor, but they could hear him.

"It's called camotape. I blend in to the couch as long as I touch the tape." Connor removed his hand from the tape and he reappeared.

Matthew took the roll and expressed his excitement. "This could really come in handy."

April looked at the piece on the couch. "I don't know; it seems a little weird to me."

Matthew noticed a pair of sunglasses lying on the coffee table and put them on. He could no longer see anything in front of him, only his bedroom. Connor jumped up and ran into the bedroom. "Can you see me?"

Matthew replied, "Yeah, I can see and hear you." Connor came back into the living room and removed the glasses from Matthew's face.

"They're called mirror glasses. All you have to do is look at something, like the clock in our room, and tap the lens."

April asked, "Then what do you do?"

"You put the glasses on and you can see and hear everything that can be seen or heard from that object." Connor tapped the lens again and gave the glasses back to Matthew. Matthew placed the glasses back on his face and he could see normally through them.

April had an idea. "Matthew, you need to take these to the Currys' house and set them."

Chapter 12

Matthew replied, "Yeah, that's a good idea; we may need to know what's going on there after I leave."

"Hold the phone. You're going over to Amanda's tonight?"

Matthew smirked and moved away from his brother. "Yeah, I've got a little date with one Amanda Curry tonight."

Connor shoved Matthew against the wall. "So I get the girl interested and now you swoop in and get to spend all the time with her?"

April got between the two boys and reminded them both of why they were there. "We're not here to get a girlfriend, boys; we're here to complete a very important task." She handed the glasses back to Matthew and said, "I don't care who gets the charm from her. Right now, it looks like Matthew has the best chance."

Connor turned and made his way back into his bedroom and mumbled to himself, "I'm the best Chance."

April saw a folder lying on the table that read, "For April Only." April recognized the folder as the same one that she had seen before going through the tunnel. Walter didn't want her to read it until she arrived in the past. She had almost forgotten about it.

"Connor, where did you find this folder?"

"I found it under the bed. It must have fallen out of one of the bags when we first got here." He went on to proclaim his innocence before it was questioned. "I didn't open it up. I figured it was special woman instructions or something."

April opened the folder with Matthew standing behind her. He tried to get a peek. "You go on and get ready for your date. I need to see what this is." Matthew agreed and made his way to join Connor in their room.

She found one piece of paper and an old newspaper clipping. She spent the next twenty minutes reading and then rereading the handwritten letter from Walter Wainright. The last line on the paper said to destroy the page when complete, so April took it out back and threw it into the garbage can that leaned against the back of the home. She kept the newspaper clipping and placed it into her jacket pocket.

April mulled around the home for a few hours and looked back through all of the instructions that were sent along from Walter. Matthew emerged from his room around 4:30 p.m. and asked what she was doing. "I'm just making sure that we didn't miss anything that Walter needed us to do."

Matthew was surprised by the response and replied, "You've been over his instructions and notes a hundred times. We know what we have to do."

April looked to her son and said, "Do you?"

Matthew pulled the fake attribute charm from his pocket and said, "We need to get Amanda to hand over her charm, of her own free will. We give her this one in its place to give Evan Elliott or whomever he sends to get it."

April said, "Go on."

"We get back to the tunnel, Amanda goes on with her life, and Evan Elliott is none the wiser."

April had a somber look on her face and asked Matthew if he was ready to head to the Currys' home. Connor stayed behind, still upset with how things had gone with Amanda. He spent most of the night playing with the camotape and the memory boots. In fact, he had a lot of fun out back walking between trees. He was levitating between the limbs.

April dropped off Matthew just before five at the home of the Curry family. Their home was twenty minutes out of town and isolated from any neighbors. It took Matthew and his mother only ten minutes to drive there, since they lived out of town as well.

Large oak and Bradford pear trees dotted the front and back yards of the two-story home. "Look at the columns of this place, Matthew." The driveway was a long winding stretch in itself. By the time the Chances made it to the front door, it was as if they had been on a backwoods adventure.

April asked her son, "Do you want me to walk up with you?"

Matthew replied, "Of course not! Are you crazy? It's bad enough that you brought me here. I'm supposed to be sixteen, remember?" Matthew opened the door to the car and started to get out. "I should have driven here myself."

April passed Matthew a ten-dollar bill and, with a smile on her face, said, "Take this to pay for the movie tonight, and if we have time before we head back to Georgia, I'll teach you to drive."

Chapter 12

Matthew walked up to the big green door at the front of the house and rang the bell. He waited for just a few moments before the door flew open. He looked down to see a boy, no more than eight or nine, staring back at him. Matthew wanted to break the silence and said, "Hello, my name is Matthew."

The boy continued to stare at him until he blurted out, "Amanda, your boyfriend's here!" Matthew tried to explain that he was not Amanda's boyfriend, but the young boy slipped away and paid no further attention to him.

"Come on in, son; you can take a seat at the table." The dining room looked as if it had been pulled from a magazine spread of country furnishings. Matthew saw a very nicely dressed gentleman, blue suit, without the jacket, but still wearing a tie. "I'm Amanda's father, Steve. You can call me Mr. Curry." Matthew reached out his hand to shake Mr. Curry's, but the gesture was not returned. "From the announcement, I could hear that you have met Amanda's little brother, Steven Jr."

Matthew replied, "Yes, sir," as he took a seat at the table.

As soon as Matthew sat down, he saw Amanda and her mother coming from the kitchen with several plates of food. "Hey, I see you met my father. This is my mother, Laura."

Matthew began to tell her that it was nice to meet her, but Mr. Curry stepped in before he could and said, "You can call her Mrs. Curry."

Matthew grinned and said, "Well, it's very nice to meet all of you." Steven Jr. came careening into the dining room, and Matthew added, "Even Steven Jr."

It was a feast of spaghetti, meatballs, salad, and breadsticks. Mr. Curry said a quick blessing before they started eating and then the interrogation of Matthew began. Amanda's parents asked every question imaginable to Matthew from where were you born to what type of soda do you drink. Matthew did a great job answering their questions without hesitation, even though he made up the majority of the answers.

After fifteen minutes of getting grilled, Matthew attempted to change the subject. "So, Mr. Curry, what do you do for a living?"

Mr. Curry said that most of the boys Amanda invited to dinner never asked anything about her parents, so this was a pleasant surprise. "I'm in real estate, my boy. How do you think I was able to get such a great piece of land here?"

Mrs. Curry interrupted. "Don't let him fool you; he is very good at what he does, but this land has been in his family for over a hundred years. He can thank his great-great-grandfather for this land."

Mr. Curry explained that his family had lived in the area for several generations. The home itself had been built back in the mid-1800s. "We just keep updating it and adding to it." He looked at Steven Jr. and said, "Who knows, maybe one day this little guy will be living with his family here." Amanda rolled her eyes and asked if Matthew was full.

"I am *completely* full," replied Matthew. It was still an hour before the movie was set to begin, so Mr. and Mrs. Curry asked Matthew if he would like to come into the living room. Matthew agreed but helped Amanda clean up some of the plates on the table first.

While Amanda was alone with Matthew, she told him, "You're doing great; just don't let them see you sweat."

Before he went into the living room, he asked where the bathroom was and Mrs. Curry pointed him in the right direction. As Matthew made his way down the hall, he noticed a large mirror that pointed directly into the living room. The rest of the family couldn't see Matthew or what he was about to do. Matthew grabbed the sunglasses from his pocket and put them on. He looked up to the mirror and tapped one the lenses, linking the mirror and glasses together.

He took off the glasses and saw Steven Jr. staring at him from the side stairs. "What are you doing?" asked the young boy.

Matthew knew that Steven Jr. saw him with his glasses so he made up the most logical story at the time. "I saw that mirror up there and wanted to see how cool I look in my new sunglasses."

Steven Jr. shrugged his shoulders and said, "Teenagers are weird."

Matthew arrived in the living room and turned his attention to the one thing he needed most. "Mr. Curry, I couldn't help but notice that lovely necklace and charm Amanda's wearing; was that a gift from you?"

Chapter 12

Mr. Curry, proud of his own accomplishments, couldn't take all of the credit for Amanda's necklace. "Well, Matthew, I did in a roundabout kind of way. You see, there is a very interesting story that goes along with that particular stone."

Mrs. Curry set the stage. "That particular stone has been in the Curry family for well over 150 years. There is a sort of legend that goes along with it."

Mrs. Curry went on to explain that the stone had been given to one of Steve's relatives way back in the early 1800s by a drifter. It seemed that this relative of Steve's had helped this drifter with some sort of debt that he owed and the drifter told him that he would give him this stone as payment on that debt.

Mr. Curry continued, "The real interesting thing about the stone was that no one had ever been able to determine exactly what it was. Was it some type of jade or discolored quartz? No one really knows, but it's been a family heirloom ever since."

Mrs. Curry held her cup of coffee and added, "Steven gave it to me on our honeymoon, and Amanda had her eyes on it from the first day she could talk. Her grandmother wanted us to give it to her then, but we decided to give it to her on her sixteenth birthday. She knows that it has to come back to Steven Jr. someday, to make sure it stays with the Curry family name."

Mr. Curry elaborated on the drifter. "There's some legends or tall tales about this drifter. People had accused him of being some sort of magician or prophet."

He explained that there had been stories of this man saving people from illness and protecting other people from all sorts of bad dealings during that time. "To make a long story short, people in my family think the stone has some magical traits." He looked to his daughter and said, "I was hoping it would magically get my daughter through Chemistry, but no luck so far."

Amanda stood up at that comment and said, "Enough stories; we're going to be late for the movie."

Matthew stood and made his way to the door. He thanked Mrs. Curry for dinner and for everyone having him in their home. Amanda walked out the front door and Matthew followed.

Mr. Curry hollered to Matthew, "You make sure nothing happens to my little girl."

Matthew shook his head and promised that he'd watch over her. At that, they climbed into Mrs. Curry's car and they were off.

The young couple reached the theater and Matthew paid for them both to see the movie. During the scary parts of the picture, Matthew was enthralled that Amanda would reach down and grab his hand; at one point, she buried her head into his shoulder. Matthew came out of the theater thinking that horror movies were the best thing ever invented.

Matthew and Amanda decided to take a walk on the downtown sidewalk before heading back home. "Maybe we could go get some ice cream at the Snack Shack."

Amanda was trying to find ways to keep the night going, and Matthew had no issues staying out as long as she wanted. The more time they spent together, the better the odds were of getting the charm. Matthew enjoyed the time with her. She wasn't just a pretty face, although it was easy to get hypnotized by it.

"I really want to help people someday. Maybe I'll become a doctor or someone who can help kids."

Matthew replied, somewhat sarcastically, "It sounds like you'll have to do better in Chemistry to work that doctor angle."

The two laughed, and Amanda asked Matthew an unexpected question. "Are you and your brother for real?"

Before Matthew could answer, he noticed three men walking toward them. Matthew also noticed that he and Amanda had walked to an area that was isolated from the rest of the downtown. He recognized one of the men as Keith Kellington and he started to panic. Amanda asked if he was OK.

Keith made the first move. "Little Amanda Curry. It's been so long."

Amanda replied, "Do I know you?"

Chapter 12

Keith answered with a pleasant demeanor. It was like talking to the local Baptist preacher. "I can't believe you don't remember your Uncle Keith. I've known your dad for years."

He told Amanda that he's known her since she was a baby and that he was in town to talk to her dad about some new real estate opportunities. Matthew stayed quiet while Keith made generic small talk with her and realized that the other two men had formed a small circle around them.

Matthew grabbed Amanda's hand and said, "Look, sir, we really need to be going, so if you don't mind."

Keith became agitated and said, "I'm just trying to catch up with this young lady here, son. I'm sure wherever it is you're going can wait a few minutes."

Keith asked Amanda if she still had that lovely yellow stone her father had given her for her birthday. Amanda asked how he knew about it, and he explained that her father had told him about it. "He also says that you may be interested in selling it to me."

Amanda grabbed a hold of the chain around her neck and said, "I can't believe he would say something like that. I can't sell this!"

Keith Kellington pulled five thousand dollars from his coat and offered it to Amanda for the necklace and stone. "You're seriously going to give me five thousand dollars for this stone?"

Keith put the money in Amanda's hand and said, "It's yours; all you have to do is give me the necklace."

Matthew stepped in between Keith and Amanda. "You can't sell that stone, Amanda; it's an heirloom."

Amanda attempted to hand the money back to Keith and said, "He's right. I can't sell you the necklace. You'll have to talk to my father."

Matthew recognized a change in Keith from this happy exterior to the man he had met two hundred years in the future. Keith took the money, placed it back in his pocket, leaned down to Matthew's ear, and said, "If you know what's good for you, you'll tell your little girlfriend here to sell me that stone."

Matthew saw Keith Kellington reach for his Hathmec. Matthew had noticed the outline of the pendant under his shirt. Matthew started to reach for the snap ring in his pocket. If he had to, he would throw Keith Kellington through the window of the pawnshop they stood behind. Keith looked ready to make a move.

Chapter 13

ALIENS AMONG US

Matthew was blinded by sharp blue lights that seemed to have appeared from nowhere. He took his hand from his pocket once he saw Keith Kellington pull his hand down from his chest. Keith shielded his eyes from the piercing glare.

Matthew focused on the object projecting the lights and determined that a police car had pulled up on the sidewalk. Both the driver's and passenger's doors opened and Amanda recognized one of the occupants. "Officer Charles, is that you?"

Matthew recognized the other passenger. "Mom?"

April flanked Officer Charles and said, "Hey kids, we thought it was you over here. I see you've met, Keith, right?"

Keith looked at April and said, "You're the one who thought I was from Georgia."

"Yeah, that was me. Looks like you've met my son and his friend."

Officer Charles asked the men in Keith's group to back up. "Y'all kids need to be careful wandering down these dark streets by yourselves. You never know who you might run into out here."

He turned his attention to Keith and his men. "So, what exactly's goin' on here?" Keith explained that he was old friends with Amanda's father and was simply trying to see if she remembered him. "I haven't seen her in a long time and just wanted to see how she was doing." Two more police cars pulled up behind Officer Charles's cruiser.

Chapter 13

Officer Charles removed the flashlight from his belt, shined the light into Keith's eyes, and said, "I get nervous when I see two of my kids surrounded by three grown men that I've never seen in this town."

Keith agreed and said, "I'm sure this looked a little strange, but we meant no harm to the kids."

Officer Charles pointed his light down the street and suggested that Keith and his friends just head on down the road. "I'm fixin' to head to the house and don't much feel like dealin' with you boys tonight, so get on outta here."

Keith responded, "I assure you that we meant no harm, officer, but you're probably right—we'll just be on our way. By the way, I love your accent. It fits you well." Keith turned to Amanda, one last time, and said, "I'll let your father know I ran into you when I talk to him."

Keith glanced at Matthew as he walked away. His quick stare shot a hole through Matthew. He knew they would meet again. Officer Charles yelled to one of his men, "Make sure they're outta here in the next few minutes or we'll have another talk with 'em.

Officer Charles asked Amanda, "Did you know any of those men?"

Amanda explained that she had never seen any of them before. "He acted like he knew my father."

April asked, "Did he want anything or was he just talking to you?"

"He offered me five thousand dollars cash for my necklace."

Officer Charles looked at the necklace and replied, "It's a nice charm, but he could buy a nice diamond for five thousand bucks."

Amanda told them that she could never sell it. "I don't think my dad would take any amount of money for it. He would kill me if I sold it."

Keith and his men were already out of sight when Officer Charles asked, "What did he say his full name was?"

Matthew replied, "He said his name was Keith Kellington."

Officer Charles wrote the name in his little black tablet and told Amanda that he would do some checking on the name.

April took the kids to the side and said, "It's getting late. Maybe we should all call it a night." Matthew told his mother and the officer that he didn't want Amanda driving home by herself. Officer Charles put his worries to rest and promised that he would follow her all the way home.

Amanda pulled Matthew to the side and told him that she had a wonderful time. "I'm sorry we have to end the night so early."

Matthew responded, "Yeah, nothing like a few police cars to put a stop to a fun night."

Amanda chuckled and reassured Matthew that Keith was probably a buddy of her father's. "He has people to the house all the time; I'm sure I just didn't recognize this one."

Amanda didn't want to plant a kiss on Matthew with his mother standing four feet away, so she grabbed Officer Charles by the arm and they walked to his car. She turned and blew a kiss Matthew's way as the door closed. Officer Charles waited just a moment before starting his car to see if April would do the same.

She looked to him and waved good-bye and said, "Thank you."

He rolled down his window and replied, "Not a problem. I'll scoot on over to this young lady's vehicle and make sure she gets home OK." He put the car in gear and added, "I'll be seein' y'all."

Matthew turned to April and said, "You realize I could have had my first kiss if you hadn't shown up."

April put her arm around her son and said, "You realize that Keith may have hurt you and Amanda if we hadn't shown up." It wasn't clear what would have taken place had April and Officer Charles not arrived, but for now, everyone was safe and the charm still belonged to Amanda.

The two walked a couple of blocks to April's car and headed home. Matthew asked, "How about teaching me to drive on the way home?"

April grunted and moved to the driver's side door and said, "Not tonight—let's just go home and get some rest."

Matthew replied, "If you teach me to drive, I'm sure I can convince Mrs. Curry to teach you to cook. Takeout and school lunches are ok, but it can't beat a home cooked meal."

April rolled her eyes and said, "I don't think we'll be here long enough to need cooking lessons."

Matthew asked, sarcasm on full display, "So, did you get a kiss from Officer Hottie?"

April blushed and explained, "I'm here to help you get the attribute charm, not flirt with Officer Hottie—I mean Charles."

Chapter 13

Matthew grinned and said, "Enough said."

Saturday night melted into Sunday morning. Connor and Matthew were in a deep sleep, but that would be short-lived. A loud pounding at the front door resonated in both of their heads.

"You gonna get up and get that?" asked Connor.

Matthew rolled over and said, "I thought I would let you get it."

Connor, quite groggy, explained, "I'm supposed to be all beat up, remember?"

Matthew lumbered out of bed and put on a pair of jeans. "Fine, I'll get it."

Matthew walked by the kitchen table and noticed a note from April that read, "Had to go out for some supplies. There's cereal in the cabinet." Matthew looked at the clock, rubbed his eyes, and stretched his arm into the air. The clock read 7:30 a.m. He reached the front door and opened it to see Jack and Cassie Jenkins. "Hey, guys. It's a little early, don't you think?"

Jack positioned himself just outside the door and responded, "We wanted to make sure we talked with you before we head to church."

Matthew looked to Cassie and asked, "What's up? You wanna come in?"

Cassie stepped back down the front steps, legs trembling, and responded, "No, I think we'll just stay out here."

Matthew saw how serious both Jack and Cassie were by their lack of eye contact and nervous twitches. They both seemed energized and scared at the same time. He asked, "Is there something wrong with you two?"

Jack took out a small vanilla envelope and explained why they were there. "We have proof that you and your brother are not of this world and we want to know what's going on."

Cassie added, "If you don't tell us what's going on, we'll report you to the proper authorities."

Matthew looked to the awkward girl and said, with a sheepish grin, "Is this 'cause I didn't go to the dance with you?"

Cassie furled her brow and responded, "Of course not!"

"Look, Matthew—if that's your real name—my sister and I are well versed in the scientific laws of the universe."

Matthew responded, "OK, what's your point?"

Jack went on to explain that he and his sister had come by the Chance home yesterday morning and saw Connor doing some very strange things. Cassie added, "In fact, we had our camera with us and got this shot of your brother, levitating."

Matthew opened the envelope and saw a picture of his brother standing fifteen feet in the air between two of the trees in the backyard. Matthew handed the picture back to Cassie and said, "That's a real nice picture, but you must have taken it while he was jumping. Maybe he was falling out of the tree when you snapped it. It's not possible to levitate."

Jack explained that the miraculous takedown of half the football team on Friday night was not the act of some normal sixteen-year-old kid. "You threw guys twice your size like you were tossing horseshoes. I wanna know how you did it. Do you have superhuman strength, mind control abilities, or are you an alien with special powers?"

Matthew laughed and shook his head. "You're both crazy. You both need to stop watching so many movies."

Jack pulled out a book of Georgia maps. "The place you talked about in class, Hathmec, doesn't exist." Cassie pulled out a copy of Matthew and Connor's transcript from school.

"How did you get that?"

Cassie explained that she was a very trusted office aide and she stole a copy of the transcripts when the secretary wasn't looking.

"I was just curious about you two, but after what we saw yesterday, I decided to call an administrator at your last school, in Grover, Georgia. It turns out no one there remembers any Matthew or Connor Chance."

The two siblings felt quite proud of what they had found and looked to Matthew for answers. "We're waiting, or do we need to bring this to the sheriff's attention?"

Matthew tore the envelope in two and threw it back at the brother and sister. He thought a show of anger would back off the two of them.

"I guess we'll just have to show 'em, Matthew." Matthew looked up to see his brother standing on the roof of their small home. Cassie and Jack looked up to see Connor levitating off the side of the roof, fifteen feet in the air.

Chapter 13

He walked closer to the siblings and Jack yelled to him, "Stay away from us."

Connor dropped to the ground and said, "So, you've figured us out? What do you plan to do with this information?"

Cassie put her hand up to block Conner and said, "People know where we are, so just keep your distance."

Connor walked to a tree located behind Cassie, and with a piece of the camotape on his hand, he placed it on the tree trunk. At once, he vanished and Cassie screamed.

Jack yelled out, "Oh my god! Where'd he go?"

Connor spoke, in his invisible state, "Do you really think your puny Earth technology and law enforcement can keep me from melting your face off? You would never see me coming." Cassie and Jack tried to run to the road, but Matthew blocked their path.

Jack began to plea and bargain for him and his sister. "We're sorry; we won't say a thing to anyone."

Cassie looked to Matthew. "Please don't melt our faces off!" Both Cassie and Jack were on their knees in the front yard of the home.

Matthew grabbed both of them by the arm and pulled them into the house. He told them to sit on the couch. Both Cassie and Jack were hyperventilating, so Matthew told them, "Calm down; no one's melting anyone's face off." Matthew had to think on his feet and come up with a story that would both calm the Jenkins kids and keep their own cover intact.

He explained that they were right. He and his brother and mother were all aliens sent to this world to investigate the human condition. "We're also on a very important mission to find out as much as possible about Travis itself. I must say I am very impressed that you figured out who we were. Connor and I knew that you two had a higher intellect than others in this town. We're not here to hurt anyone. We're good aliens."

Connor entered the living room and apologized for scaring them. "Sorry, guys, but you are so serious about everything." Cassie and Jack started to relax and felt a sense of pride that Matthew and Connor thought so highly of them.

Matthew continued, "We can't really tell you anything about where we're from, for your own protection. We only have a week left to acquire all the data we need, and we'll need your help to get it all."

Connor put his hands on Jack and Cassie's shoulders and asked, "Will you help us?"

Jack and Cassie both stood up and shook the hands of Matthew and Connor and asked, "What exactly do you need information on?"

Matthew grabbed a piece of paper from the kitchen and wrote the address to Amanda Curry's home. "We need to know everything about the house at this address and everything you can dig up on the Curry family."

Cassie took the address and said, "That's why you couldn't go to the dance with me; you're researching the area around the Currys' home."

Jack looked to his sister, snatched the address from her hand, and said, "We just met two aliens and all you care about is why one of them wouldn't go to a dance with you?"

She replied, "I just want to clarify it."

Matthew asked the brother and sister if they had a deal, and they agreed. "We'll find out everything there is to know about this address and the Currys."

Connor told them that they needed everything by the end of the week. Jack replied, "That shouldn't be a problem, we're good at digging up data." He motioned for his sister to leave and asked one last question. "Do we get to see your spaceship before you leave?"

Connor shook his head no and told them to get going before their mom got back.

As Jack and Cassie went out the front door, Cassie turned back to the brothers and said, "Welcome to our planet."

Matthew looked to Connor and threw a pillow at him. "You idiot! You had the memory boots on outside the house."

Connor threw the pillow back and said, "It all worked out and now we have some help finding out about the Currys. Just don't tell Mom about it." Matthew agreed and the boys headed back to their room.

Monday started as any other day at school would have started, except for a few obvious differences. Five members of the football team

Chapter 13

had been suspended from school for a few days for fighting, which was great for Matthew and Connor. Their last week in Travis would be bully free. The boys' prowess on the dance floor had spread through the school, and it seemed that more students knew their names. Cassie and Jack were nowhere to be found, as they were busy gathering information.

Matthew wasn't sure what to expect from Amanda on Monday morning, so what he got was a pleasant surprise. As Matthew rounded the corner to his locker, there she was. What a beautiful sight first thing in the morning.

"I thought you were never gonna get here. Do you wanna walk me to class?"

Matthew was overjoyed to walk Amanda to class. This gave him multiple chances throughout the day to talk to her and try to figure out a way to get the charm from her.

Connor was still embarrassed that Matthew was able to get the girl from him. Several students asked him why his brother was with Amanda. He focused more of his time with Jack and Cassie Jenkins. Amazingly, they had already researched a ton of information on the Curry home, and they shared it with Connor and Matthew.

"Look at all the paths that lead from the house," said Connor.

Jack explained that the main road that ran in front of the house had only been there for twenty years. There was an old service road that ran right up to the rear of the house, back in the day.

Matthew asked, "Where does that road lead now?"

Jack replied, "Basically, it's an old side road that was shut down, but it can still get you to the main highway, as long as you don't mind crossing a small ditch." Jack pointed out the side road and ditch on the map.

The roads weren't the only findings of the gifted Jenkins kids. They also explained that the house was constructed back in the days of the Civil War. Cassie began to speak at an accelerated rate, as her excitement couldn't be contained.

"There are hidden rooms all over this house. Some are behind bookcases, some behind staircases, and then the basement." She circled spots on the map that illustrated general locations of the rooms.

"This entire area here is located under the main floor of the house, but it can only be accessed from the outside through this door."

Connor and Matthew strained to see what she was pointing at and asked, "What door? All I see is the ground."

Jack sported a big grin and told his sister to tell them. "It's hidden under some fake brush, right about here."

Connor asked, "Is it still there?"

The brother and sister didn't know. Cassie continued, "If it's still there, it's an easy way into the house."

The twins continued to disclose what they had found about the construction of the home, its history, and who had lived in it. They only broke the pattern of information long enough to ask the boys questions about their alien race. "So, what does your spaceship look like? How long does it take to get to Earth from your planet?"

Cassie focused more on the biology. "Are you two anatomically similar to us humans?" The boys decided it was better to keep those questions unanswered for now, for the twins' own protection. For the anatomically correct question, both boys blurted out, "Yes!"

The days passed by, and Matthew felt that he was no closer to getting the charm than he was when they first fell out of the tunnel. He tried a local custom of giving her his new letter jacket, just to see if she would give him something in return. Both Connor and Matthew were awarded the jackets during a practice from Coach Dane. Little did Coach Dane know that Matthew and Connor would never play a snap in a real game.

It was already Friday morning, and April had to have a talk with the boys before they headed to school. "We're down to the last couple of days, boys. You have to get that charm today."

Matthew didn't seem overly confident. "I don't know what else to try, besides telling her the truth."

Connor jumped in. "You know you can't tell her the truth. She'll know that the future is going to get messed up and then we end up changing the past."

April took a seat on the couch in the living room, and Matthew asked what he should do next.

Chapter 13

"You have today at school to get the charm from her. If you don't, I want you to tell her that her family will be killed if she doesn't give you the charm."

Matthew was stunned by his mother's comments and asked, "So, you want me to scare her into giving me the charm?"

April dipped her head and said, "If it's the only way to get it, then that's what you have to do. Tell her whatever it takes to get it, give her the fake charm, and we're on the road to head back to Georgia."

The boys left in April's car. They had learned to drive with their mother teaching them after school. They discussed what April had told them and decided they would do what was needed, but only after trying every other avenue first.

Matthew spent as much time with Amanda on Friday as he could. Lunch was a good time to talk with her. There were pep rallies in the afternoon, and Amanda was wearing her cheerleading uniform in preparation. Matthew tried to convince Amanda to give him the necklace before the pep rally so that it didn't get damaged.

"If you wanna give it to me for a little while, I'll hold it so it doesn't get messed up during the pep rally."

She replied, "I wear it all the time, even during games. It'll be fine."

Just before the pep rally, Matthew tried another approach. "You know, my uniform would look really cool with your necklace around my neck. That way everyone knows that you're my cheerleader."

Amanda sported a confused look and asked, "What is your deal with this necklace today? Don't worry; everyone knows that we're together."

She popped a kiss on his cheek and said, "They'll really know after the game tonight when I run out to you and give you a big wet one on the fifty-yard line." She flashed Matthew a wink and ran out to the center of the gym to start the rally.

Matthew and Connor sat together on the bleachers during the pep rally as the cheerleaders jumped around, chanted some catchy slogans, and got the crowd of students and faculty fired up for the game that night. Connor leaned over to Matthew and said, "Let's try to catch Amanda at her car after the rally's over and we'll have the talk with her."

As the pep rally ended, the school gym became a maze of students and teachers just trying to get out of the building and head to their vehicles or buses for the ride home. Matthew and Connor were held up for a moment but were able to make their way to the school parking lot where Amanda's vehicle was still sitting. The boys waited for over half an hour, but there was no sign of Amanda.

Finally, another cheerleader, by the name of Brittany Thigpen, walked onto the lot. Matthew rushed to her and asked if she had seen Amanda.

She replied, "Oh yeah, she left about thirty minutes ago with Beth. I think they had to run some errands before the game." She smiled at the two boys. "It's so sweet you were waiting for her."

The boys rushed back to April's car and decided to head out to the Curry homestead to catch Amanda before the game. Connor told Matthew, "I'll stand off to the side while you talk to her. I don't want her to think we're ganging up on her."

The boys were coming down the road that led to the Curry home and noticed three men blocking the road. There was one quite large man in a black on black suit. He had a scar that ran the length of his face and greasy hair. He was flanked by two smaller men in similar suits.

They pulled up and asked what was going on. One of them asked Matthew if they were headed to the Curry home and he told them no.

"We live on down the road a few miles from the Currys. Do you need us to help you with anything?"

The man replied that they were just having some engine problems and already had help coming. The boys pulled away slowly and continued toward Amanda's house.

As they got closer, they realized that there were even more cars parked in front of the home. Matthew pulled the car on down the road and parked behind a tree. "I think the best thing to do is come up on the house by foot to see what's going on."

Connor agreed and the boys walked through a side lot that was heavily covered with foliage. Connor pulled out the mirror glasses. "Maybe we can see and hear what's going on in the house."

Chapter 13

Using the mount that Matthew had placed in the house the week before, Connor was able to hear what was being discussed in the living room of the home. Matthew asked, "What do you see?"

Connor put his finger to his mouth and said, "Shut up so I can hear."

Connor saw that Keith Kellington was in the Curry home with several other men wearing black or gray suits. He heard, "Listen, Mr. Curry, we simply need to speak with your daughter and then we'll be out of here."

Mr. Curry replied, "She's just running a little late from school. I just don't understand what you could possibly need to talk to her about. I'm her father and I have a right to know what the government wants with my kid."

Keith responded, "We simply think that she may have something that belongs to us, and we just need to question her about it."

While he got up and moved toward Keith Kellington, Mr. Curry told his wife and son to stay in the dining room. "I want to talk to your superior," he said. Keith pointed to an adjoining room and Mr. Curry made his way toward it.

Connor couldn't see into the adjoining room, but he could faintly pick up what was being said. "You just need to stay calm, Mr. Curry, and this will all be over quickly."

Connor concentrated as much as possible and heard one more comment from the hidden man. "Control is only what we make of it."

Connor thought, "Do I know whose voice that is? It sounds awfully familiar."

Connor removed the glasses, and Matthew asked him what he saw.

"The three guys up the road are probably there to make sure Amanda is led into the house. They're acting like they work for the government and need to talk to her."

Matthew scratched his head and said, "This can't be right. Walter said that the necklace was taken on Saturday, not Friday."

Connor replied, "I don't care what Walter said. If we don't get to Amanda before those guys on the road do, we're not gonna get the charm."

Matthew agreed and said, "We need a plan."

Chapter 14

TRUST ME

"You think we'll get paid extra for actually gettin' that girl in the house? Did you see the picture of her on the mantle? I know she's only sixteen, but I wouldn't mind having some alone time with that."

The three men waited at the end of the driveway for Amanda to show up and passed the time by making rude comments and suggestions about Amanda and her family. "The mother's pretty hot, too." They all shook their heads in agreement, and the largest of the three men pulled a pistol from his coat. He rubbed the end of the barrel along the scar that divided his face.

"I wish I knew how Kellington does it."

One of the others asked, "How he does what?"

The largest of the men continued, "I've only been working with the guy for a few months, but he isn't what he seems to be."

The scarred man explained that he'd had an altercation with Keith Kellington a few weeks after he started working for him. There had been a disagreement between the two, and Keith told him that if he wanted to do something about it to take a swing at him.

"I'm at least twice the size of Keith Kellington, and that man threw me down like I was a sack of crap." He pointed to his scar and said, "He gave me this and told me that his orders were nonnegotiable. I won't ever mess with that guy again. I think he could take all of us at the same time."

Chapter 14

The man with spiked hair and a strong Italian accent said, "I heard he treats some guys different. If you're in his circle, you get certain perks."

The scarred man replied, "Well, he's one dude I don't question when he asks me to do something. Between him and those Elliott guys, you just keep your mouth shut and do as you're told."

An engine revved in the background, and the three men looked up to see a car coming down the road. It pulled to a stop where all three men could see inside. The larger man looked into the window and only saw Matthew at the wheel.

"You headin' back out already?"

Matthew grinned at the man and said, "I see your buddies haven't shown up yet."

The man smirked and replied, "They'll be here soon enough, son. Why don't you head on down the road."

Matthew shut off the engine and started to get out of the car. "You guys could really help me out with a problem."

The three men walked to the side of the car and told Matthew, "You need to get back in your car and get going—now!"

Matthew replied, "Really, this won't take but just a second. I just need you to help me get something out of my trunk."

One of the men responded, "Look, kid, if you don't get out of here, we'll dump you in the trunk."

Matthew chuckled and said, "Real funny, guys. It will literally take a minute to help me here. I'm just not big enough to pick it up by myself." The scarred leader of the men could see that Matthew was not a threat. He was no bigger than his own left leg, so he gave in. He told the other two to go help him with the trunk.

"I'll make sure you don't get run over."

The two men followed their leader's direction, but grumbled as they did. They reached the back of the car and Matthew popped the trunk open with his key. The two men looked into the trunk and didn't see anything.

"What's your game, kid? Trunk's empty—there's nothin' in it."

Matthew replied, "Of course there is. You just have to look deeper into the trunk."

Both men stuck their faces in and could smell the residue of the road and rank carpet of an older vehicle. They did see something, but the surrounding darkness confused them. "What's that little round thing floating there?"

A quick snap was heard and the two men felt a crush, like a large tidal wave had barreled into their chests. It took their breath and their consciousness and launched them onto the hard gravel at the center of the road. At that moment, Connor released the camotape that he was touching on the back of the trunk. He immediately appeared to Matthew.

On the other side of the car, the largest of the three men yelled out, "What the hell's going on back there?" He made his way to the back of the car, toward Matthew.

Connor emerged from the trunk and Matthew said, "Don't worry. I got this."

The scarred man saw his two comrades lying motionless in the road and reached out his hand toward Matthew.

Matthew pressed a button on his watch and raised his hand to block the man from his approach. Matthew heard a beep and realized that he had hit the wrong button. Before he knew it, the large man had his hand around Matthew's neck and had picked him up off the ground.

Matthew, gasping for air between words, motioned to Connor and rasped, "Connor...help...hit...wrong...button."

Connor knew that he couldn't use the snap ring without hitting Matthew, so he tried to tackle the large man. Connor gave the man a good shot but ended up knocking himself for a loop. The man laughed, grabbed Connor, and tossed both of them onto the ground by the car.

"You OK, Matthew?" Matthew couldn't catch his breath and shook his head no. He pointed to the large man who had now pulled his pistol and pointed it at the boys.

The scarred man said, "I don't know who you boys are, but I bet my boss will want to find out."

Chapter 14

A noise was heard in the distance and the large man and both boys looked to the other end of the road. They could hear the tires throwing gravel to the side of the road. The boys realized that it was Beth Perry's car.

Matthew motioned to his brother to use the snap ring. The gun flew from the man's hand from the force of the shockwave. Another snap and he was pushed up against the boys' car. He wasn't knocked out, as the other two men were, but he was stunned and struggled to get up. Connor ran over and kicked the gun down the road as Matthew rushed out to stop Beth's car.

Matthew jumped up and down in the middle of the road and tried to get Beth's attention. She finally hit the brakes, just feet in front of him. The girls saw the men lying in the road and watched as Connor ran toward them. Both girls got out of the car and ran to Matthew, but Matthew was only concerned with Amanda.

"What's going on? Where are my parents?"

She noticed the gun lying in the road and began to lose her composure. Matthew stopped her and said, "Amanda, you have to trust me and come with us—right now."

Amanda pulled away and replied, "I'm not going anywhere until I see what's going on here. Where's my dad?"

Connor realized that the largest of the three men was making it to his feet and yelled to Matthew, "We have to leave now!"

Matthew pleaded with Amanda: "*Please* trust me! We have to *go!*"

Amanda again resisted and pushed Matthew away. "I'm going to the house."

Matthew yelled to Connor, "Just grab her!"

Connor grabbed Amanda and threw her into the backseat of the car. Amanda struggled and yelled at Connor, "Stop it! What are you doing? Let me go!"

Matthew jumped in, started the car, and sped off, with Beth Perry banging on the window. She avoided the flying gravel and jumped back into her car to follow the boys. As she pulled away, she could see the large man in the background stumbling over to his pistol.

"Get off me, Connor!"

Connor kept a tight hold around Amanda's arms as he held her in the backseat of the car. "I'm sorry. I can't do that. You'll slug me the second I let go." Matthew steered the car onto the highway and made his way back home.

"Something happened to my parents, didn't it?" she exclaimed, as a small tear rolled down her cheek. "Answer me, Matthew!" Matthew tried to calm her, knowing that these next few moments would make the difference in getting the charm or complete failure.

"Listen, your parents are OK for now, but we couldn't let you go into the house. Those men you saw lying in the road are bad news, and the men that are in the house are even worse."

Amanda began to calm herself and told Connor that she wouldn't slug him. He slowly released her from his clutches, and she rolled to the side of him and slapped him in the face.

"Jerk!"

Connor could feel the sting of the cheerleader's hand across his face. He rubbed the exposed area with his hand and pleaded his innocence. "I only did it because Matthew told me to. Why don't you slug *him*?"

"What's going on?" she demanded. "Who are they?"

Matthew explained that the man in the house was the same one they had run into after the movie the other night.

"You know how he wanted to buy your necklace? Well, he's upping the ante on getting it."

"That doesn't make any sense; it's just a novelty."

Matthew pulled the car into the driveway of his home and said, "You better come inside for a minute. I'll let you know everything we know." Matthew reached into the backseat and caressed Amanda's hand. "I promise everything's gonna be OK."

They arrived at the boys' home and walked to the front door. The red patch on Connor's face had subsided. Another car came screeching into the driveway and Connor realized it was Beth Perry. Connor expressed his frustration. "This is all we need."

Beth emerged from her car and said, "What the hell are you guys doing? Amanda, are you OK?"

Chapter 14

Amanda assured Beth that she was fine and told her that she needed to go home.

Beth replied, "I'm not leavin' you here alone with these two weirdoes." Beth invited herself into the Chance home and stood there waiting for an explanation.

April emerged from the kitchen and saw the boys and two girls. "It looks like we have some things to talk about, don't we?"

Beth Perry gave her an earful. "We sure do. Who do you people think you are? You kidnap Amanda, scratch up my car, and then act like it's not a big deal."

April looked to Connor and said, "We really need to speak to Amanda alone."

Connor replied, "Say no more." He picked up Beth Perry, threw her over his shoulder, and carried her to April's room.

"Put me down! Let me go!" Connor pulled April's door closed and locked it from the outside.

"I'll let you out after we get done talkin' to Amanda." The muffled sounds of a very irate teenager could be heard coming from April's bedroom. Connor said, "She knows some flashy words, doesn't she?"

April looked at Amanda and said, "Sorry about that, but she doesn't need to hear what we're gonna tell you."

Amanda examined the boys and their mother and said, "Just tell me what's going on. Why can't I go home?"

Matthew wanted to let Amanda know as much as he could, without giving away too much. "This Keith Kellington has figured out a way to use that charm as a weapon and he wants it. It's nothing you did or your parents did. He'll do whatever he has to do to get that necklace."

Amanda walked around the room and grabbed a hold of the charm that dangled from her neck. She asked, "Why didn't he just come after me and take it from me? Why's he holding my parents and my little brother?"

Matthew knew he had to be careful and decided to focus on the how and avoid the why. "The only way Keith can actually get the charm from you is to have you actually hand it over to him. If he simply takes it from you, it can't be turned into a weapon." Amanda shook her head, both confused and in disbelief.

Matthew continued, "He'll threaten to hurt your parents, or maybe your brother, if you don't give him the charm."

April jumped in before Amanda could respond. "You have to understand that this man will kill your family just to get that charm. He'll have no remorse and he will torture them until you give it to him."

Amanda had tears streaming down her cheeks. She looked to Matthew and asked, "What am I supposed to do?"

Matthew put his hands on Amanda's shoulders and walked her away from Connor and April toward the kitchen. He took a moment to wipe the tears from her cheeks, making sure to take a mental picture of her beautiful face. He knew this would be the last time he spoke with her. He slowly took the charm in his hand and said, "I need you to give me your necklace."

Amanda backed away from Matthew and glared into his moist eyes. Matthew took the fake stone that Mr. Wainright had given to him and said, "You need to give Keith, or whoever else wants the necklace, this fake one. If you give this to him, he'll think he has what he needs and leave your family alone."

Amanda took a step closer to Matthew and said, "How do I know you and your family aren't after the weapon, too?"

Matthew shook his head slowly and simply said, "You don't. All I can ask you to do is trust me and know that I only want to keep you safe."

Amanda didn't hesitate and made her decision. She reached behind her neck and unclasped her necklace. She held the charm and necklace out and dangled it in front of Matthew's face. She quietly said to him, "I do trust you. You take the charm."

A yellow light emitted from the charm as it pulled from the setting of the necklace. It was thrust from the small setting and Matthew's Hathmec was exposed from under his shirt. The charm maneuvered its way into a rectangular spot at the top left of the pendant. Within seconds, Matthew felt that something was different.

Chapter 14

Amanda couldn't believe what she had seen but had enough sense to place the fake charm into her necklace setting. She reclasped the necklace and asked Matthew, "Are you OK? What just happened?"

Matthew assured her that he was fine and everything was going as expected. In reality, Matthew was pretty freaked out by what had happened, too. Walter had never said anything about floating or glowing charms.

Amanda reentered the living room. Connor let Beth out of his mother's room. She bypassed Connor, found Amanda on the couch, and whispered, "Don't worry. I called your parents from that room; they'll be here any minute."

Connor heard what she said and yelled to April, "She called Amanda's parents! They'll be here any minute!"

April immediately signaled to the boys. "We've got to get out of here, right now. Matthew, do you have the charm?" Matthew patted his chest and glanced at Amanda. April knew that he had what they had come for.

Connor had already made his way to the front door, but quickly turned back. "It's too late, they're already here." Everyone in the Chance home heard the doors slamming shut from three black vehicles that now blocked their exit.

April looked to Amanda and said, "No matter what happens, just give them that fake charm when you get home. You're gonna be just fine."

Matthew stood as close to Amanda as he could when the door to his home burst open and three men entered, led by Keith Kellington himself. Connor took a position in front of his mother as Keith walked by him and approached Amanda Curry.

"Well, Ms. Curry, you have been a hard one to find today."

Amanda slowly backed away from him and asked, "Where are my parents?"

"Oh, you'll see them soon enough. You need to come with me now, and then you'll get to see them."

Beth Perry got between Amanda and Keith. "I don't know who you are, mister, but Amanda isn't going anywhere until her parents get here."

Keith Kellington took his hand out of his jacket pocket and made a quick tossing motion toward Beth Perry. A light mist hit Beth in the chest and Keith said to her, "Sit down on the couch and don't move."

Immediately, Beth Perry moved toward the couch, sat down, and became a statue. She was straining with everything she had just to wiggle a finger, but she was unable to. Keith finished, "You can continue to breathe."

Amanda looked to her friend, unaware of the power that had full control over her body. "Beth, what's wrong? Look at me!" Keith focused on Amanda as Matthew stepped over and blocked his path.

"Just leave her alone."

Keith took an overview of the room and said, "You people just keep sticking your noses in my business. I'll just have to take care of that, this time."

He flung carrier stones at all three of the Chance family and said, "Don't move." The family knew that they couldn't let on that they had the health charm protecting them, so they became motionless. Keith put his mouth up to April's ear and said, "I don't think your cop friend can save you tonight."

He walked back toward Amanda and said, "I have a way of getting people to do what I want them to do. Watch this." He looked back to the Chance family and said, "Walk over to the kitchen window and stare out of it." The family made their way to the window, as instructed, while they fought every temptation to turn around and fight the awful man. The boys were confident that if they just let Amanda go with him, Amanda would be all right. Once he had the charm, she would be all right.

"OK, Ms. Curry, now to you. Am I going to have to ask you again to come with me?" The two men who had entered with Keith Kellington snickered and opened the door to walk out. Amanda turned toward the back door to make a run for it, but Keith had already tossed the carrier stone onto her back. "Walk with me to the car," he ordered. Amanda made her way with Keith out the front door, and he shut it behind him.

As Keith and Amanda got into a black car, he turned to one of the men accompanying him and said, "Burn it down."

Chapter 14

The remaining men began tossing gasoline onto the home's structure and even walked back into the house to lead a stream from the kitchen. The boys and April had actually started to move until they heard that the door was opening again. The men didn't notice that they were no longer looking out the window. As the last man left the home, he flicked a match and yelled, "It's gonna get hot in here!"

The inside of the home started to burn. Connor and Matthew headed toward the bedroom to get their backpacks, but April screamed out, "Connor, you get Beth! Matthew can get the backpacks!" The home started to fill with dark smoke and some of the structure began to give way. April was able to grab her most-needed belongings, including her bag and some prestored food.

Connor picked up Beth Perry, who had started to regain some power over her own movements. "Don't worry, Beth. I'll get you outta here."

She tried to say something, but didn't have enough control over her lips to get the words out. Connor raced from the back door and cleared the home to find April waiting by the stretch of woods behind the house. Just then, a loud explosion rocked the home as a main gas line ignited.

April desperately looked around. "Where's Matthew? Connor, where's Matthew?"

Connor still held Beth Perry in his arms and began turning his head from side to side. "I don't see him."

April began crying out, "Matthew! Matthew!" April's pulse quickened and a panic gripped her like she had never felt before. Her child was missing or hurt or even dead. She started to rationalize in her own mind, *He has the health charm; he'll be fine.* She called out again, "Matthew!"

"I heard you!" Matthew emerged from the smoky corner of the house. "Don't worry, I made it out the bedroom window." Matthew walked up from the end of what used to be the east side of the house, carrying all of the family's backpacks.

April rushed over to her son and gave him a big hug. "Don't you ever scare me like that again!"

Matthew grinned at the outpouring of emotion and looked over to his brother. "I see you got the most important item from the house."

Connor stood motionless and looked down to see Beth Perry trying to catch her breath.

"You can put me down now!"

Connor replied, "You're welcome for saving your life." He immediately dropped her into the cold grass. He couldn't believe a girl so cute could be such a pain.

Beth regained her composure as she regained the function of her body. "What in the hell's goin' on here? Who were those guys? What are they doing with Amanda? Why couldn't I move?" She looked to the corner of the burning home and said, "What are those nerds doing here?"

Matthew turned to see that Jack and Cassie Jenkins had arrived at the burning remains of the Chance home. April looked to her sons and said, "What are they doing here?"

Matthew replied that he had no idea, but he would get to the bottom of it. April turned her attention to Beth Perry.

"Look, dear, everything's gonna be OK, but you need to go home and forget any of this ever happened."

Beth Perry pushed Connor to the side and replied, "I'm not going anywhere until I have some answers, and when I call the police, believe you me, I'll get answers." She got directly into April's face and said, "Or maybe I'll just have my father, a county judge, take care of you people."

April nodded her head in agreement and said, "Just wait here for a minute."

April slipped over to Connor and asked him if there was any room in the shed behind the house to store some extra baggage. Connor understood the question and replied, "There's plenty of room." April walked back to the opinionated cheerleader and asked her to take a walk with her.

"I'm not going anywhere with you crazy people. You're all going to jail." So Connor once again threw Beth Perry over his shoulder. Beth, once again, began crying out, "Put me down! My dad is gonna kick your ass for this!"

Cassie and Jack seemed shaken by what they saw. They looked to Matthew and he calmed their nerves.

Chapter 14

"Don't worry; you can let her out after we're gone. Just give us a ten- or fifteen-minute head start."

Profanity continued spewing from the shed as Jack replied, "We'll give you thirty minutes, just to make sure."

Cassie looked to Matthew and told him that the fire department would be there any minute. "We can tell them that no one was home when the fire started." She asked, "How did the fire start?"

Matthew told her it would be better if she didn't know that. He asked, "So what are you two doin' here?"

Jack replied, "We weren't sure about you guys at first. You could have all been evil aliens plotting to take over the world." Matthew raised his eyebrows and waited for the point. Jack continued, "Of course, we know differently now." Jack smirked as he paused after the last statement. "Anyway, we had done some digging around your house and in your garbage cans, and we came across something you probably don't want found by the wrong people."

Jack presented Matthew with a large envelope that was addressed to April. He looked the envelope over and could see that it was from Walter Wainright. "I saw this the other night."

Cassie interrupted and said, "I think it may be something about Amanda. Is she gonna be all right?"

Matthew opened the envelope and began to read what Walter had specifically written to April. As he moved his eyes down the page, he started to understand why he wanted only April to see it. He patted Jack on the back and gave Cassie a small peck on the cheek. He told them to hide in the woods until the fire department got there. "You need to make sure that Beth gets out OK. It's time for us to get back where we belong."

Cassie could barely contain her excitement from the peck, so she lunged at Matthew and planted a good long wet kiss right on his lips. Matthew staggered and regained his composure long enough to say, "OK, then."

Cassie asked, "Will we ever see you again?"

Matthew looked at the setting sun, partially blocked by the smoke that billowed from the house. "I don't know, Cassie. Only time will tell."

Cassie dropped her head and grabbed her brother's hand. The brother and sister made their way into the woods and took up a position where they wouldn't be seen.

April and Connor had made their way back from the shed. April told Connor, "I hope that door can hold her. She's strong for a little cheerleader."

April saw Matthew standing with his back to the blaze and said, "OK, boys, we got what we came for; it's time to get back to the tunnel."

Matthew held the envelope in the air for his mother and brother to see and responded with a resounding, "Sorry, April, plans have changed. We're not going anywhere!"

Chapter 15

THE STRENGTH OF MANY

April looked at Matthew and realized what he held in his hand. "Where did you find that?"

Matthew separated the paper from the envelope and handed it to Connor before he replied, "It doesn't matter where I found it." Matthew walked over to his mother and stared deep into her eyes. A small tear formed in the corner of both their eyes and Matthew, with a broken voice, asked, "How could you keep this from us?"

Connor finished reading the letter and said, "She's gonna die? That can't be right; we gave her the fake charm. That was the plan; give her the fake charm and it's like we were never here."

April couldn't look her son in the eye but tried to explain her actions. "You don't understand. We had to get the charm, but we can't change history; it's just too dangerous."

Matthew couldn't believe what he was hearing and replied, "We *have* changed history; she's not supposed to die!"

"She dies regardless, Matthew! Whether she gives Keith the real charm or the fake one, she dies either way. That's why Walter sent me the letter. He wanted to make sure we were gone before you found out what really happens."

Matthew took a piece of wood that was lying at the edge of the woods and threw it into the fire. Anger built in his gut as he asked his mother, "So was the family thing a big lie too, April!" April realized that Matthew had called her by name.

Chapter 15

Matthew continued, "I've seen what a real family is, and they would do anything for each other—like the Curry family. We came here to stop someone who has no compassion or feelings toward human life, but you're no better. These are people we know don't deserve what's happening to them. How does that make us any different from Minister Hathmec?"

April dried the tears from her eyes and defended her decisions. "We're not responsible for everyone in the world. We can only do what we can do to make things better, and if that means a few good people have to die, then that's what has to happen."

She took the letter from Connor and threw it into the fire. "There will be and have been many others that have died fighting against the minister. Amanda and her family are just a few of the many."

April picked one of the bags from the ground and continued, "We *are* a family. We are the Chances and you are my sons and if there is one thing that I have learned while living in Travis, it's that I will do anything to protect my family. Now this discussion is over."

April tossed the first bag in the car as sirens blared in the background. Connor paused and said, "I hear the fire trucks; we need to get out of here." Matthew bypassed his mother and proceeded to Beth Perry's car, still parked at the front of the house.

April yelled out, "Just leave her car there!"

Matthew replied, "I'm going to help Amanda and her family."

April ran over to the car and grabbed Matthew by the arm. "No you're not! I'm the adult and your mother and you will do as I say!"

Matthew peered at his brother, and with one glance, Connor knew that he needed to help him. Matthew put his hand on April's shoulder and placed a small carrier stone. With the help of the new attribute charm, he stole every ounce of strength from April and said, "Catch her."

April felt the loss of the ground below her as Matthew picked her up and tossed her back toward Connor. It was like an afterburner had been lit as the background of the house in flames created a silhouette around her frame. Connor caught his mother and they both fell to the ground. Matthew yelled back, "Sorry, Mom, but I have to try."

Matthew jumped in the car and started the engine. April yelled to her son, "Stop! You can't!" The car was already down the driveway before April could make it to her feet. She glared back at Connor and said, "Why didn't you stop him?"

Connor brushed the grass from his pants and replied, "Because he's right."

April walked back to her car and pounded her fist on the hood. She had lost her composure and needed a moment to clear her head. She opened the driver's side door and said, "Fine, we'll go to the Curry place and help him." Connor grabbed the last of the bags and threw them in the car.

She started the car, only to be blocked by the fire trucks that had arrived to put out the blaze that still raged behind them. April told Connor to stay in the car while she talked to one of the firefighters.

"Oh, thank goodness you're here. Our home is being destroyed." The firefighter promised that they would do everything they could to save what was left of the house.

"Please, ma'am, you need to stay back." April turned around and saw the familiar face of Danny Charles.

"Danny, over here," she yelled. Officer Charles was relieved to see the lovely single mother and ran over to her location.

"You OK, April? I heard over the dispatch that there was a fire in this area and I just wanted to check on ya." April knew how Danny felt about her and she had some fairly strong feelings toward him. She hated to ask him what she was about to ask him, but again, she would do anything for her family.

"Danny, I need your help." April explained that Matthew had taken off and she needed his help to find him. "Would you mind following me out to the Curry place?"

Officer Charles asked, "You wanna go looking for Matthew while your house is burnin' up?"

April replied, "There's nothing I can do here, and I'm really worried about Matthew."

Officer Charles relented and said, "OK, I'll follow you out there."

April jumped back into her car and Connor asked, "What's going on? Why were you talking to Officer Charles?" April shifted the car into drive and sped down the driveway.

Chapter 15

She put her hand behind her neck and replied, "We have to get to your brother. Don't worry about Officer Charles."

Three figures emerged from the woods as the fire department continued their battle with the house fire. Cassie and Jack had listened to all of the talk between the Chance family, and Jack had set Beth Perry free. They walked to the front of what was left of the house and Beth screamed, "They took my car too! I've gotta find a phone and call my father."

The twins chuckled but were quickly brought back to reality when Jack asked, "Do you think Matthew can get to Amanda fast enough to save her?"

Cassie looked to the sky and replied, "Do you think we'll ever see Matthew or Connor again?"

Jack paused and reassured his sister, "I don't think we've seen the last of Matthew or Connor Chance. Maybe they'll come back to Earth someday."

Matthew sped toward the Curry home as fast as he could. He almost ran off of the road a couple of times. He decided to take the back route that Jack had told him about earlier in the week. It was faster and would allow him to sneak up on the house if Keith and his men were still around. As he approached the back of the house, he could already tell that something wasn't right.

It was getting later in the day and the air around the Curry home looked darker than the sky around it. He made his way down the old back path to the house and it became obvious that one of the oldest homes in all of West Tennessee was going up in flames.

Matthew could see the smoke pouring from the house as he jumped out of the car. He would never forgive himself if he was too late to save her. All Matthew could hear was the voice of Mr. Curry from the weekend before: "You take care of my daughter."

The back door of the home was engulfed in flames, so he had to find an alternate path into the house. He didn't see any of Keith's men around, but was still careful to keep a low profile around the grounds. He remembered that there should be a door behind the house, around a large bush, that would lead him into the basement.

Jack had told him to go from the east corner of the house at a forty-five degree angle. He found the door, just as Jack had told him, and he followed the dark path to the basement. The basement was full of old family mementos, but the fire had not reached it. Once there, he found the door that led into the house.

He yelled out, "Amanda! Amanda!" He didn't hear a reply, but he forged on. He made it to the edge of the kitchen and noticed a slight gap in the flames. He yelled out again, "Amanda!"

"We're in here! Help!"

Matthew barely made out the faint cry for help that resonated from the adjoining room. He knew that if he could just run past the ridge of fire, he would be in the main living room. Matthew mustered some courage and jumped through a ridge of fire just outside of the kitchen. As he oriented himself, he realized the magnitude of the problem.

"Matthew, is that you?" cried out Laura Curry from the corner of the room, closest to the stairs.

She was tied up, back to back, with her husband. Mr. Curry screamed out, "Get Amanda and Steven Jr. out of here!" Matthew turned his head and saw both Amanda and her little brother tied up and lying on the floor. Both of them were passed out from the smoke.

Matthew ran over to Mr. and Mrs. Curry. "I'll get you loose; don't worry."

Mr. Curry shook his head and said, "No, you have to get the kids out first. Don't worry about us."

Matthew stopped and reassured Amanda's father, "OK, I'll get them first, but then I'll come back and get you."

Parts of the ceiling started to fall in around Matthew as he rushed over to Amanda and her little brother. He could feel the heat against his skin. Burns were healing within seconds due to the Hathmec. Matthew was able to get Amanda up on his shoulder, but when he tried to pick up Steven Jr., he ended up dropping them both.

Mr. Curry yelled to him, "Come on, you can get them! Matthew looked to Mr. and Mrs. Curry and saw the panic that engulfed their faces. Both parents feared their own deaths, but the thought of their children dying in this hellacious inferno was unbearable.

Chapter 15

Matthew opened his hand and revealed to Amanda's parents the stones that he had created. He dropped a couple on both Amanda and Steven Jr. and then tossed the dust over to Mr. and Mrs. Curry. The mother and father had no idea what Matthew had just done, but Matthew reassured them again. "I'm getting them out of here."

Matthew felt the rush of borrowed strength from the Curry family. He easily lifted both Amanda and Steven Jr. and threw each of them over a shoulder. He dodged the falling debris and flames that surrounded the path to safety. He kicked open the front door with one mighty thud and ran the children of Steve and Laura Curry to safety.

Steve Curry turned his head toward his wife and tried to kiss her cheek. He said, "They're out; Matthew got them out." He could feel the tears from his wife's eyes on his lips.

Laura Curry asked, "Are you ready?"

Her husband responded, "The lord will protect our children and we will watch them from heaven."

Matthew made it far enough away from the house that he knew Amanda and Steven Jr. would be safe and he put them in the cool grass. They were a little worse for wear, but the fire couldn't get to them. Matthew oriented himself and headed back for the parents.

Matthew ran back toward the front door when a giant explosion erupted in the house and large flames jetted into the early evening sky. Matthew was tossed onto the hard sidewalk of the home. He landed on his side and turned back to see a house that looked more like a fireball than a home.

Matthew could still make out the door that he had kicked open and he began to crawl to it. The heat from the flames pierced Matthew's skin as he came ever closer to the home. He began to realize that something else was wrong. The incredible strength that he had gained from Amanda's parents started to leave him. Within seconds, the same strength that had helped Matthew save the lives of the Curry's children was completely removed from Matthew's body and in turn, from Mr. and Mrs. Curry's bodies.

Matthew walked away, as flames continued to billow out of windows, the walls of the home, and the roof. The stark reality of the situation encompassed him as he staggered back to Amanda and Steven Jr. Steve and Laura Curry had died in the house fire that had been set by Keith Kellington.

Matthew fought back the tears that began to well up in his eyes. As he reached Amanda and Steven Jr., he began to realize that both of them were suffering from the smoke. Neither of them was breathing well and each had several burns on their arms and legs. Matthew took his Hathmec pendant and held it in his hands. He asked for two copies of the pendant and they started to form around his own.

They were copies of his pendant, just less powerful. He made a copy of the health charm and placed one into each pendant. He placed the pendant over the little boy's and young girl's necks. He could tell that their breathing started to improve, and he could see the burns on their arms start to heal, ever so slightly.

Matthew sat on the ground while flames continued to erupt in the background. He removed the ropes that bound Amanda and Steven Jr. He held Amanda and Steven Jr. in his arms and rocked back and forth, waiting for one of them to wake up. Matthew thought, *What am I gonna do now?* He yelled out in anger, "Keith Kellington's gonna pay for this!"

"Oh, I don't think that is going to happen."

A harsh voice pierced the smoke and fog around the home and Matthew turned his head to see none other than Keith Kellington himself. Matthew responded, "I figured you were too much of a coward to stay here and watch what you did."

Keith lit a cigarette with the same lighter that had set fire to the house, and replied, "It looks like it was a good thing that I did. Seems there are a few loose ends that need to be cleaned up." He slowly walked over to Matthew, who still caressed the girl that he had both saved and, in his mind, destroyed. Keith towered over him and explained himself, in his own sick and twisted way.

"Once you realize that you can't die, the entire idea of death becomes something of a mystery. The terror that I saw in the eyes of Steve and Laura Curry at the thought of burning alive in that house—now that's power." Matthew gently put Amanda's head back onto the ground and stood to his feet.

Chapter 15

"The power that I have to control death and control lives—it takes all the fear away." Keith took a drag from his cigarette and looked at the wreckage of the Curry home. "You cannot even begin to understand what it feels like to control everything." He flipped his cigarette on the ground and said, "I no longer fear death, so I create it, just to make sure I always remember one thing."

Matthew asked, "What's that?"

Keith placed his hand on his chest and replied, "That I'm the top of the food chain."

Amanda and Steven Jr. were still prone at the feet of Matthew. Keith rested against a large oak tree and asked Matthew, "So, you were able to save the girl and the boy? I guess Mom and Dad are charbroiled pretty thoroughly by now."

Matthew could feel the anger building in his gut, but he had no idea how to repel the larger, more experienced man. Keith looked at the Curry kids and then back at Matthew and said, "I don't know how you got them out of that house, but it's not gonna happen again."

Keith began to move his hand toward his coat pocket when a siren went off behind him. He turned and saw a red sports car barreling up beside him. Then a police car ran right in behind it. April and Conner jumped out of the first car and rushed over to Matthew. Keith recognized each of them and said, "You people are a real pain in my ass."

Officer Danny Charles popped out of the police car. His pistol was pulled and he yelled to Keith Kellington, "Put your hands where I can see 'em, right now!"

Keith raised his hands and smirked at the country officer. Officer Charles reached into his car, pulled out his CB transmitter, and spoke into it. "Need the fire department at the old Curry home; send backup."

April reached Matthew and the Curry kids and made sure that Matthew wasn't hurt. April told the boys, "We have to get out of here, now."

Matthew could barely speak, but he told his mother, "He killed Mr. and Mrs. Curry."

"I know, son, but we can't help that now. How do we get out of here?"

Matthew pointed to the back of the blaze. "The car is in the back. We can take the back road."

"Get down on the ground, right now!" Officer Charles continued to yell to Keith Kellington. Keith began to slowly move to the ground, talking as he did.

"Are we really going to play this game again, officer?"

Danny Charles replied, "You shut your damn mouth and get your face in the dirt!"

Matthew picked up Steven Jr. and Conner picked up Amanda. They slowly made their way to the back of the house. Officer Charles called out to April, "What are you doin'? You need to leave those kids there until the medics can take a look at 'em."

April didn't react to Danny's calls. He again yelled out, "April, where are you goin'?"

April yelled back, "Thank you and I'm sorry."

He replied, "Sorry for what?"

Keith Kellington replied from the ground, "She's sorry because she knows that I'm about to kill you."

Officer Charles looked down at Keith Kellington and started to speak, but before he could, Keith said the following, "Don't move a muscle." Keith had taken control of Danny Charles with the use of a carrier stone.

Officer Charles was unable to move at all as Keith Kellington got up from the ground. Danny strained and grunted as he tried to make even the simplest of movements, but he couldn't. He was only able to shift his eyes as Keith walked around him.

"You see officer; you just thought you had everything under control here. You may be a big fish in this little pond, but I'm one of the biggest sharks on the planet."

"Put your gun to your head." Officer Charles put his revolver to the temple of his head as he was instructed. "Now, put your finger on the trigger." Officer Charles put his finger on the trigger as he was instructed. He tried to fight the commands but it was no use.

April turned to see the gun pointed at Danny Charles's head, but she couldn't help him. Keith yelled out to April, "Don't make me kill him! Come back now and we can work something out!"

Connor and Matthew had loaded the still unconscious Curry kids into the car, and April screamed, "Hold on, we're gettin' out of here."

Chapter 15

The car started and she tore off down the dark back road. She looked in her rearview mirror just long enough to see Keith standing there and then he was gone.

Keith approached Officer Charles and started to mock him. "Such a little country bumpkin." Keith tapped the top of Danny's head and said, "Did you know I was in here? I know your memories and your thoughts. I know about your poor wife who lost her life and how you struggle so hard to just get by from day to day." Keith lit another cigarette and said, "I'm just curious—how does it feel to know that you're about to die? You can answer."

Danny Charles regained the use of his mouth and replied, "Just leave my family alone."

Keith interrupted, "I didn't ask you that. I want to know how you feel."

Danny responded, "Y'all can go to—"

Keith stopped Danny before he could finish. "I will miss that lovely accent of yours, Mr. Charles. I may keep it for myself."

Keith could hear the sirens of more police and fire trucks coming down the road. He plucked the badge from Danny Charles's shirt and said, "Well, I guess our time is up. Pull the trigger."

A shot rang out and the body of Officer Danny Charles fell to the ground. Keith watched as more police cars and the fire department arrived at the Curry residence. He began to slowly disappear, as if he was evaporating into thin air. The view of the flames from the Curry home fell away from Keith as a new image of a warehouse wall, filled with pictures of Amanda Curry and her family, took shape in his eyes.

He walked up to the wall and placed slashes through the pictures of Steve and Laura Curry. He looked at the pictures of the Curry children, first Amanda and then Steven Jr. A familiar voice echoed in the background that asked, "What about the kids? Did you take care of them?"

Keith replied, "No, I think we have a bit more work to do on that one. Don't worry about it; we'll find and take care of them. They have nowhere to go."

Keith signaled for one of the several large men standing around the room to come over to the wall. "Did you get all of the information that

I requested about April Chance and her boys?" The large man handed Keith a stack of papers, and he began to review them.

"You see, this family is supposedly from somewhere in Georgia, but based on what we've found, they've only existed for a couple of weeks. That means they have either changed their identities or they never had identities."

Keith continued to go through the papers and explained how they would catch up with the family. "I guess she thinks that just because she was using cash to buy everything that we can't track it. Bus tickets in Atlanta, a car in Memphis, and look, the whole trail begins at a little place called Spicewater Lake. That's where they're headed boys, to a familiar location."

The familiar voice asked, "How do you know they'll go back there?"

Keith pointed to the Hathmec around his neck and said, "I read the girl's memories while I was in the house with her. She had a very distinct memory of a discussion that she had with the boy about the time that he had spent with his mother and brother at this same lake. Now why would a family that is moving from Georgia to Tennessee go on a lake vacation the day that they move from one state to another?"

Keith put his hands up as if to question the question and said, "The answer is that they don't. For whatever reason, April, Matthew, and Connor Chance were in this town for a particular reason. It obviously has something to do with the Curry family, but I think it all started and will now end at that lake."

Keith gathered up some supplies and grabbed three of his best men to make the trip to Georgia. "We'll find out who these people are, and we'll make sure they don't ever come back." Keith Kellington and his men headed out that night on a mission to find the Chance family. "This time, I won't leave a fire to do the job. I'll do it myself."

Chapter 16

ROAD TRIP

"You see what happens when you don't do as I say?" A distraught and tearful April Chance lectured her son as she tried to keep the car on the road. "A good man is dead because you think this is some sort of game." Matthew sat in the backseat of the car with Amanda and Steven Jr. as his mother sped down the back road that led away from the Curry home.

Matthew replied, "I couldn't just let them die, and I know this isn't a game."

April composed herself and fought back any remaining tears. She said, "They were supposed to die. That was the way that it was supposed to be."

She looked over to the passenger's seat and saw Connor with his face cupped in his hands, leaned over toward the floorboard. She continued, "We wouldn't have blood on our hands right now if you had just listened to me."

Matthew asked, "Whose blood do we have on our hands? We just saved two people."

Connor raised his head and said, "She's talking about Officer Charles." Connor looked to his mother and asked, "That's why you wanted him to follow us to the house? You knew he would distract Keith and give us a way out."

April wiped a final tear from her cheek and said, "I did what I had to do. I didn't want anyone else to get hurt, but I knew if Keith was still at the house, we would need a distraction to get away."

Connor replied, "So Officer Charles was the distraction?"

Chapter 16

Matthew said, "You didn't have to do that. We could have taken care of Keith."

April shot the car over to the side of the road. The car slid along the loose gravel and the headlights bounced off the highway sign that was nearly plowed over. She turned to the backseat and looked her son in the eyes.

"Look, I'm sorry I didn't tell you about the letter; I should have told you. You have to understand that you're not some kind of superhero, son. You can be hurt." April pointed to the burn marks on Matthew's arm that were still healing. "Keith Kellington and the men that he works for are not gonna go easy on you because you're a kid; they will kill you." Matthew began to reply to his mother, but before he could, she pulled her own Hathmec from her shirt.

"Keith has all the powers of this pendant, every one of them. You have two charms, and the only advantage you have over him is that he doesn't know that." April turned back to the steering wheel and put the car in gear. She finished her thought. "That's just not enough of an advantage; so now I have to live with the fact that someone who should still be alive is gone."

April pulled the car back on the road and hoped her words had made an impression. Matthew pondered her words for a few minutes and finally replied. "I'm sorry I ran off like I did, but I'm not sorry about the result." Matthew placed his hand on Amanda's head and continued, "I think Officer Charles would say the same thing."

Matthew was sitting behind the passenger's seat, with Amanda situated between Matthew and her brother. Matthew positioned himself between the two front seats and put his hands on both his mother's and his brother's shoulders. He said, "I know we're not superheroes, but we did save two people's lives tonight."

April put her hand on her son's hand and replied, "But at what cost?"

Matthew slid back into his seat and asked, "Do you want me to go ahead and copy over the new charm for your Hathmec?"

April reminded them both, "Walter said we shouldn't copy the new charm until we get back home."

Matthew said, "I wonder why."

April replied, "I really don't know, but I'm sure he has his reasons."

Connor stuck his head through the gap in the front seats of the car and examined the Curry kids and told Matthew, "They're gonna wake up any minute now, you know." Their burn wounds had almost healed and their breathing had returned to normal.

April looked into her rearview mirror and asked, "Did you give them a healing charm?"

Matthew replied, "It's not like I could take them to the hospital."

"Take those pendants back before they wake up and start asking questions."

Conner responded, "I'm pretty sure they're gonna have questions regardless." April agreed with Connor's assessment, but she nevertheless wanted Matthew to retrieve the pendants.

Matthew wasn't sure that the Hathmec copies had done all they could, but he reluctantly agreed that it would be for the best. Matthew clutched his own Hathmec pendant and uttered a few simple words: "I take back what I have given." The two pendants around the necks of Amanda and Steven Curry Jr. evaporated. It was as if they had never existed.

Matthew and Connor looked at one another, still astonished at the mystic and magical qualities that they possessed. What was even more astonishing was that they just seemed to know how to do these things. The pendant and charms themselves were now a part of them.

Matthew asked, "So now what?"

April responded, "We're heading back to the R tunnel. We have a whole day and a half to get there before it closes. We'll find somewhere in Georgia to spend the night, and then we'll finish the drive tomorrow morning."

Connor asked the question that was the most difficult to answer: "What about Amanda and Steven?"

April replied, "We'll find somewhere we can drop them off. I'm sure they have other family that can take care of them."

"We can't leave them here. Keith knows they're alive. He'll be looking for them."

Connor agreed. "Yeah, they're the only ones who know he killed their parents; he's not gonna let them live."

Chapter 16

Matthew added, "They have to come back with us. It's the only way to keep them safe."

April shook her head and replied, "We have already screwed up history enough tonight. We can't drag them into the future with us. They don't belong there."

Matthew pointed out that the three of them didn't belong in the past either. "This is the right thing to do, Mom. We can protect them. If they stay here, it just puts more people in danger."

April relented in her objections and said, "I'm sure Walter will know what to do with them when we get home."

The cheap vinyl seats in the back of the car started to creak as Amanda shifted her body toward Matthew. Connor looked over his shoulder and saw that Amanda was beginning to wake up. "Head's up, Matthew! She can get pretty irate when she feels pinned up." Matthew braced himself for what came next.

A groggy Amanda opened her eyes and saw the interior stains of an older vehicle. Her feet were rolled up underneath her legs and she tried to stretch them out. She struck the center console and planted a knee into Matthew's side. The lights from oncoming cars blinded her for a moment before she recognized who was sitting beside her.

"Matthew, I had the weirdest dream." She gave him a quick hug and a peck on his cheek. She paused for a moment and realized that she was in a car with Matthew's entire family. The memories of the hours leading up to this spot started to materialize and she knew that they weren't a dream.

She began to panic and frantically started asking questions, "My brother! Where's my brother?"

Matthew tried to hold and comfort Amanda and replied, "He's just to your side there—see?" She saw her brother curled up in a ball, oblivious to what had happened.

"What about my parents? Where are my parents?" Matthew tried to stay calm and just looked into the eyes of the girl that he would have given his life to save. He knew that nothing could save her from the pain that he was about to inflict upon her. "Matthew, where are my parents?"

Matthew collected himself and said, "They didn't make it out of the house. I'm sorry, but they're gone."

Amanda looked into the watery eyes of Matthew and knew that he was telling her the truth, though she couldn't keep herself from questioning it. "What are you talking about? They're not dead! They can't be dead!"

Connor poked his head back through the front seats and said, "It's true. I'm really sorry about your mom and dad." Amanda began to sob uncontrollably and she laid her head on Matthew's chest. Tears ran down her cheeks and soaked Matthew's shirt.

Matthew did all he could to console the young girl. Her entire life had been turned upside down, and the weight of the world seemed too much to bear. Amanda cried off and on for the next two hours as the car with the Chance family screamed down the interstate headed for Georgia. Steven Jr. had stayed asleep the entire time. He had slept through the frantic cries of his older sister as she tried to come to terms with the loss of her mother and father.

As Amanda began to dry the tears from her eyes, she started to question how she and her brother ended up with Matthew and his family. "I don't understand what happened, Matthew. I remember giving you my necklace and you gave me that fake one to give to those men. You said everything would be OK if I just gave them that necklace."

Matthew replied, "I know I did." He looked to April and added, "You were all supposed to be fine."

Amanda looked at her wrists and could still see the marks where she had been bound earlier in the night. She started to remember what had happened at the house. "Oh my god; that man, Keith, he had a gun to my mother's head." Matthew found it hard to listen to Amanda, but he needed to know what he was up against. She continued, "He said he would kill her and my dad if I didn't give him the charm. He said he would let us all go if I did what he wanted."

Matthew tried to grab Amanda's hand, but she pulled it away. "I gave him the charm, like he wanted, and then he tied us all up." She went on to describe the scene as Keith Kellington and his associates left the house with trails of gasoline all over the floor. They were laughing,

Chapter 16

and Keith was taking bets on how long it would take for the whole house to burn.

"My dad was struggling so hard to get loose, but he couldn't. The smoke got really thick where they had me and Steven." Amanda began to lose her composure again as she described the last thing she remembered. "My dad told me that everything would be OK and my mom just kept yelling to us that she loved us." She wiped her eyes and said, "I can still hear her yelling. I still hear her!"

April struggled to drive the car as she listened to Amanda Curry talk of the love that her parents had for her and her brother. April was from a different time and world, but she could understand the helpless feeling that Amanda's parents must have felt.

Connor's reaction was muted. He heard the entire story and he truly felt sorry for Amanda and her family, but he didn't react to it. He thought about the fear and frustration of the last few hours and wondered if it was worth it. He was relieved that Matthew and Amanda were safe, but he still wondered if he could have done more than his brother in the same situation.

Amanda stewed for a bit and started to question Matthew about his family's role in what had happened. "This is all your fault. If you hadn't told me to go with that lunatic, none of this would have happened." Matthew slid away from Amanda and determined that she had gone from sad to angry.

Matthew tried to explain. "You don't understand; we weren't sure what was gonna happen."

Amanda replied sharply, "You weren't sure if my parents would get killed! You just play with other people's lives." She kicked the driver's seat in front of her and said, "Who the hell do you people think you are? *You* should have died, not my mom and dad!"

April veered over to the shoulder of the interstate and stopped the car for a second time. She understood that the girl was upset about her parents, but she also felt the need to set the record straight. "Look, I get it. We're here and your parents are gone, but this is not our fault. Both of you would be dead if it wasn't for Matthew."

Amanda shook her head. "I don't believe you."

Connor interrupted, "It's true. Matthew got to your house quick enough to get you and your brother out."

Matthew slid over to the door and gave Amanda as much physical space as possible. He extended his hands out to her and said, "I tried to get your parents out too, but I just didn't have time."

Amanda looked to the boy who only a week ago had begun to win her heart and asked, "How does this make any sense?" Connor and April looked back at Amanda and she asked, "You all knew what would happen if I gave that man my charm and you just let it happen, didn't you?" She turned back to Matthew and said, "You just felt guilty about lying to me. Now my parents are dead because of you and your family."

April grew frustrated and blurted out, "That's enough! Neither of these boys knew what was going to happen to you or your family. They both thought that if you didn't give Keith the charm, he would kill you." Amanda didn't trust April, but she continued to listen to her.

"I was the one who knew what would really happen. Your entire family should be dead, but for Matthew." April turned to the steering wheel and pulled the car back on the road. April was upset and confused, and she blamed herself for everything that had gone wrong.

She couldn't hold her tongue and said, "He should have let history repeat itself." Amanda was crushed at that comment, and Matthew was disturbed that his mother could say such a thing.

The next hour of the trip was made in complete silence. Amanda rode with her head directed to the floor. Matthew tried to get some type of reaction from Amanda by staring at her, but she was oblivious. The only sounds in the car came from the radio that Connor had quietly turned on. April focused on the road and tried to determine where the group could stop for the night.

Amanda pondered everything that the Chance family had explained to her and was more confused than ever. She asked the next obvious question. "How did you know what was going to happen?" Matthew knew Amanda's trust in him had waned, but he wanted to tell her the truth.

"I know this is going to sound crazy, but you need to keep an open mind. The reason we knew what was going to happen to your family is

Chapter 16

because we aren't from this time." Amanda looked at Matthew like he was crazy. He continued, "We're from the future—two hundred years or so."

Amanda chuckled and cried at the same time. Matthew asked, "Are you OK?"

Amanda looked up. "You're right; I do think you're crazy." She laughed and rolled her eyes. "These crazy time travelers came two hundred years into the past because they wanted my necklace." She put her finger to her ear, made a circular motion with it, and said, "That doesn't sound crazy at all."

"He's telling you the truth." Connor had wanted to tell someone about their secret ever since they'd arrived in the past.

"We are from the future and now we have to get back to our big tunnel of time to get home."

Amanda refused to believe such nonsense and asked, "OK, so if you're from the future, what number am I thinking of?"

April had been quiet but chimed in with a sarcastic tone. "We're from the future; we're not mind readers."

Matthew desperately wanted Amanda to believe him and began spouting off facts that he had learned from Walter's history textbooks. "A man named George Bush will be president after Ronald Reagan. Then later on, another man named George Bush will be president. I think it's his son."

Amanda, unimpressed, shook her head and said, "Well, if two George Bushes become president in my lifetime, maybe I'll believe you, but until then, you're all nuts."

Amanda was troubled about the answers she got from Matthew and his family, but she was really concerned about where this potentially crazy family was taking her and her little brother. "Look, why don't you just drop me and Steven off at the next police station or even a hotel and I'll call my uncle or my aunt to come get us."

April continued down the road with no reply to Amanda's comment. Amanda cleared her throat and again asked, "Is there any reason why we're making this trip with you? We can just call my family and they'll come and pick us up."

Matthew tried to explain the situation. "We can't let you call your other family. In fact, I think you and your brother will probably have to come back with us."

Amanda asked, "What do you mean, back with you?"

Matthew continued, "Keith Kellington knows that you and your brother survived tonight."

Connor jumped in. "That is the real crazy person in this whole thing, and he won't stop until he knows that you and Steven are dead."

April added, "I'm sure you don't want to put any of your other family members at risk. If you call and get them involved in all of this, he won't hesitate to hurt them as well, just to get to you."

Amanda replied, "You people are insane. Where are you really taking us?"

April took an exit just north of Atlanta. "Look, I'm not real excited about taking you two back with us either, but for now, I just don't see any other way."

Matthew put his hand on Amanda's hand and said, "The only way that you two will be safe is with us. April doesn't want you to get hurt."

April replied, "They're both liabilities to us, son. They already know too much, and if Keith got hold of them, he would be able to pull anything out of their heads that he wanted. That includes everything she knows about us."

Matthew couldn't understand why his mother was acting like this. Why was she making Amanda feel worse than she already did? He was trying to console her, and his mother was talking like she was a prisoner of war.

April pulled the car into a hotel parking lot. "I think we'll just stay here until morning." Amanda could see that the parking lot was well lit. She decided that it was a good time to get away from the Chance family.

As everyone began to get out of the car, Amanda pulled on her little brother. "Steven, wake up. We need to go. Steven, wake up. It's time to get up."

Amanda continued to pull and tug on her little brother with no response from him. She started to panic as the realization that something was wrong with him invaded her thoughts. "Steven, wake up! Wake up!"

Chapter 16

Matthew heard the terror in Amanda's voice and sprinted to the far side of the car, along with Connor and April. Matthew asked, "What's going on? What's wrong with him?"

Amanda's voice and body shook uncontrollably as she said, "He won't wake up. I can't wake him up." She fell to her knees and said, "He can't be gone, too. Somebody do something!"

April helped pull Steven Jr. to the ground, just outside of the car. "His breathing is shallow."

Amanda screamed out, "Someone call an ambulance! We need help over here!"

April looked to Connor and told him, "Get her quiet or we're all gonna be in trouble here."

Connor grabbed Amanda and tried to calm and quiet her down. "You have to be quiet; we'll help him."

Matthew held the boy's head and said, "I took the charm off of him too soon. He must have inhaled more smoke than Amanda did." Matthew created a new copy of the Hathmec from his own and copied the health charm to be placed in it. He put it around the neck of Amanda's little brother.

April tried to stop Matthew, "You can't let her see that."

Matthew backed away from the young boy and told his mother, "Do you really think it matters at this point? You want his death on your conscience, too?"

Amanda, still being restrained by Connor, yelled to Matthew and April, "You're both crazy! You're gonna let him die! We need to get him to a hospital." She began to cry and imagined the loss of yet another family member. It was just too much to bear.

Amanda struggled to free herself from Connor when she noticed some movement from her brother. She began to calm down and could see that he was waking up. He was coughing and his eyes were still heavy, but he was waking up.

He looked to his sister and said, "Mandy, where are we?" Connor let go of Amanda, and she lunged toward her little brother and hugged and kissed him right there in the parking lot of the Moon Over Georgia Hotel.

"How did you do this? What did you give him to wake him up?" She could see the Hathmec pendant and charm that her brother was now wearing. She recognized it as the same one she had noticed on Matthew a week earlier. "This looks just like yours. What is it?"

Matthew shut the car door and said, "There are a lot of things we need to explain to you, but for now, just be glad that your brother's OK."

He walked over to his mother, who had leaned up on the front of the car and said, "What's wrong with you? Can't you show a little compassion?" April could see the disappointment in her son's eyes, but couldn't bring herself to respond to him.

Steven Jr., still groggy, stood up with the help of his sister. April walked toward the registration office and said, "We'll stay here and get some sleep and then go on to the park."

Steven Jr. asked his sister, "What park?"

Amanda responded, "I'm not sure, but I think we need to do what she says for now, OK?" Amanda was doing a good job keeping her brother calm in the face of something that neither of them could have ever prepared for.

Amanda held her brother up and whispered into Matthew's ear, "I still don't know what your family's up to, but if you do anything to hurt me or my little brother, I swear I will make you pay."

Matthew could see the fear and hurt in Amanda's eyes and responded the only way that he knew how. "I know you don't believe me right now, but the last thing we want to do is hurt you or Steven." He looked into her eyes and added, "It will all make sense when we get back to 2185."

Amanda handed Steven over to Connor, but she wouldn't back down from Matthew. She replied, "Cut the crap. I don't know how you know what you know, or how you helped Steven, but this whole future thing is ridiculous. Maybe you just want to plead insanity when you and your whole family are sent to jail."

April could hear the end of the conversation between her son and Amanda Curry, and it suddenly occurred to her that she had the proof of their time travel with her all along. "Let's get to the room, kids." She stopped Amanda and handed her a folded piece of paper and said, "Maybe this will help. Read it."

Chapter 16

Amanda unfolded the paper to see that it was a newspaper clipping dated four days from the current date. It was a copy of the Travis Tribune and under the heading for obituaries it displayed the names and dates of the death of her mother, father, brother, and herself.

Amanda had trouble believing what she saw, but it was real. April had placed the newspaper clipping in her pocket after she had read it several days ago. Walter wanted to make sure she believed the future that he had written to her about. Now she used that same clipping to try to convince Amanda Curry of a future that would have existed. Amanda still had her doubts, but there was at least the slightest hope in her mind that it could be true.

Matthew and Connor carried the few bags that the family had into the hotel room and took a quick stock of what was left for the final push back to the park. Connor asked, "Do you think we'll have any problems getting back to the tunnel tomorrow?"

Matthew replied, "We've had problems ever since we got here; we're due for an easy finish."

Matthew placed his bag on the bed and told his brother, "I just wish I could have saved her parents."

Connor agreed and said, "Yeah, too bad I wasn't the one who had the attribute charm."

Matthew was confused by Connor's comment and was about to ask for clarification, but he was stopped by April's arrival.

"Let's get some rest. Tomorrow is a big day."

Chapter 17

WHAT ARE YOU THINKING?

"You rolled into me again." Matthew pushed his brother's leg away from his back and tried to roll over.

Connor mumbled, "The floor's too hard; can't get comfortable."

The hotel room the Chance family and what was left of the Curry family occupied was nothing to get excited about. April, Amanda, and Steven Jr. shared the one bed. A potent odor emanated from it and burned the nostrils of its occupants. The boys just wanted to get a few hours of sleep, but the hard floor at the side of the bed didn't allow for much comfort.

The group was only three hours away from the park that hid the R tunnel. The beacon to the future would be open for another eighteen hours, so the family had plenty of time to complete the trip. April had spent much of the previous two weeks worried about the time needed to retrieve the attribute charm; she never dreamed they would be early.

The only noises coming from the hotel room were the on and off roar of the room's air conditioning system and the beats and bangs that came from the surrounding rooms. Beyond that, it was quiet. This type of quiet had everyone sinking into the recesses of their own minds. What they found was a doubt and fear that could lead them all to ruin.

April lay on the right side of the small bed located in the center of the room, closest to the door. The last few hours had not gone as planned. Not only was she worried about her own sons, but she had the added burden of Amanda and her little brother. She knew the harm that this could cause and worried about Walter's reaction to the Curry

Chapter 17

kids. Her memory flashed back, years before, when she first met Walter Wainright. She questioned herself and the decisions that she made back then.

From the moment she and the boys arrived in the park and made their way to Travis, her eyes had opened to a world that she could not have imagined. A world where people could choose their own path and raise their families how they saw fit, all in a world without boundaries. She could eat what she wanted and talk to whomever she wanted. She could brag about her sons, her own sons. It could be so perfect here. This place in history was so wonderful; it was possible to fall in love with a man she barely knew.

April also saw a world of loss. She saw people who were on their own and needed help. They were normally passed up by others who were so wrapped up in themselves they couldn't spare the time to aid a fellow human being. There was a class of citizens that had more than they needed, and a class that could barely get by. There was the loss that a young girl now felt, as her parents had been taken away from her. There was the loss that an even younger boy would have to come to grips with as his world would change forever.

April was also dealing with the potential loss of her emotions and sense of humanity. It just continued to run through her head, over and over. "I brought a man who I had feelings for to his death. I killed a man. I killed a man. I killed a man. I didn't just kill any man—I killed a good man."

April wiped her eyes and watched the ceiling fan as it went around and around. She remembered the few conversations that she and Danny Charles shared. She remembered the stories that Danny told her of the times he would go hunting with his father and the delicious food that his mom cooked for him.

She pondered the effect that his death would have on his young daughter. He had told her, "She's the light of my life. She's a little four-year-old miracle who keeps me going every day." Danny had revealed to April how her mother had died during childbirth and the pain that he had gone through just trying to get out of bed in the mornings after it happened. "I didn't have a choice. I'm her father and it's my responsibility to take care of her. Don't matter how bad I feel."

What Are You Thinking?

Danny's southern accent and charm echoed in April's head as the realization of that little girl's world without her father flooded April's thoughts. She saw her going to school for the first time without him. She saw her celebrating a birthday without him. She saw her crying, back to a wall, knees around her face, and the anger that would surely build up in her as the years passed.

She started to realize that Matthew was right. Her regret and hatred for herself was being projected onto Amanda Curry. She wasn't to blame for the position that she and her little brother had been put in. It was ultimately April's responsibility, and she knew it.

The boys were the most important things in the world to April Chance. She was willing to give her own life for them, so why would she not give someone else's? She never wanted to hurt Danny Charles or the Curry kids, but the mission was still the most important thing. Or was it?

April pondered one more question. *What if we just stayed here and enjoyed life for as long as we can? Just miss the window back home and try to survive in the past.*

It entered her mind that it would be another thirty or forty years before they would have to worry about the minister or the Hathmec. It could be a good life for April and her kids. School for the boys and a job for her sounded like a dream. They could be anything they wanted to be and with the Hathmec charms they already had; they would be healthy and protected.

April contemplated her options and allowed those thoughts to drift into sleep. She dreamed of the perfect life for her and her boys and tried to forget the dreadful results of the past day.

Connor Chance, on the other hand, was nowhere near nodding off. He dealt with the bumps and muffled words coming from the rooms around them. He dealt with the stray cat meowing outside of their door. He even dealt with the hypnotic rotations of that same ceiling fan.

Connor was starting to have issues dealing with his newly confident brother. Matthew had become the alpha male in the family and Connor wasn't comfortable with that. Matthew, of all people, controlled the attribute charm, saved two people from certain death, and worst of

Chapter 17

all, Amanda thought he hung the moon. At least she did a few hours ago. None of it was right. That's a description for Connor Chance, not Matthew Chance.

He glared over at his brother and could see the attribute charm lighting up for brief moments at every turn of the fan. He imagined the amount of power that Matthew must have felt when he used that charm to save Amanda and Steven Jr. He imagined what it must have felt like to have two, three, or more times your normal strength. He whispered to himself, "I would be unstoppable."

Matthew whispered back to Connor, "What did you say?"

Connor sharply replied, "I didn't say anything; you're hearing things."

"I was just making sure you were OK."

Connor's mind raced with a mix of anger and envy as he replayed that last comment. *He wants to make sure I'm OK? He isn't my keeper.* Connor began to open his mouth to respond to his brother, but he decided to hold back. He thought, *Just because he gets to look like the hero and he's able to talk Amanda out of the charm doesn't mean he has any say over me.*

Connor thought back to his life in 2185 and wondered what would change when they got back. He wanted to know what Walter Wainright had in store for them next. He wanted to know how Amanda and Steven Jr. were going to react to the future and what Walter would do with them when they got there. For the most part, Connor Chance wanted to know if anything they had done over these two weeks would make any difference in his own life.

While Connor's mother and brother seemed to think that 1984 was a great place, Connor was not convinced. It was nice to lead the football team, and the girls in 1984 were a lot more fun to look at, but was that enough?

He liked calling April Mom. He liked telling people that Matthew was his brother. He liked the idea of being allowed to be outside of his home at any hour of the day or night, without being questioned about it.

The experience had opened Connor's eyes, but in his heart, he still questioned the merit of it all. Sure, he enjoyed the freedoms that he had in Travis, Tennessee, but should everyone have those freedoms? It was good for him, but maybe it wasn't good for everyone.

Who decided that? Surely, there were people in the world who knew what was best for other people. He thought, *Maybe I could be one of those people.*

As he pondered that question, it reminded him that Matthew was not one of those people. He remembered that he was the leader of the two brothers. He remembered that he was always the one who stuck up for Matthew. He remembered that he was the best beamball player, the strongest brother, and the starting quarterback. He thought, *Matthew wouldn't have even talked to Amanda if I hadn't done it first.*

Connor convinced himself that things were going to return to normal once they got back to 2185 and Sector 37. He dreamed of a day when he had liberated the world from the likes of Keith Kellington and the minister. He dreamed of crowds carrying him in celebration.

They would see the good that he had done and they would want him to lead them into the future. The dreams finally overpowered the anger and the angst of the intense Chance boy and he fell off to sleep.

While Connor dreamed of the future, Amanda struggled to wrap her mind around her current circumstance. This was a girl who less than twenty-four hours ago had absolutely everything in the world going for her. She was very popular in school. She had a loving family. She was falling for a new guy who seemed lost at times, but who also seemed to have all the answers she had been looking for. She was going to get out of Travis and see the world. She was going to be more than just one of the leftovers from a small town.

Now she thought about what was to come. Based on what the Chance family had told her, she was definitely going to get out of Travis. Two hundred years into the future out of Travis was a bit more than she had planned for. The newspaper clipping had shocked her, but she knew there had to be a trick to it. She thought, *It's a fake.* She could explain the clipping but she struggled to explain the pendant around her brother's neck. How did Matthew do that?

Amanda thought about that charm for a while—that stupid charm. She concluded that this was the cause of all her problems. If only she had never given Matthew that charm.

Chapter 17

She convinced herself that she could have saved her own family if she just would have kept the charm she had given to Matthew. She thought, *That's why they wanted to kill us, because they knew that the necklace I gave them was a fake. If I had given them the real one, they woulda let us go.* She felt like she had been played by Matthew Chance, and any feelings that she thought he had for her were obviously faked.

Determining blame for the death of one's parents was not an easy process to go through, especially for a sixteen-year-old girl. The laid-out plans for her life had been gutted and there was no longer a clear path to take. Her little brother lay beside her, still asleep, and, for the most part, oblivious to what had happened to his mother and father.

She wondered, "What will his life be like now?" She began to realize that she had been forced into a role of mother for little Steven Jr. Mother was not a role that Amanda wanted to play until much later in her life.

At a much younger age, she had promised herself that she would not become a local young girl who ventured into motherhood too early. This was different, though, and as scared as she was, she knew that it was her responsibility to take care of her brother.

Amanda's thoughts were disturbed by a sound coming from the bathroom. A continuous drip, drip, drip, could be heard from the faucet. She thought, *Can't anyone else hear that? It's so annoying.*

She thought about her parents. She thought about the times that her mom and dad had taken her and Steven on vacation. They always wanted everything to be so perfect. Her mom would tell her dad, "This trip is for the kids. I wanna make sure they have a great time. We won't get to have these times with them forever."

A small tear formed in the corner of Amanda's eye as those words played over and over in her head. Amanda told herself, *Mom wouldn't let that sink keep dripping and wake up the kids. I won't either.*

She didn't want to wake up either Steven or April, so she slithered her body down to the end of the bed until she could get her feet planted on the floor. She tiptoed to the bathroom and turned on the light. The problem was quite obvious as the drip was catching a loose piece of plastic attached to the sink drain. It vibrated every time the drip hit it, so Amanda simply took a small towel and placed it between the plastic and the drip.

As Amanda turned to switch the light back off, she was startled to see Matthew standing in the doorway. Amanda took a step back from him. Matthew raised his hands to show that he meant no harm and asked, "Are you OK? Do you need anything?"

Amanda slowly made her way to the bathroom door and clicked the light back off. As she passed Matthew, she whispered into his ear, "My parents."

Matthew stood at the door to the bathroom and watched Amanda carefully crawl back into the bed with his mother and Steven. She had done an excellent job making sure that she didn't wake either of them, but her comment to Matthew guaranteed he would get no sleep.

Amanda grinned and closed her eyes. She was happy with herself. She wanted to make Matthew feel as bad as she felt. Whether it was justified or not, Amanda had convinced herself that everything bad happening to her was Matthew's fault, and she was going to make sure that he knew it. In her mind, he didn't care about her anyway.

Amanda didn't know if the Chance family was completely nuts or not. If the time came that she and Steven Jr. needed to make a run for it, she was going to be ready. With that on her mind, she finally began to fade away and get some much-needed sleep.

Matthew stood at the doorway to the bathroom for a few minutes and tried to process what Amanda had said to him. Matthew didn't need the power to read someone's mind to know that she was very upset with him. Even though he had saved her and her little brother, it didn't seem to make up for those he couldn't save.

Matthew took his spot back on the floor and stared at the stained ceiling of the hotel room. He couldn't sleep. He couldn't talk to anyone. He just stared at the ceiling and thought. He thought about his mother, his brother, and the decisions he had made.

It was difficult for Matthew to quantify what he had done over the last two weeks. He went from the brother who no one really paid much attention to, to the one who was dating the most beautiful girl in school. He went from the brother who followed Connor's lead, to the brother who took the

Chapter 17

lead. Ever since he put on the Hathmec, and even before they came back to 1984, he had felt different. It wasn't just the healing charm and attribute charm's power; it was something else that just felt right.

This feeling of right had engulfed Matthew for weeks now. He felt it when he made the decision to save Amanda and her family. He felt it when he thought about protecting his mom and his brother. He felt it when he thought about all the things that he had seen since he came through the R tunnel. He knew the things happening back home were wrong and regardless of how he knew it, he knew that things would never be the same.

He had found someone to care about in a way that he had never cared before. This same girl now hated his guts, or at least, he thought she did. He tried to convince himself that he did the right thing. Two people were alive who wouldn't have been otherwise.

He tried to legitimize what happened to Officer Charles. *I never asked for his help. He's a cop; things happen to cops all the time.* He was losing the argument with himself and he started to doubt his decisions.

Doubt was a powerful emotion. It could, at times, be either a good thing or a bad thing. In this case, it could only be a bad thing. Doubt filled this small hotel room just outside of Atlanta, Georgia. Matthew doubted his own decisions. Amanda doubted her own abilities and her future. She also doubted the Chance family's sanity. Connor doubted his experience in 1984 and April doubted her duty to Walter Wainright and her own humanity. It would be a long night.

April awoke first and began to mill around the room. She wanted to make sure nothing was left behind before completing their run to the park. The dreams of staying in 1984 had all but evaporated from her mind as she reverted back into the leader of the family. A leader had to deal with the realities of the situation, not dream of one that was impossible.

Connor and Amanda woke up and started to get their things together. No words were spoken between Amanda and Matthew, so Connor was more than happy to fill in the silence. "Did you get any sleep?"

Amanda replied, "I got a little, but it was hard to sleep with all the noise."

Connor pointed to the bathroom. "That dripping sound was driving me nuts. I guess somebody got up and fixed it during the night."

Amanda noticed that Matthew was eavesdropping on her and Connor's conversation and mustered up a little giggle and said, "Well, someone had to make sure we got some sleep. There's a lot of time traveling today."

Connor shot a grin back and said, "We're really not crazy. We are going into the future." He threw a blanket back onto the bed and added, "All of us."

Matthew became jealous of Connor and Amanda's discussion and tapped Connor on the shoulder. "Make yourself useful and take these backpacks to the car; we're gettin' outta here as soon as possible."

Connor turned to his brother and said, "There's nothing wrong with your arms and legs; you take the bags."

Matthew grabbed the bags and snapped, "Absolutely, your highness. I would hate for you to break a sweat."

Connor threw a bag on the floor and rushed after his brother. He slammed him against the wall, knocking down a picture hanging over the bed. "You don't talk to me like that, little brother! I can still kick your butt." Connor had his hands on Matthew's arms as he pressed him against the wall.

Matthew seized Connor's hands and said, "You wanna bet?"

Matthew began to push Connor's arms away from him and Connor lowered to one knee. "You have to use your little charm to take me down, you wuss."

April saw what was going on and stepped in. "Both of you stop it right now!"

Matthew released Connor and he stepped back. April got in between them and said, "We're not going to do this. We've come too far to fall apart now." April put her hands on each of their shoulders and said, "You two are brothers, and we need each other to get home."

Steven Jr. woke up from his long sleep amid the commotion. As the young boy looked around the room, he saw nothing familiar. He saw ugly dog pictures hanging on the wall and an old ice bucket at the foot

Chapter 17

of the bed. The boy began to panic and started calling out to his mom and dad.

"Mom, Dad! Where are you?"

Amanda rushed over to her brother's side and said, "It's OK, I'm here."

Steven looked to his sister and asked, "Where are we? Where's Mom and Dad?"

Amanda tried to keep her brother calm and told him that everything was going be OK. "I'm here and we're gonna be fine."

The young boy started to remember what had happened to him the night before. He remembered the fire and the sound of his parents yelling to him. He remembered how scared he had been and the men in his house. He came to the realization that his parents were gone. His young voice strained to utter the words, "They're dead, aren't they?" Amanda put her arms around her brother, not knowing what to say, and just held him.

Steven had tear-filled eyes and asked again, "They're dead, aren't they? Aren't they?" He began to struggle to get away from his sister, and Amanda realized that she didn't know what to do.

"Yes, they're gone. I'm sorry."

Matthew and Connor halted their squabble as they realized the magnitude of the situation. They saw the distress in Amanda and had no idea how to help.

April could see that Amanda was having problems, so she took Steven from her. April knelt down so that she could look into Steven's eyes. "Steven, my name is April. I'm Matthew's mother." April knew that Steven had met Matthew, so she hoped that would calm him.

"Your parents were killed in the fire that happened at your house last night. Do you remember that?" Steven nodded his head that he remembered it. April continued, "Your mom and dad were able to get you and your sister out of the house before you were hurt. They did everything they could to get out themselves, but they just couldn't."

"Your parents love you so much that they gave their own lives to make sure that you were OK." April began hugging Steven and told him that his parents asked her to take care of him and his sister. "I promised them that I would take care of you and Amanda from now on, and I promise that I will." Steven's eyes continued to fill with tears but he seemed to be calming down. She added, "Isn't that right, Amanda?"

April and Steven looked up to Amanda for her blessing. Amanda knew why April was saying these things and agreed with her. "Yeah, Ms. Chance is going to take care of us for now—just like Mom and Dad wanted." Steven heard this reassurance from his sister and grabbed April around the neck and hugged her as hard as he could.

April was shocked by Steven's acceptance and started to let her guard down. A faint smile popped onto April's face as she squeezed the young boy. She gathered herself and let him go. She said, "Now we have to get going, so go get ready, OK?" The boy made his way to the bathroom and Amanda went with him to make sure he was all right.

A rush of love filled April's heart as memories of her two boys at Steven's age flooded her mind. She realized that Steven was no different than Matthew or Connor when they both came into her life. This was a child who needed to be taken care of and it was her job to do so.

Connor asked his mother, "Why did you tell him that his parents got him out of the house?"

April said, "It was important for him to think that his parents wanted him with us. It will just make things easier."

Matthew grabbed his mother's hand and said, "You didn't lie. His mom and dad made sure I got their children out before letting me help them."

Connor observed, "I guess you have three sons now."

April started to reply but didn't know how to, so she simply put her arm around both of her boys and said, "We'll see. Now go ahead and take everything to the car."

She grabbed Matthew's arm before he rushed off and said, "You did the right thing yesterday. I'm sorry for how I acted."

Matthew smiled at his mother and replied, "You just want what's best for us. I knew you'd come around."

The boys filled the car with the backpacks and did a quick look around the parking lot to make sure they didn't see anything out of

Chapter 17

place. Connor said, "I don't think anyone in the world knows we're here or where we're going."

Matthew closed the trunk of the car and replied, "I hope not."

April closed the hotel door behind them and exclaimed, "We're only three hours from the park, so let's get going."

Amanda asked Connor, "Will you sit in the back with me and Steven?"

The Chance family and what was left of the Curry family loaded into the car in search of the R tunnel. April and Matthew sat in the front seat, while Connor, Amanda, and Steven filled up the backseat.

As their car cleared the front of the building, another vehicle, a black van, made its way around the corner of the hotel. The occupant of the black van pressed down on the CB trigger and said, "They're on the move, but I'm tracking them."

A voice from the other end of the CB radio echoed, "Let them get to the park, and then you know what to do."

Chapter 18

HIT LIKE A GIRL

"This is it, Spicewater Park." April pulled into the deserted parking lot of the largest public park in the state of Georgia. "It doesn't seem very full this morning, does it?"

Connor replied, "I guess no one else woke up early to see all the nature."

Amanda asked, "What exactly are we doing here?"

Matthew turned to the backseat and answered, "This is where we left the tunnel that brought us here and will get us back to 2185."

Amanda rolled her eyes, still unconvinced that the Chance family was from the future. Steven tapped his sister on the shoulder and asked, "Are we gonna go into the future?"

Amanda whispered into her brother's ear, "Don't worry, everything will be fine."

Steven looked out the window and asked, "Are we gonna go fishing?"

April stopped the car and told the kids to get everything out of the trunk. "We're not coming back to it, so don't leave anything behind." The boys grabbed the backpacks and slung them over their shoulders.

Matthew asked Connor, "Do you have the bag with the camotape and the boots?"

Connor peeked into his bag and replied, "Yeah, I've got 'em."

April told little Steven to stay close to her. "We're gonna go on a little hike and then you're gonna come home with us."

Chapter 18

Steven began to walk toward April, but Amanda grabbed his hand and said, "I think I should stay with him. I'll make sure he doesn't get lost."

Connor sensed the tension and asked Amanda if she wanted him to walk with her and Steven. Amanda checked to make sure Matthew had heard his brother and then answered, "I think that would be a great idea." Connor took her hand and she took the hand of her brother. The three of them walked toward the main office of the park with April and Matthew following behind them.

April saw a sign that stated the office would be closed until noon. "I guess they weren't expecting many people today." She looked over her crew of kids and explained that they would go ahead and make their way to the tunnel. "It will probably be a little slick on the paths, so everyone watch their step."

She asked Matthew to lead the way since he still wore the watch that would lead them to the tunnel. Matthew told his mother, "With the watch leading the way, we'll find the tunnel in no time."

The watch displayed a simple arrow that pointed him in the right direction. It was like playing a video game. Matthew waved his hand in the air and said, "Follow me, everyone." April was on Matthew's hip as they made their way down the hill and up a path next to Spicewater Lake. Connor, Amanda, and Steven brought up the rear.

Steven was excited to see all of the boats at the dock and the birds that played in the water. The wind popped the water on the bank of the lake and the sun shot rays of light through the dense edges of the woods. He almost tripped over his own feet due to the distractions. "Pay attention, Steven," barked his sister.

It was a nice morning by the lake. It wasn't too warm, but wasn't too cool either. It was perfect hiking weather. The Chance family was in no mood to do any sightseeing. Their only goal was to get back to the tunnel with everyone in one piece.

Connor asked Matthew, "How much farther do we have? It's starting to look a little familiar now."

Matthew was confident that his watch was leading them in the correct direction. He realized they were to the break in the woods that led to the tunnel. He replied, "Not far at all. Actually, all we need to do is follow this path into the woods, get up over that hill, and we'll be there." Matthew pointed to a path that led much deeper into the woods. "This is where we came out last time."

Connor let go of Amanda's hand and headed to Matthew. He wanted to make sure Matthew knew what he was doing.

"Are you sure this is right? I thought we were farther away from the lake when we came out of the woods last time." He grabbed Matthew's wrist to look at the watch. "We should be going this way."

Matthew pulled his arm away from his brother and replied, "You don't know what you're talking about."

As Connor and Matthew argued about the location of the tunnel, Amanda motioned to her little brother to stay quiet. She moved her finger to her mouth and whispered to Steven, "Follow me, but be quiet." Amanda slowly backed away from the Chance family. She was careful not to shuffle her feet in the fallen leaves. She turned around with her brother to make a run into the woods. She didn't care where she ran, as long as it was away from the Chance family.

She noticed a shadowy figure at the end of the path they had just traveled. The figure started calling out, "Amanda, Amanda!"

Amanda dug her feet into the soft ground and yelled back, "Dad!"

Matthew, Connor, and April all turned back to see a man approaching Amanda and Steven. They knew it was not her father. The boys raced to cut off Amanda and Steven. Matthew told them, "That's not your dad."

The figure came closer and stopped ten yards in front of the boys. Amanda realized who it was and screamed out, "You were at the house! You killed my parents!" Connor held back Amanda as she tried to lunge toward the man.

The man wore camouflage pants and a black shirt. He replied to the panicked girl, "My goodness, you're a scrappy one, aren't you?" He looked down at the scared young boy who had huddled behind Connor's leg, and said, "Remember me, little man?"

April moved past the boys and blocked the path. She glared at the man in camouflage and exclaimed, "Stay away from these kids!"

Chapter 18

The man replied, "I'm sorry, but I can't do that. I was sent here to do a job and it's gonna get done, whether you like it or not."

Connor reached in his pocket and grabbed the snap ring that he and Matthew had prepared the night before. He puffed his chest and said, "It's gonna take a lot more than you to finish that job."

The man nodded his head, affirming what Connor had said, and he dropped three small rocks on the ground. He said, with a smirk and light chuckle, "You're right." As soon as the rocks hit the ground, the air around each of them began to distort and the figures of three other men formed. It was clear that one of the men was Keith Kellington.

Keith opened his eyes to see April, the boys, and what was left of the Curry family all standing in front of him. "Excellent job, Mr. Tate; they're all here, just like you promised."

Keith put his hands together and rubbed them slowly before making his next comment. "You know, I really only want the girl and her brother. If you just want to pass them over to me, I'll let you and your two boys go." Keith pointed at the path to the side of the lake trail and said, "Take your sons and start walking into the woods."

Keith pulled a piece of paper from his pocket and explained his findings to April. "You see, Ms. Chance, I know you and your sons didn't exist until a few weeks ago. I know you aren't who you say you are. I know this park has something to do with it." Keith tore the paper, threw it in the air, and said, "I don't care about any of it."

He pulled a knife from his belt and said, "I do care about tying up loose ends." He pointed to Amanda and Steven and said, "They are loose ends. I would sure hate to gut your sons, due to some loose ends." He returned the knife to his belt and smiled. "Of course, that would be a last resort." April noticed that the four men had kept their distance. Keith took just one step closer to April and asked, "So what's it gonna be?"

April looked at the scared Curry kids. Steven trembled behind Connor and Amanda couldn't believe what she had heard. It amazed April how quick she had changed her mind about them. Twenty-four hours ago, she would have left both of them for Keith to do as he wanted, but not now. She saw them all as her responsibility.

April saw that Matthew had raised his hand to his Hathmec. She suddenly felt the power that came from the attribute charm. He had shared it with her and Connor. April stared into her son's eyes and said, "Well, Mr. Kellington, you really haven't left me with much of a choice." She took Connor and Matthew by the hand and said, "I can't risk losing my family."

Connor smiled at his mother and released her hand. She turned back around, with a snap ring in hand, and blasted a snap toward the four men. The leaves on the trees shook and fell with the strength of the blast and all four men skidded across the ground. They were only stopped by the hard tree trunks that blocked their path.

April turned to her kids and yelled, "Get to the tunnel—run!" Connor grabbed Amanda by the hand and ran down the wooded path. Amanda had Steven by the arm as he struggled to keep up.

Matthew stayed by his mother's side. April told him to go, but he wouldn't. "I'm staying with you."

Keith got up and ordered the other three men to follow Connor and the Curry kids. The three men ran off into the woods after them. April pushed on her son and said, "You need to go help Connor. If he doesn't reach the tunnel, he'll need your help. I'll take care of Mr. Kellington."

Matthew agreed with his mother and ran off after the three men. He told his mother as he ran off, "I'll come back for you."

April kept her focus on Keith Kellington and yelled to her son, "No matter what happens to me, you get them to the tunnel!"

Keith Kellington began walking back toward April. He was cocky and asked, "So, you're going to take care of me?"

April replied, with the snap ring still pointed at him, "I'll die before I let you hurt those kids."

Keith replied, "I agree."

Keith dove out of the way as April sent another snap his way. As he dove, he delivered a handful of carrier stones into April's direction. While kneeling down, he motioned toward the ground under her. Stones, dirt, gravel, and earth shot straight up beneath April and the snap ring was dislodged from her hand. The force of the earth was strong enough to knock April to the ground and cut her right hand. A small stream of

Chapter 18

blood ran between her thumb and forefinger as she searched frantically for the snap ring covered by the dirt.

"It's just a little blood, my dear. I'm sure there will be more before we're done." Keith shuffled leaves on the ground as he came closer to April. She popped up and threw her fists in the air. Keith didn't notice that she had thrown a portion of carrier stones in his direction. He passed right through them.

Keith raised his fists and mocked April. "Oh, you want to go the way of fisticuffs, do you? This might tickle."

Keith leaned in toward April with his face in a lowered position. "Go ahead, sweetheart, let's see what you got."

April had captured Keith's strength. She reared back and blasted the unsuspecting face of her foe. Keith staggered back, as if being hit by a sledgehammer, and fell to the ground.

He gathered himself and saw April approach. He attempted to throw another carrier her way, but she was too fast and lifted him from the ground with a wicked shot to the stomach. He rolled precariously close to the water's edge and struggled to regain his footing.

"What's wrong, Keith? Never been beat up by a sweetheart before?" Keith, no longer mocking or smiling, tossed his carrier stones at April again, much like a mist of water.

"You think you're so cute, don't you? Let's see what type of statue you'll make." Keith, thinking he had control over April, told her, "Don't move a muscle."

April used this to her advantage and pretended she couldn't move. This deluded Keith into a false sense of safety and brought him in to an attack location for her. Keith recovered from the initial shots he had taken from April, meandered up to her nose, and said, "You're not so tough when you can't move, are you?"

April raised her knee into the crotch of Keith Kellington and punched him in the face until he fell back to the ground. Keith writhed in pain as April moved in for the finish. He bled from his nose and his eye swelled. Keith mumbled, "That's impossible! It's not possible!" He backed away from April as he slithered along the ground. April followed him but her steps were stopped when something wrapped around her leg.

She couldn't move as tree roots wrapped each ankle into place. She had walked through a bed of carrier stones that Keith had placed while sliding along the ground. They wrapped so tight, she was unable to move any farther. She started to reach down to cut the roots, but Keith had moved in and grabbed her around the waist. Her arms were pinned.

"Your strength is incredible, Ms. Chance." Keith struggled to hold April's arms down as their two attribute charms battled to steal the other's strength. Keith was able to control two more roots as they wrapped around April's wrists and pulled them toward the ground. April pulled with all of her might to break the roots, but was unable to.

Keith placed one of his hands down the neck of April's shirt. He exposed the Hathmec from inside of her shirt and exposed the charms. Keith stepped back from the fiery blonde and the light bulb went off in his head.

"I knew it! You have a Hathmec!" He was stunned to see the tool that he had used for years to get what he wanted. "Where did you get this?" Keith ran through a list of associates who he knew had access to a Hathmec.

"You must have received it from Evan or Daniel." Keith studied the pendant shining in the drops of sunlight that penetrated the foliage. "You only have two charms and one of them is the health charm." He walked to the edge of the lake and threw a carrier stone into the water. The stone made a single *kerplunk* in the water.

"That's why you can match my strength and why I can't control you."

As the madman moved the lake water around with his hand, April replied, "You will never control me or my boys, you bastard!"

He nodded and said, "So your boys have the same charms as you?"

April feverishly shook her head no. She knew that she had mistakenly given Keith information that could hurt Matthew and Connor. He responded, "Oh, I think they do."

April tried to convince him otherwise. "No, it's just me. I'm the one that's here to stop you."

Chapter 18

"Let me ask you something, Ms. Chance. It occurs to me that you have some knowledge of the power that these pendants can wield." Keith was standing to the side of the still-bound mother of two. He started to run his hand down April's face. "You knew the power that I had. You knew you couldn't match me, yet you brought that poor police officer to me."

April turned and spit at Keith Kellington, just missing his face. Keith suddenly changed his accent to match the late Danny Charles. "Guess y'all just don't care bout the common man." He walked back to the water's edge and said, "Reckon I'll have to teach y'all a lesson."

Keith released April from the roots that were wrapped around her ankles and wrists, grinned, and said, "You know, Ms. Chance, you should always load your gun before a showdown. If not, you never have enough bullets to win the fight."

With that, a roar was heard behind April that sounded much like the tidal waves that flow from Niagara Falls. April turned to see a huge wall of water that engulfed her whole body. She struggled to move from it, but it was too late. The wall of water had rushed her into the lake, several yards from the shoreline.

Keith stood on the shore and watched April struggle to reach the water's surface for short breaths of air. April could only get a glance of him as he yelled to her, "The element charm is one you should probably pick up! I would love to stay here and play around with you some more, but I need to find those two brats that you call sons. I have to make sure that the Curry kids get a bullet from my gun." He thought, *I should have shared my Hathmec with my men.*

April struggled to reply, "No! Leave them alone!"

He turned to leave, but he stopped and made one more gesture toward the lake. "Don't worry, Ms. Chance. I won't kill you yet. I'm sure my associates would love to get that Hathmec from you, and I know the best way to get it."

Keith walked off toward the trail that the boys had taken, leaving April pinned in the lake. She was being wrapped in arms of water, keeping her from getting out of the lake. She was being dunked, pulled, and tossed, but she wouldn't give up. She knew her boys needed her and she would die trying to get to them.

While April battled Keith, Matthew was hot on the trail of two of Keith's men who were closing in on the R tunnel. Matthew was worried for his mother, but he was frantic in his attitude toward protecting Amanda and Steven. He knew they were with Connor, and he was hoping that they had already reached the tunnel and were out of harm's way.

Matthew reached a small clearing about one hundred yards from the tunnel. He heard the racking of a pistol to his left. One of Keith's men appeared from the edge of the tree line with it pointed at Matthew.

"I hate to shoot a kid, but I can't have you gettin' in my way either." Matthew could see that the man was large, muscular, and confident in his physical prowess. His Italian accent was thicker than the cloud of cologne that he wore.

Matthew asked the man, "You look like a pretty stout fellow, but I bet you can't take me down."

The man put his gun back in his holster and yelled to his cohort on the other side of the opening, "Hey, Max! This kid thinks he can take me down."

Max emerged from the other tree line. He had a few leaves resting on his large shoulders. "Damn, Marco, we don't have time for this; just shoot the kid and let's get outta here."

Marco cracked his knuckles and told Matthew, "I have a black belt and I was a bouncer at one the toughest clubs in New York City for six years." He removed his coat and placed it on the ground.

Matthew never moved from his location and said, "You shouldn't have any problems with me then."

Max leaned by the nearest tree and asked Marco, "Why do you wanna beat down this little kid? That's pretty messed up."

Marco replied, "I don't get the opportunity to try out my skills on people very often." He pointed to Matthew and said, "Don't worry kid; I'll snap your neck quick; you won't feel a thing."

The clearing was surrounded by trees, but the sun had made its way high enough into the park sky to shine a natural spotlight on the open

Chapter 18

area. Nature had created a center stage for a modern-day David versus Goliath.

Matthew removed the light jacket that he wore and threw it toward Max. He asked, "Do you mind holding this for me?" Max took the jacket and noticed a sandy substance on the outside of it.

"Sure kid, we'll make sure and bury you in it."

Marco moved toward Matthew and asked, "Are you ready, kid?"

Matthew cracked his knuckles and said, "I am now."

Marco moved in on Matthew quickly and threw a barrage of punches and kicks, each one blocked by the much smaller and seemingly weaker boy. Max watched in shock as Matthew avoided each of Marco's attacks. It was as if Matthew was toying with the man.

Finally, Marco rushed Matthew and grabbed him around the arms. Matthew smiled at the much larger man and grabbed his wrist. Matthew twisted Marco's arm behind his back and thumped him on top of his head. Matthew looked in Max's direction and asked, "You were special forces at some point, weren't you?" Max, stunned at the boy's knowledge, reached for his side arm.

Matthew spun Marco around and laid a wicked shot across his face with a sweeping kick. You could hear his jaw break as Marco went careening back into the woods. Matthew saw that Marco wasn't knocked out, so he moved over him and cracked him in the face with the front of his boot.

Marco and Max had failed to realize that Matthew had used his Hathmec against them. Matthew was smart and had added carrier stones to the jacket he had thrown to Max. He had also thrown a few carriers to Marco when he cracked his knuckles. He not only had the strength and skill of a karate and bouncer expert, but he had taken the strength and skill of a former mercenary for hire.

While Matthew had neutralized Marco, he still had to deal with Max, who had pointed his gun in Matthew's direction. "I don't know how you did that, kid, but I won't make the same mistake."

Matthew thought, *Wonder if I can survive a bullet.*

Max pointed the black-tipped gun and started to pull the trigger until he heard something above him in the tree. He looked up to the sky and saw a boot just above his eye line. The boot reared back and crushed the side of his face, knocking him to the ground. Matthew rushed over to kick the gun into the woods. Max was groggy but appeared to be getting up. Matthew grabbed a limb that was lying on the ground and, as Max stood, shattered the limb across his back.

"That did the job," said a voice coming from the tree.

Matthew looked up and saw Connor wearing the memory boots and standing in midair off a tree limb. Connor reached down and shut off the boots to fall to the ground.

Matthew asked, "Were you there the whole time?"

Connor explained that he heard the fight from just down the hill. "I put the boots on and made my way through the trees. I figured you would need my help. I already took care of that other guy."

Matthew asked, "Did you use the attribute charm?"

Connor responded, "The guy was a bodybuilder. One good shot and he was out."

Matthew looked around and asked, "Where are Amanda and Steven? Did you go ahead and send them through the tunnel?"

Connor shook his head no and said, "I gave them some of the camo-tape and hid them down the hill." Connor took a pair of sunglasses from Marco and asked, "Where's April?"

Matthew replied, "I'm not sure. She was trying to stop Keith, but I don't know what happened."

Matthew and Connor made their way down the hill and Matthew asked his brother, "Do you think we should go back for her? I don't know if she can stand up to Keith by herself."

Connor skidded to the bottom of the hill and replied, "She wants us to get to the tunnel, and that's what I plan on doing."

Matthew reached the bottom of the hill and called out for Amanda and Steven. "Amanda, it's all clear; you can come out now." He called out again, "You can come out now; Steven, where are you?"

Matthew turned to Connor. "Where did you leave them?"

Connor had a blank look on his face and said, "It was somewhere around here." They started touching various areas around the bottom of the hill. They tried to feel for an arm or leg, with no luck.

Chapter 18

On the other side of the ravine, Amanda Curry held her little brother tight and whispered in his ear, "You have to stay quiet. When they leave, we'll get outta here." She watched as Matthew and Connor searched for her and Steven, and waited for her chance to run away. She didn't trust the boys or their mother to protect her or her brother.

Connor, frustrated with the search, told Matthew, "I think they're gone. Maybe they shouldn't come back with us anyway."

Matthew threw down a rock and replied, "We're not leaving them. If they stay here, they'll die and none of this would have been worth doing." He continued to shuffle leaves and searched the bottom of the hill.

Connor restated, "They're gone. We should do the same thing and get out of here before more of Keith's men show up."

Matthew threw his arms in the air and said, "If you're too scared to stay, just go on."

Connor pushed his brother away and said, "I just saved your life and now I'm a coward. I'm not scared of anything, but I'm also not so stupid as to stay here and get killed."

Matthew pushed Connor back and said, "You don't care for anyone but yourself."

Connor grabbed Matthew by the arms and threw him to the ground. "She doesn't care about you, but I do, so get up and let's get out of here."

The two boys noticed several rocks and stones rolling down the hill to their sides. Both boys looked at each other as if to signal that something was wrong. Before they could react, Keith Kellington had grabbed Matthew from behind and torn his Hathmec from his neck.

Keith had Matthew around the neck with his forearm as Connor looked on. He didn't know what to do. Keith held the Hathmec up in the air away from Matthew. The pendant was trying to pull away from Keith and return to Matthew.

Keith said, "It's amazing how these things know who to go back to. You should really get one of these transport charms; they come in handy when you want to sneak up on somebody."

Keith threw Matthew to the ground and pulled out a gun. He pointed it at Matthew's head and said, "Now I really want to know where you boys came across these, but I have a little business to finish first." He called out, "Amanda Curry! Amanda Curry, show yourself or I will kill this young man."

He pressed the barrel of the gun into Matthew's forehead and said, "After I shoot this one, I'll shoot the other one, too."

Matthew yelled out, "Don't do it, Amanda; just stay away!"

Keith took the butt of his pistol and popped Matthew across the face. Matthew fell to the ground. His face was now smeared with the mud at the bottom of the hill.

He cocked the gun and pointed it to his head again. "You have to the count of five or his brains will get splattered across this lovely landscape. One." Keith looked around for Amanda, but there were no signs of her. "Two." He looked around again, with no movement. "Three." Matthew looked to his brother, who was frozen with fear, and closed his eyes. "Four." Keith waved the gun for a moment and said, "I guess saving her life isn't enough for her to save yours, kid. Five!"

Chapter 19

CHANGE OF HEART

Amanda Curry knew what it felt like to be loved. Amanda knew her parents gave up their own lives to save her and her brother's life. Amanda knew how much her parents loved her. Amanda had known the juvenile love of her youth and the empty feelings that those left behind.

What Amanda didn't expect was how she felt about a young boy she had only known for two weeks. He felt strong enough for her to give his own life. Now she knew it.

As Keith counted ever closer to five, Amanda began to shake. The shaking was not out of fear. Amanda Curry feared what was about to happen, but it was not fear that held her back. Amanda had cried for the last day remembering her parents and wondering how she was ever going to be able to take care of her brother. This time there were no tears. There was a fire in her eyes she had never felt before. This feeling was a realization that this was all real. This emotion was different. This was anger.

The count reached five and Amanda Curry jumped up from her position, only fifteen yards from Keith and Matthew. A shaken, rage-filled young lady yelled out, "Stop!" Keith turned to his left to see Amanda Curry, arms wide open. "If you want to kill me, then go ahead and do it! You've already taken my family, but you won't take this one."

Keith turned the gun in Amanda's direction. He was ready to pull the trigger but couldn't help himself. He made one more bone-chilling, evil, and honest comment: "I'll end up killing them, too."

Keith began to pull the trigger but was suddenly thrust up into the air. He landed between Matthew and Amanda. His gun flew off toward

Chapter 19

the mound of leaves at the bottom of the hill. Matthew's Hathmec flew off toward the tree line. The Hathmec turned in midair and returned to its rightful owner, Matthew.

Keith oriented himself to see the youngest of the Curry kids, Steven Jr., standing there with a round disk in his hand. Connor looked to the young boy who had used the camotape to work his way around the tree line without anyone seeing him. Connor told Steven, "I told you that would come in handy." The boy grinned with a sense of accomplishment, but there was no time to waste.

Matthew yelled out, "Connor, get him outta here!" Keith jumped to his feet and threw a barrage of carrier stones toward Connor and Steven, but his attempts to stop them with his control charm wouldn't work. Both Connor and Steven wore Hathmec pendants and ran out of sight.

Keith started to pursue them, but Amanda would have none of it. She leaped at Keith and jumped onto his back. She clawed at his face and tried to put her fingers into his eyes. She was holding on with all of her strength, but Keith grabbed her arms and flipped her onto the hard ground. He jumped on top of her and put his hands around her neck. He squeezed and exclaimed, "I don't see a Hathmec around your neck, young lady."

Matthew got his Hathmec back around his neck and ran to Keith and Amanda's location, just yards ahead of him. He released some carriers in both Keith's and Amanda's direction and grabbed Keith's hands. He used the attribute charm to gain both Keith's and Amanda's strength. He pried away Keith's hands and pulled him away from his position on top of Amanda.

Amanda struggled to catch her breath and her hands went directly to her throat. Keith turned to face the much smaller Matthew and said, "You really think you can match my strength? I can feel your strength, your brother's strength, even that little kid's strength."

Keith wasn't able to stop Connor and Steven, but the carriers that were linked to them allowed Keith to pull their strength.

Keith and Matthew threw each other around from tree to tree. Matthew called out to Amanda, "Run, Amanda! Get out of here!" Amanda continued to lie on the ground and struggled to catch her breath. She could see Keith and Matthew as they struggled on the ground.

Keith rolled on top of Matthew and moved his hands to Matthew's throat. "I told you, kid, even with that pendant you can't match me." The interesting thing was that Matthew was matching the larger man's strength. He started to move Keith's hands away from his throat.

Matthew looked on in amazement as he pushed the larger man away from him. *How is this possible?* he thought. Regardless, he was beginning to overpower Keith Kellington. Keith realized that he didn't have the advantage he thought he did, and he jumped away from Matthew in shock. Matthew picked himself up from the ground and said, "Had enough?"

Keith tossed a handful of carrier stones to the ground and grimaced from the pain left on his wrists from the smaller Matthew. "You know, kid, I bet you're just like your mother. She was pretty strong too." Matthew stared a hole in Keith Kellington as he prepared himself for the filth to come. "She didn't have a complete Hathmec either."

Keith motioned to the ground and a large log plowed into the side of Matthew. Matthew realized that multiple rocks that were lying at the base of one of the trees were now zeroed in on him. He tried to duck and dodge out of the way, but he was pelted by multiple, large, sharp rocks. Matthew's face was cut and blood started to drip from his forearm. The rocks had struck him in the side, the legs, and in the back of the head.

Matthew was knocked for a loop but he began to get his senses back. He saw that Keith had moved back toward the location of the gun. Matthew gazed to his right and saw Amanda running toward him. "Matthew, are you all right?"

Matthew pushed Amanda away and said, "You have to run; go find Connor and go with him. I'll hold off Keith as long as I can." Amanda knelt down to Matthew, who struggled to get up from the pummeling of the rocks.

Amanda helped him to his feet and stuttered, "I won't leave you."

Keith had found his gun and pointed it directly at Amanda. Matthew pushed Amanda behind him and yelled, "Run!" Amanda got up and began to run toward the far tree line, but Keith stopped her.

Chapter 19

"Don't move!"

Amanda stopped, unable to move.

Matthew realized that he had not given Amanda a copy of his Hathmec, so she had no protection against the controlling charm of Keith. "Turn toward me!" Keith ordered. Amanda fought the urge to turn but couldn't. She faced Keith and the weapon that he planned to use in her death. Amanda couldn't move or talk, but her mind was racing with anger, fear, and a sense of regret that she wouldn't be able to tell Matthew how she felt about him.

Matthew jumped in front of Amanda and told Keith, "I won't let you shoot her." This was the first time that Matthew's voice had trembled. He knew that he couldn't stop a bullet, but maybe he could break the contact between Keith and Amanda.

Keith replied, "You just don't give up, do you?"

Matthew felt a gust of wind come from the west and Keith cupped his hands. "You see, when you have the elements charm, you can control all of the elements." He released his hands and a massive wave of wind and air crashed into Matthew. It knocked him into a pile of dirt more than twenty yards from Amanda.

As he lifted his head, he heard Keith say, "Time's up, Ms. Curry."

Matthew thought, *Time? The watch!*

Matthew reached down to the watch on his wrist. Walter Wainright had said to only hit the red button for an emergency and this was certainly one of those. Matthew pressed the red button and he heard the shot of the pistol. He screamed out, "No!"

The scream of "no" echoed in the background like someone in another state shouting it through a bullhorn. Matthew got up from the ground and realized that there was no movement. The wind wasn't blowing, the trees weren't swaying, and Keith Kellington stood as still as a statue, just as Amanda had been left. Matthew could see the bullet that had come from Keith's gun stuck in midair, just five feet from Amanda's head.

Matthew peered at his watch and saw a countdown on the face. It was already at fifty and going down from there. "I only have a minute." Matthew realized that the countdown was telling him how long time would stay frozen. Matthew ran to Amanda, picked her up, and carried her to just inside the tree line, well away from the bullet's trajectory.

He saw that he only had thirty seconds left, so he ran over to Keith's location and removed the Hathmec from his neck. Matthew knew that the minute he released it, it would try to return to Keith, so he locked the chain around a small limb of a tree. "Only ten seconds left." The only thing to do was get the gun from Keith's hand. Matthew used his own strength to pry Keith's hand from the gun.

Just as Matthew got the gun from Keith's hand, a bright light flashed over the area. Time was no longer frozen and Amanda was no longer under Keith's power. Keith looked to the sky at the flash of light and realized that Matthew now stood in front of him. He staggered backward with a look of disgust. Matthew threw the gun as far as he could down the hill and grinned at Keith. Keith's eyes opened as wide as they physically could as he yelled out, "That's it!"

He rushed Matthew with a closed fist and attempted to punch him square in the face. Matthew caught Keith's fist and squeezed. Keith went to his knees in pain as he realized that he was no longer wearing his Hathmec. Matthew closed his fist and with the added strength of the Hathmec, knocked Keith out.

Amanda emerged from the tree line and ran to Matthew. "I thought I would never see you again."

Matthew tried to calm her. "We're gonna be all right. I don't think Keith will be a problem anymore."

Amanda looked into the eyes of the boy that was willing to give his life for hers. She had been so wrong about him.

"We need to get to the tunnel." Matthew took Amanda's hand and began to lead her through the foliage and back to the main trail. It would lead them to the R tunnel. They ran past stumps, insects, and birds singing in the trees. Matthew thought of his mother and what Amanda had said to him. Maybe she cared for him as much as he cared for her.

"There it is!" Matthew saw the low light that radiated from the tunnel coming from a small clearing just down a hill.

Amanda looked at the tunnel and asked, "This is the tunnel you were talking about?" She put her hand over her mouth and said, "You're

Chapter 19

not crazy. Do you think Connor and Steven have already gone through this thing?"

Matthew looked around and replied, "I hope so."

Matthew made another copy of his Hathmec with the health charm and gave it to Amanda. "You'll need this for the trip home." Without warning, a voice came from the tree line and startled Matthew.

"You didn't think we would leave without you, did ya?"

Matthew turned to see his brother and Steven standing behind them. Amanda picked up her little brother and said, "You were so brave; I knew you could do it."

Steven replied, "Yeah, I got that jerk good."

Connor said, "We were using the camotape. I knew you would make it."

Matthew shook his head and replied, "We just barely made it." He looked around one more time and asked, "What about Mom?"

Connor shook his head no. "I was hoping she would show up like you two did. I don't know where she is."

Matthew took Amanda by the hand again and told her that he was going to look for his mother. "You and Steven go with Connor through the tunnel, and I'll come later with Mom."

Connor stepped in and said, "You can't go after her; she wants us to get back, no matter what."

Matthew pushed his brother away and said, "I can't leave here without her. We're a family." Suddenly, the boys heard a rustling coming from the trees.

Connor said, "That must be her."

A figure emerged from behind a large tree and rustled the leaves on the ground. He was spinning a loaded pistol in his hand. "No, boys, it's not your rotten mother."

Connor yelled out, "It's Keith!" Keith walked clear from the tree and the boys could see that he had found his Hathmec and his gun.

"When you take someone's Hathmec, you need to make sure you attach it to a really sturdy branch." Connor and Matthew stood in front of Amanda and Steven as Keith cracked his knuckles. "Now, who gets to die first?"

Connor tilted his head to the right, grinned, and said, "I don't think it's any of us."

Keith felt a small tap on his shoulder and turned to see April Chance holding a large piece of broken wood. "Try this one, sweetheart!" April reared back and blasted Keith with the block of wood. It knocked Keith across the clearing and square into a boulder. April dropped the wood and ran to her kids. "We don't have time to chat. Everybody grab hands and walk into the tunnel."

April grabbed Steven's hand and said, "Don't worry—it won't hurt a bit."

Matthew and Connor both took Amanda's hand and the group walked into the tunnel. Matthew looked back just as he entered and saw Keith getting up and making his way toward them. That was the last image Matthew saw in 1984. He was plunged, once again, into a sea of lights, images, and colors.

Keith reached the tunnel just as it closed. A quick snip of light was all that remained where the tunnel had been. He placed his hand in the area where he had last seen the Chance and Curry families, but there was nothing there. Keith was irate and confused, but he knew what to do. He followed the trails back out of the park and reached the main park station, where he found a pay phone. He ran through the numbers quickly and waited for a response from the other end of the line.

"Hey, it's Keith."

The person on the other end of the line replied, "Did you take care of it?"

Keith replied, "We have bigger problems than just those two kids. I think you need to come to Georgia." Keith cleared his throat and said, "They just vanished."

There was a long pause on the other end of the line and then, without warning, Keith felt a hand on his shoulder. The same voice followed it, saying, "Show me."

Keith walked the man to the former location of the R tunnel. The man watched as Keith's helpers reached the area. They were all beaten and bruised from their interaction with the Chance family. Keith explained, "They were right here one second and gone the next."

Chapter 19

The man reviewed the area and stared at the small speck of light that was starting to flicker out. He put his hand on Keith's shoulder and said, "I know what to do."

Back in 2185, Matthew started to regain consciousness from the latest trip through the tunnel. He looked to his side and saw April and Connor coming to as well. He asked, "Where's Amanda and Steven?" As he staggered to his feet, he realized that this room was not the same room they had left from. "Johnson, Walter, where are you?"

A door opened from behind the R tunnel and Matthew made his way to the sound of the creaking door. "Walter, is that you? Hey, we need to talk about something."

The figure closed in on Matthew and replied, "Don't you worry about them. I'm taking care of it."

Matthew caught a glimpse of the man and stumbled backward. "It can't be."

The man replied, "Surprised to see me?"

Matthew yelled out, "Run! It's Keith!"

TO BE CONTINUED IN
LAST CHANCE, VOLUME 2:
THE LEGEND OF THE HATHMEC
PLANTING THE SEED

ABOUT THE AUTHOR

Bradley Boals is an industrial engineer by day and an author by night. He lives in west Tennessee with his wife of nine years and has always wanted to write a story that can be enjoyed by all. He hopes that everyone who reads *The Legend of the Hathmec* will want to continue the story with subsequent books.
"All things are possible through the Lord."

Made in the USA
San Bernardino, CA
24 September 2014